Bodies in the Boatyard

Bodies in the Boatyard

A MOLLIE MCGHIE SAILING MYSTERY #2

ELLEN JACOBSON

Bodies in the Boatyard
Copyright © 2018 by Ellen Jacobson

All rights reserved. This book or any portion thereof may not be reproduced or used in any manner whatsoever without the express written permission of the publisher except for the use of brief quotations in a book review.

This book is a work of fiction. Names, characters, places, and incidents either are products of the author's imagination or are used fictitiously. Any resemblance to actual persons, living or dead, events, or locales is entirely coincidental.

Print ISBN: 978-1-7321602-4-8
Digital ISBN: 978-1-7321602-3-1

Editor: Chris Brogden, EnglishGeek Editing

First Printing: November 2018

Published by: Ellen Jacobson
www.ellenjacobsonauthor.com

For cats everywhere who hate wearing collars

CONTENTS

	The Crew	i
1	Mr. Oblivious	1
2	That Sinking Feeling	9
3	The Dating Game	30
4	The Most Annoying Eyebrows Ever	40
5	Mystery Ingredient	60
6	Oompa-Loompa vs. Smurfs	74
7	Sugar Cravings	87
8	The Case of the Missing Collar	102
9	Stage Fright	118
10	How Not to Climb a Ladder	126
11	Fun with Markers	142
12	Another Mystery Ingredient	158
13	Snowbirds	166
14	Seeing Ghosts	182
15	Harassing Seagulls	195
16	Bling for Mrs. Moto	206
	Mollie's Sailing Tips	220
	Author's Note & Acknowledgments	223
	About the Author	225

THE CREW

MOLLIE MCGHIE—When she isn't investigating murders, Mollie spends her time educating the public about UFOs and alien abduction.

SCOOTER MCGHIE—Mollie's husband. Passionate about boats, he dreams about selling everything and sailing around the world.

MRS. MOTO—Mollie and Scooter's Japanese bobtail cat who has a talent for finding clues.

NANCY AND NED SCHNEIDER—Owners of the Palm Tree Marina.

KATY AND SAM—Nancy and Ned's grandchildren.

PENNY CHADWICK—Runs the local sailing school and boat brokerage.

ALEJANDRA LOPEZ—A young waitress at the Sailor's Corner Cafe.

BEN MORETTI—A wannabe pirate who works at the marina.

CHIEF DALTON AND OFFICER MOORE—Local law enforcement officers.

TIFFANY AND CHAD—Two teenagers who work part-time at Penelope's Sugar Shack and Melvin's Marine Emporium.

ALLIGATOR CHUCK—Mollie and Scooter's neighbor. Owns a local barbecue restaurant.

KEN AND LEILANI CHOI—Young couple living aboard their sailboat in the boatyard. Ken is a marine biologist. Leilani works as a virtual assistant.

NORM AND SUZANNE THOMAS—Norm owns a number of local businesses, including a fishing charter business. Suzanne is a real estate agent.

LIAM THOMAS—Norm's nephew. Works for his uncle's fishing charter business.

XANDER CARLTON—Suzanne's son.

MELVIN ROLLE—Originally from the Bahamas. Owner of the local marine store and a fishing charter business. Mollie and Scooter's neighbor.

DARREN ROLLE—Melvin's nephew. Works for his uncle's fishing charter business.

SIMON—Does volunteer work with Mollie investigating UFOs and alien abduction.

CONNIE AND FIONA—Do volunteer work to protect sea turtles and other marine wildlife.

MABEL—Does volunteer work at sea turtle sanctuary.

HANK AND VIOLET—Snowbirds looking to buy a home in Coconut Cove.

ALAN—Aspiring photojournalist.

CHAPTER 1
MR. OBLIVIOUS

WHAT WOULD YOU DO IF your husband announced over a romantic Valentine's Day dinner that the two of you were going to sell the house, do some extreme downsizing, get rid of all your belongings—including your beloved collection of boots—and move onto a dilapidated sailboat? Would you:
    (a) see about arranging for a little "accident" that causes the boat to sink;
    (b) suggest downsizing his comic book collection and watch him have a panic attack;
    (c) roll your eyes—this isn't the first harebrained scheme your husband has come up with; or
    (d) skip the rest of the main course and crack open the gift-wrapped box of chocolates sitting next to you?

    I have to confess, it wasn't the first time that (a) had crossed my mind. Ever since Scooter had presented me with a sailboat named *Marjorie Jane* a few months ago for our tenth anniversary, I had been trying to figure out how to get rid of her. She was run down, in need of serious repairs, and was costing us a ton of money. Sometimes I even thought my husband paid more attention to her than to me. But before I resorted to something so drastic, I would need to check our insurance policy and see if we'd be covered if she "mysteriously" sank.

Scooter had an unnatural attachment to his comic books, so (b) was seeming like a real possibility. It would probably put downsizing into perspective if he realized he'd have to give up Batman, Superman, Spider-Man, and Cotton-Candy Man. Okay, I totally made that last one up, but could you imagine how awesome his superhero getup would be? Some sort of fluffy pink wig and a cape made out of white crepe paper. I could just picture him stopping criminals in their tracks by wrapping them in sugary strands of cotton candy while shouting out his trademark line, "I'm going to fluff you up, man!"

I definitely did a bit of (c). Harebrained schemes are par for the course when it comes to Scooter. Like the time he thought building a carport out of straw bales and Popsicle sticks was a good idea. I don't think I'd ever rolled my eyes so much before.

I seriously thought about (d), but my mother had always told me to finish my dinner before I had dessert. Hey, stop laughing out there. Yes, I know I have an unnatural love of chocolate and other sugary treats, but I can show some restraint at times. Like in this case, where I was perfectly happy to finish eating my greasy french fries before opening the box of chocolates.

I nibbled on a few fries while I thought about how to respond to Scooter's announcement.

"Why are you rolling your eyes, Mollie?" he asked while he tried to steal some food off my plate.

I batted his hand away. "Eat your own, mister." I put my arm in front of my dish to act as a defensive barrier. "Why am I rolling my eyes?" I asked. "You casually mention that you want to sell our cute cottage on the beach and move onto *Marjorie Jane*. Did you really think I'd be okay with that?"

Scooter furrowed his brow. "But we've talked about this before."

"No, *you've* talked about wanting to sell the house and sail around the world, but I never said I was on board with the idea."

"Hang on, I don't understand. Just the other day I mentioned getting a real estate agent out to look at the cottage."

"Was I even in the room at the time?"

"What do you mean? Of course you were." He chewed on his lip. "At least, I think you were."

"Sometimes you have entire conversations with people, but it turns out they happen only in your head." I sighed. "I know, you can't help it. That's what I get for marrying one of those introverted, nerdy computer types. You might have a high IQ, but your EQ could use some work."

"EQ?"

"Emotional intelligence. You know, being able to read and understand emotions." He looked perplexed. I squeezed his hand and smiled. "I guess that's why people call you Mr. Oblivious."

He frowned. "Mr. Oblivious? Who calls me that?"

I busied myself putting more ketchup on my plate. When I glanced at Scooter, he was staring at me and drumming his fingers on the picnic table.

"Well?" he asked.

I pointed over at the public docks, where commercial boats tied up to offload their catch, pick up and drop off charter passengers, and wash down their decks. "Hey, a couple of fishing boats are coming in."

"Don't try to change the subject. Now, 'fess up. Who calls me that?"

"Well...Mrs. Moto does."

He snorted. "Mrs. Moto is a cat. She can't talk."

"Of course she can talk. Don't you hear her meowing when you forget to fill up her food bowl? She's saying, 'Hey, Mr. Oblivious, I'm hungry. Snap to it.'"

"I feed her all the time, yet she always seems to be hungry." He smiled. "She even dragged her bowl into the center of the kitchen the other day to get her point across."

Despite his objections to adopting the calico Japanese bobtail a few months ago, I think he'd become rather fond of her, which was probably due to the fact that she had black markings on her face that resembled eyeglasses. Since Scooter was as blind as a bat without his glasses, I suspect he liked seeing someone else always "wearing" a pair as well.

He leaned across the table. "I think *you're* the one who calls me Mr. Oblivious."

I shrugged. "Maybe, but with good reason." I took a sip of my soda. "I mean, come on, buying a boat for our anniversary, knowing that I had never even been on one before—unless you count the log ride at Disney World."

"But you love *Marjorie Jane* now, don't you?"

"Love's a strong word. I love Mrs. Moto and I love you." I untied the red ribbon from the heart-shaped box and peeked inside. "And, of course, I love chocolate."

"Aren't you going to eat the rest of your fish first?"

"Nah, let's take that home for Mrs. Moto. She'll be starving by the time we get back."

I popped one of the chocolates into my mouth. "Mmm...delicious." Scooter stared at me with those dark-brown puppy-dog eyes of his that I have trouble resisting. I pushed the box toward him. "Go on, you can have *one*, provided you agree that we're *not* selling the cottage and that I'm *not* giving up my collection of boots."

Scooter started to take one of the chocolates out. I pulled the box back toward me. "Promise first."

"Okay, I promise," he said, snatching it back and quickly grabbing a cherry-filled one. "But I still don't understand why you have all those boots. We've been living in Florida for almost a year. The only thing I see on your feet lately are flip-flops."

"You never know, it might snow here. You know what they say about climate change."

Scooter laughed. "I'll remind you about that the next time you're complaining about being too hot."

"See, another reason why we shouldn't sell the cottage—air conditioning. All *Marjorie Jane* has going for her is some really disgusting mold growing on her deck."

"Pass me a coconut-filled one," Scooter said. "It seems appropriate, since we live in Coconut Cove."

"No problem. You can have them all." Scooter's eyes lit up. "No, not all the chocolates, just the gross ones. I still can't believe they couldn't come up with a more original name for this town."

"I don't know, the tourists like the name. Plus, it kind of fits, considering how many accidents there are each year with coconuts falling down and injuring people."

I shuddered. "Let's not talk about that. It reminds me of how I was attacked after we first got *Marjorie Jane*. I still can't believe everyone thought it was just a coconut that fell off a tree and hit me on the head."

Scooter slid off his bench and sat next to me on mine. He pushed a lock of my frizzy mousy-brown hair behind my ear, then kissed me on my forehead. "I'd be happy to never talk about that again or the fact that you were almost killed. Swear to me you won't get mixed up investigating any more murders."

"Coconut Cove is a small town. What are the chances that anyone else would get murdered here?"

Scooter put his arm around my shoulders, and we snuggled while watching the moonlight dancing on the water. We had decided to have a low-key Valentine's Day celebration with our picnic of fish-and-chips in the waterfront park. From our vantage point, I could just about make out the mooring field, with boats bobbing gently up and down in the water, and the Palm Tree Marina, where our sailboat was berthed.

Despite the fact that *Marjorie Jane* and I weren't exactly BFFs, I did enjoy watching other boats out on the water and when they came into port. *The Codfather*, a large blue charter fishing boat, had tied up at the dock a few minutes earlier.

A lanky young guy with short red hair and a sunburn to match was busy carrying a cooler over to a fish-processing station, while an older man wearing a floppy hat and long-sleeved shirt helped two couples disembark. One of the women seemed grateful to be on land again.

"Liam, do you mind getting Lisa's backpack from the boat?" the older man asked, his nasal voice ringing out across the waterfront. "She's not feeling well."

"Sure thing, Uncle Norm," he replied.

As he walked back toward *The Codfather*, another charter boat, *Nassau Royale*, inched into the slip next to theirs. It was captained by a short, wiry black man with dark-gray hair. "Hey, Liam, do us a favor and take that line from Darren," he yelled out, pointing to the bow of his boat. His accent reminded me of past vacations in the islands. A young man with dreadlocks, who appeared to be the same age as Liam, was poised to toss the line down to the dock.

Liam scowled. He leaned over the side of his boat, grabbed the backpack off one of the bench seats, then walked up the dock, ignoring the cries from *Nassau Royale*.

The captain shook his head in disbelief. "What is wrong with that boy?"

"Don't worry, I've got it," Darren said. He jumped off the boat, quickly tied the bow line to the cleat on the dock, and secured the stern.

The older man handed him some gear. "Looks like Liam's uncle's bad habits are rubbing off on him. No respect for his elders. No nephew of mine would have an attitude like that. Isn't that right?"

Darren smiled. "Of course not, Uncle Melvin."

"I can't believe he treated you like that. You two are supposed to be friends."

Darren shrugged. "We are, I guess."

"I imagine things have changed since you were in high school." Melvin wiped his brow with a towel. "Help an old man down," he said. Darren pulled the side of the boat closer while his uncle stepped onto the dock.

I nudged Scooter. "Did you hear him call the older man 'Uncle Melvin?'" I whispered. "Do you think he's the same Melvin who runs your favorite store, Melvin's Marine Emporium?"

"Hmm. Could be. Which reminds me, I heard they're having a sale."

"Shush, I want to hear what they're saying."

Scooter poked me in the ribs. "No, you just don't want to talk about spending money on boat equipment."

We watched as Melvin walked to the end of the dock. He pointed at Norm chatting with the two couples. "If he thinks he's going to be the only charter business in town, he's got another thing coming," he said to Darren. "Especially after this morning when he poached *our* customers, getting them to go out on *his* boat instead of ours. He's been trying to sabotage my business ever since I got back from the Bahamas." He rubbed his temples. "It was foolish for us to go out fishing today without any paying customers. We barely caught anything. Think of all that money we spent on diesel. It would have been easier just to pour it down the drain."

"Don't be like that," Darren said. "You needed a break from everything. Besides, it was nice to spend time with my favorite uncle."

The older man smiled. "You're just saying that so you don't

have to wash down the boat." He wagged his finger. "But you're still going to."

Norm and Liam waved goodbye to the two couples, handing them a bag full of cleaned and filleted fish. As they made their way back to *The Codfather*, Norm elbowed Melvin in the stomach. Melvin seized him by the arm and shoved him backward, knocking the hat off his head into the water. Norm pulled his arm away and made a fist. His nephew gripped him by the shoulder.

"It's not worth it," Liam said. He pointed over at where Scooter and I were sitting. "Especially with witnesses."

Norm cupped his hand to his mouth and yelled, "Are you enjoying the show? Should I get you some popcorn? How about a couple of drinks?"

I started to hold up my empty soda can, when Scooter snatched it out of my hand. "Knock it off," he whispered. "Don't make him angrier."

After looking at us with daggers in his eyes for a moment, he turned back to Melvin. "I've told you once, and I'll tell you again—don't mess with me or my family. There's only room in this town for one fishing charter business, and it's mine!"

CHAPTER 2
THAT SINKING FEELING

"WE'RE ALMOST THERE," I SAID to the ball of fur perched on my shoulder and meowing loudly into my ear. Scooter turned into the parking lot of the Palm Tree Marina and pulled into a shady spot. I clipped Mrs. Moto's leash onto her harness, opened the car door, and set her gently on the ground. She ran toward the path that led down to the marina, pulling me along with her. You might not think a cat could drag a human behind them, but they're surprisingly strong when single-mindedly focused on their destination or chasing a lizard.

"She's a real marina cat, isn't she?" Scooter asked. "She loves poking around the docks, jumping on boats, chasing seagulls, and begging for treats from the tourists." He nudged me. "I think she'd vote for selling the cottage and moving onto *Marjorie Jane*. If she could talk, that is." The calico twined herself around his legs and made a chirping noise.

I stifled a laugh. "Allow me to translate. She said that she has no intention of downsizing her collection of catnip mice and giving up her air-conditioned house. That makes two against—and only one for—selling the cottage."

Scooter pushed his tortoiseshell glasses up his nose and glanced down at the leash twisted around his feet. "You women always stick together, don't you?"

After he untangled himself, we walked across the patio, nodding at people sipping on their coffees and enjoying the morning before it became too hot later in the day. Before we'd left for the marina, my husband had thoughtfully made me a mocha with a double shot of espresso, which would keep me going until lunchtime.

Scooter had a lot on his plate lately with work, and as a result, we hadn't been down to see the boat for over a week. This meant that there was some serious boat withdrawal going on—on his part, not mine.

I don't know if you've ever seen someone suffer from this affliction. It's not pretty, trust me. He had given up his beloved Froot Loops and had started eating Cap'n Crunch cereal practically nonstop to lift his nautical spirits. And I had caught him watching sailing videos on his laptop at two o'clock in the morning the other night while he and Mrs. Moto shared a bowl of cereal. He'd take a spoonful, then wait while she lapped up some milk. When I expressed surprise that he was eating from the same dish as the cat, he shrugged and said, "I didn't think she'd mind."

I don't know what was worse—that he had eaten an entire box of Cap'n Crunch in one sitting and would be complaining about a tummy ache the next day or that the YouTube vloggers were so impossibly young and good-looking. Seriously, who looks that gorgeous after they've been on a boat all day? No one, that's who. You inevitably end up with grease stains on your clothes, scrapes, bruises, and sweat dripping everywhere. If anyone tells you that sailing is a glamorous lifestyle, they've clearly never been on a boat. Sadly, I'd become all too well acquainted with the reality of boats over the past few months.

After spending a few minutes standing on the boardwalk and watching the tourists strolling on the beach, Mrs. Moto insisted that we remove her harness and leash. Before we'd adopted her, she had lived on a boat at the marina and had free run of the place. While she reluctantly accepted being restrained elsewhere, she refused to put up with our nonsense here.

She scurried away ahead of us toward B Dock, where we kept *Marjorie Jane*, while we trailed behind her. When the dilapidated sailboat came into sight, my husband let go of my hand, rushed past Mrs. Moto, and had what amounted to a tearful reunion with the other woman in his life. If he could have hugged her, he would have. But since she was thirty-eight feet long, he couldn't quite get his arms all the way around her.

Personally, I didn't get it. All I saw was red paint flaking off the hull, weather-beaten teak decks, and an old, rusty anchor at the bow. You would have thought that—considering all the money we had spent on her to date—she would have looked a lot better by now.

As I was thinking about our latest credit card statement, someone tapped me on the shoulder. "Hey there. I haven't seen you guys in a while." I turned and saw Ben Moretti, a wannabe pirate who lived on a sailboat that rivaled *Marjorie Jane* in the fixer-upper category. "She's sure been missing you," he said, pointing at my nemesis.

"I'd say the feeling is mutual," I said. "At least on Scooter's part. See him fawning over her?"

I tore my eyes away from the scene and looked at Ben. Something was different. Greasy brown hair tied back in a ponytail—check. Ripped khaki shorts—check. Goofy smile—check. Ah, that was it. "New T-shirt?" I asked.

"Yeah. How'd you know?"

"It's clean, and there aren't any holes."

Ben chuckled. "That's true. It's hard to keep things looking brand new when you work in a boatyard. Maybe I should change into something else and save this one for a date."

"Date? Who's the lucky girl?"

Ben gazed down sheepishly at the ground. "No one yet. But there is someone I'm thinking of asking out."

"Well, you might want to think about a different shirt before you do. I'm not sure one that says 'Pirates get all the booty' next to a picture of a scantily clad girl is the way to go."

He glanced down at his shirt and frowned. "Hmm...I hadn't thought about that."

Scooter looked over at Ben. "Just the person I wanted to see! I was over at Melvin's the other day, and I saw they had a sale on tung oil varnish. I wanted to get your thoughts on whether you think that's the right way to go."

While the two of them debated the pros and cons of synthetic wood finishes, I stifled a yawn and kicked my flip-flops off. The last time I had tried to get on the boat wearing them, one of them had fallen off into the water, and I had to scramble to get it out before it drifted out into the bay.

"I'm going to open the hatches up and air this place out," I said. I climbed up onto the boat, adding a new bruise to the collection on my shin. Mrs. Moto executed a graceful leap on board, then stretched out on a tattered cushion in the cockpit. I gave her a quick scratch behind her ears before unlocking the boat.

I cautiously made my way down the narrow ladder into the cabin below and stepped onto the floor, straight into a puddle. This was not good. While I didn't know a lot about boats, I did know one thing—water belonged on the outside of the boat, not the inside.

After turning on the overhead light to see exactly what was going on, I ended up sliding on the floor and landing on my butt with a thud. *Great, now it wasn't just my feet that were wet.*

I ran my fingers through my hair, which I realized was probably a stupid thing to do—who knew what was in that puddle?—and assessed the situation.

There was at least three inches of water above the floorboards. Or maybe it was three centimeters. My mom and I were planning a trip to Canada, and I'd been trying to get the hang of the metric system, but I had to admit that it wasn't going all that well. In any event, there was water everywhere, which wasn't good, no matter what units of measurement you used. Thankfully, she was on a trip in Europe for the next few weeks and didn't know how to use her cell phone over there. Otherwise, she'd have been texting me constantly during the day, as she usually did, so I was glad I didn't have to explain the latest issue with *Marjorie Jane* to her.

As I got to my feet, Mrs. Moto scrambled down the ladder and leaped onto one of the couches. The way she was staring down at the water, it seemed like she expected some fish to swim by any moment now.

I called out to Scooter. "You'd better get down here. We've got a problem." I put my purse on the galley counter, grabbed a dish towel, and wiped my hands.

"I'll be down in a minute, my little panda bear."

I glanced at the water again. "I'm not sure we have a minute."

The boat rocked back and forth in her slip as Scooter climbed aboard. He poked his head down the companionway. "What's going on?"

I pointed at the floor. Scooter gasped, uttered a few curse words that would have made any salty sailor proud, and scrambled down the ladder, splashing water onto Mrs. Moto. She did not seem amused.

"Ben, get down here!" Scooter yelled. "Now!" He put his head between his hands and whimpered.

"Here, sit down next to Mrs. Moto," I said as I led him to the couch. I reached into my purse and pulled out a pack of M&M'S. Scooter doesn't deal well when things get dicey. I've found that having an emergency stash of chocolate comes in handy in circumstances like these. He popped several pieces into his mouth while Ben made his way aboard.

"That's not good," Ben said. He leaned down and flipped a switch on the wall near the galley. "I wonder why the bilge pump isn't coming on."

Scooter crumpled up the empty bag in his hand and looked at Ben with a worried expression. "It isn't?"

Ben fiddled with the switch. "Nope, it isn't. I guess it's one more thing to add to your to-do list."

"Is the boat going to sink?" Scooter asked. He wrapped his arms around himself and rocked back and forth while Ben pulled up an access panel on the floorboards, peered into the bilge, and examined the pump.

"Well, the water doesn't seem to be rising, so that's a good sign." Ben ducked into the passageway and opened up the engine compartment. "It doesn't look like the water has gotten into here, which is a plus."

Scooter held up the empty M&M'S bag with a pleading expression in his eyes.

"Sorry, I'm out of chocolate," I said, squeezing his shoulder.

Ben walked back into the main cabin. "Maybe your water tanks are leaking. Or maybe it's because of those heavy storms we had last week. Water could be coming in through the deck." He glanced down at the floor. "Tell you what—why don't you taste the water? If it's salty, then you'll know it's coming in from outside the boat. If it's fresh, then you'll know it's not."

Scooter cocked his head at me.

I shook my head. "You've got to be kidding. I'm not going to do that. You do it."

"No way," he said. "Not after I ate all that chocolate." He turned his gaze to Ben.

Ben shrugged, bent down, and stuck his finger in the water. He put it in his mouth. "Can't really tell. Listen, you were saying you needed to do work on the bottom. Why don't you just get the boat hauled out now and take her into the boatyard? That way you can find out for sure what's causing the leak. Give the office a call and see if the Travelift is free. Just make sure you tell them it's an emergency."

"What exactly is a Travelift?" I asked.

"It's a big blue crane-like thing with straps." He paused and rubbed his chin. "I'm really not sure how to describe it. Basically, it lifts boats out of the water and moves them around on land."

"Sounds weird," I said.

"Well, you'll see it soon enough," Ben said.

Scooter got out his phone and had a quick conversation. "Okay, they can pull us out now," he said.

Ben clapped his hands together. "Good. Let's get this baby fired up."

As he and Scooter tried to start the engine, I began to feel pangs of guilt. What if I were responsible for the leak aboard *Marjorie Jane*? After all, just last night I had been thinking about different ways to get rid of her, including having her spring a leak and sink to the bottom of the sea. Did some vindictive mermaids use their ESP to read my thoughts? Did they decide to teach me a lesson by convincing a shark to chew a hole in *Marjorie Jane*'s hull? But, more importantly, would our insurance company pay up if she sank before we could haul her out?

* * *

Thankfully, *Marjorie Jane*'s engine sputtered to life. We hadn't fired up the boat since we'd bought her a few months ago.

Come to think of it, there were a lot of things we hadn't done since we'd bought the boat, like take her out of the slip.

"Okay, here goes nothing," Scooter said as he started to reverse the boat.

"Watch out to your port," Ben said frantically as a wood piling came precariously close. "Put it in neutral, quick!"

I shut my eyes and clutched my hands together. While I didn't see the boat hit the piling, I felt the thud. Mrs. Moto yowled and cowered in my lap.

I breathed a sigh of relief as I heard Ben tell Scooter that it seemed like a minor scrape. *What's one more dent?* Marjorie Jane *already makes us look like trailer trash at the marina with all the marks on her hull. This one will just blend in with the others*, I thought to myself.

"I guess he's a little rusty," Ben said in an effort to calm my nerves. Or maybe it was to calm his nerves. I wasn't sure.

I rubbed my temples. "I'm not sure a little rusty actually covers it. Completely oxidized would be more like it. I don't know when the last time was that Scooter drove a boat. Certainly not in all the time we've been married, and that's been ten years now."

Ben gulped. "Scooter, want me to take over?"

I watched as Scooter gripped the wheel tightly and stared straight ahead. "No, it's okay. It's a straight shot from here to the haul-out area." I think the last thing he wanted to do was admit to Ben that he was in over his head.

As we passed by other boats, people waved at us and yelled out encouragement. "Finally taking *Marjorie Jane* out for her first sail?" "You're going the wrong way—the open water is that way." "Whoa, that was awfully close." "Hey, watch where you're going! You almost hit my stern!"

"It's a shame the first time you're taking *Marjorie Jane* out is because she has a leak," Ben said. He reached down and playfully batted at Mrs. Moto's cute little rabbit-like tail, which was a hallmark of Japanese bobtails. She was so entranced by the other boats that she didn't even notice.

After we passed the dinghy dock and the fuel dock, a blue fishing boat cut in front of us and slipped into the area where they haul boats out.

"Hey, isn't that *The Codfather* from last night?" I asked. "The captain is one of the guys who got into a fight. Can you believe he just cut right in front of us?"

"I'm busy trying to steer the boat," Scooter said. "I can't check to see who that is. But whoever it is, that was a really crappy thing to do."

Ben leaned forward to get a closer look. "Yeah, that's Norm Thomas's boat. It doesn't surprise me in the least. He's such a jerk."

"I recognize him too," I said, pointing at a young sunburned guy with short red hair who was standing on the dock. "He was there last night. Norm is his uncle."

"Yeah, I know him as well. We went to high school together." Ben walked out to the bow and yelled down at Liam. "Hey, man, what's going on? These folks arranged for an emergency haul-out. Tell your uncle he has to wait his turn."

The redhead sneered. "First come, first served." He glanced at *Marjorie Jane* dubiously. "I'm surprised that thing is even floating. I still can't believe anyone would be suckered into buying this excuse for a sailboat."

Scooter looked like steam was coming out of his ears. He gripped the steering wheel so tightly that I thought he might bend the metal. "She's a great boat, bud," he snapped. "She just needs a little TLC. Now get that other boat out of the way, so we can get hauled out before we sink!"

Liam laughed. "Nah, you can wait. That's what bilge pumps are for. Besides, we're running a business. Time is money, you know."

He sauntered over to *The Codfather* and had a few words with his uncle, pointing back at us occasionally. Then he walked over to the Travelift operator and handed him something.

"What was that?" I asked. "Did he just bribe him?"

Ben shook his head. "Nah, I don't think it was a bribe, just a tip. Lots of folks tip those of us who work at the marina." He grinned. "I know I sure like it when it happens. Keeps me in beer."

"Ben, what are we going to do here?" Scooter asked anxiously.

"Hang on a bit. Let me go check down below." After a few minutes, Ben popped his head back up. "It looks okay. The water doesn't seem to be rising. Why don't we tie her off here and wait for them to come haul you out when they're done with Norm's boat?"

"Wait? Why should we have to wait?" I asked. "That Norm guy is really getting on my nerves."

"Well, don't take it personally," Ben said. "He treats everyone that way. He thinks that because he's a successful businessman, he's in charge of the town."

"Can you really make that much money from running a fishing charter business?" Scooter asked. I was relieved to notice that his grip on the wheel had loosened slightly.

"Oh, that's just one of four charter boats he owns. Plus, he has his finger in a lot of other pies in town. That guy is ambitious. If he had his way, he'd own everything in Coconut Cove."

While Ben and I got *Marjorie Jane* tied off, I thought about how Norm had threatened to drive Melvin out of business the previous night. Exactly how far would he go?

* * *

As I walked across the patio, a group of kids tore past me. One of the girls glanced back as she reached the top of the steps, which led down to the beach. "Hi, Miss Mollie! Where's Mrs. Moto?"

"She's on the boat," I said. "I'll tell her you said hi, Katy."

"Can I come visit her later?"

"Of course, anytime." I looked over at the marina office. "But maybe we should keep that between you and me. You know how your grandmother feels about cats."

She giggled and raced down the stairs to catch up with her friends.

I watched as the sailing instructor, Penny Chadwick, attempted to corral them. "All right, kids, settle down," she yelled with an adorable Texan twang in her voice. The kids bounced up and down while she briefed them on the morning's activities.

My weekly ladies' sailing lessons with Penny were very different—less youthful exuberance and more complaints about muscle aches and knee replacements. Having only recently celebrated my fortieth birthday, my joints were still working adequately, but *Marjorie Jane* seemed to be trying her best to change that. Crawling in and out of confined spaces to fix things and doing yoga-like moves getting on and off the boat were starting to take their toll.

Although we might not have showed it in the same way, I think we had as much fun as the children did. It really was exhilarating to take Penny's boat out into the bay and feel the wind in her sails. While I wasn't very fond of *Marjorie Jane*, I had learned to appreciate the joy of sailing over the past few months.

I took a deep breath and summoned up my courage to face Katy's grandmother. Nancy Schneider and her husband, Ned, owned and managed the marina. They were close to retirement age, but they loved running their own business too much to consider selling it.

While Nancy oversaw day-to-day operations with an iron fist, Ned was more easygoing, the type of guy who couldn't even hurt a fly. Not that flies would get anywhere close to the marina office these days—word had gotten out about Nancy's exceptional talents when it came to wielding a flyswatter.

As I opened the screen door to the office, I saw a sign stuck in the middle of the carefully manicured flower bed that read "Gone Fishing with Norm's Charters." I reached over and spun it around to face the wall. Yes, it was a bit petty, but I should get some credit for not ripping it out of the ground and hurling it in the trash.

"Why is that door ajar? Are you coming in or out?" a shrill voice yelled from inside.

I stepped inside and quickly shut the door behind me. Nancy peered at me over her reading glasses. The look in her intense blue eyes caused me to stop slouching and stand at attention.

"Yes, what can I do for you, Mollie?" She tapped her long, exquisitely manicured fingernails on the counter. I think she liked the slight intimidation factor her nails had on people. I'd seen large men cower when she jabbed her talons in their direction to emphasize her point. "You haven't jammed quarters in the washing machine, too, have you?" she asked.

"Huh? I have a perfectly good machine at home. Why would I need to do laundry here?" I asked. I felt guilty despite the fact that I hadn't done anything wrong.

A young woman approached the counter. "Nancy, for the last time, I'm really sorry." She tucked her long glossy black hair behind her ears and straightened her shoulders. "But it wasn't my fault that someone gave me a Bahamian quarter. They're the same size. How was I supposed to know it would mess everything up?"

"Well, dear, if it were me, I would look at the coins *before* I put them in the washing machine." She pursed her lips, then added, "But that's just me. I'm sure Mollie would agree, wouldn't you?" I reluctantly nodded. I really didn't want to get caught in a squabble over foreign coins. "You know Leilani, don't you?" Nancy asked.

The woman's glittering necklace caught my eye. "Yes. I've seen you around the marina. You're Mrs. Diamond," I said.

She cocked her head to one side. "No, it's Mrs. Choi, actually. But it feels weird when someone calls me that. I always think they're referring to my mother-in-law instead. Just call me Leilani." She smiled. "I'd shake your hand, but...well..." She held up her right arm, which was encased in a cast that extended above her elbow.

"Ouch. How did that happen?"

Leilani grimaced. "I fell off the ladder trying to get on our boat. Fortunately, I only broke the one arm, but my other one still got pretty banged up." She certainly did have a lot of bruises on her wrist.

I thought about getting on and off *Marjorie Jane* at the dock. Sure, it was a pain, but I wasn't convinced that a ladder would help. When I asked Leilani about it, she smiled.

"No, we've got a ladder because we're on the hard," she said.

"I know what you mean. I'm flabbergasted at how much it costs to have a boat. It seems like everyone is hard up at the marina." I furrowed my brow. "Although I'm not sure how a ladder would help when it comes to paying the credit card bills. Unless, of course, you're talking about climbing the corporate ladder." I shuddered as I remembered my days working as a temp in cubicles for big companies. The thought of spreadsheets, dress codes, and only getting thirty minutes for lunch was enough to make me break out in a cold sweat.

Leilani laughed. "No, we're not hard up," she said. "Our boat is out of the water and on the hard in the boatyard." I didn't have a clue what she was talking about, and I guess my expression must have given me away because she added, "You know how the boats are propped up on jack stands?" I shook my head. "You know the metal stands they place around a boat's keel to keep it from toppling over?"

Nancy gave a dry chuckle. "You'll have to excuse Mollie. She's new to boats."

"Well, there's no way you can get on a boat without a ladder or steps of some kind," Leilani said. "We're on a catamaran, so we don't have as far to climb. Only about five feet, but I'm living proof that you can still do a lot of damage from that distance. Some of the other boats in the boatyard have a ten-foot drop."

"The boatyard can be a dangerous place," Nancy said. She pointed at a series of binders on a shelf behind the counter. "That's why we have so many safety rules and regulations in place. People complain about them. I don't know why they don't realize that they're for their own good."

"Nancy, it wasn't a safety issue. It was pure clumsiness on my part. A dog barked and it startled me. I lost my grip, and well...you know what happened next." Nancy's eyes narrowed. "I'd better go get my clothes out of the dryer," Leilani said hastily.

"That's probably a good idea, dear," Nancy said.

"By the way, who's Mrs. Diamond?" Leilani asked me as she reached out to open the door.

"Oh, that's you. At least, that's what I used to call you, on account of your diamond necklace. I saw your husband give it to you over a romantic dinner at Chez Poisson a few months ago. We were sitting a couple of tables away."

The young woman smiled. "Oh, that was such a magical night. Ken really outdid himself with my birthday present this year." I put my fingers to my own necklace—a lighthouse pendant with a small diamond representing its beacon. Scooter had outdone himself as well when he'd given it to me as a belated anniversary gift. Far better than any dilapidated sailboat.

"Enough talk about jewelry," Nancy snapped. Leilani

slipped out the door while I turned back to the counter. "Why exactly are you here?" she demanded.

"It's about our emergency haul-out," I said. "What happened? Scooter called, told you about the leak, and arranged to get lifted out of the water and taken to the boatyard. But when we got there, Norm cut in front of us, and they hauled him out instead."

Nancy seemed puzzled. "What emergency haul-out? This is the first I'm hearing about it. I'm in charge of the schedule and any exceptions."

"But Scooter said he talked to you."

"Are you saying I forgot a conversation with your husband?"

"It doesn't really matter. The important thing is to get *Marjorie Jane* out of the water before she sinks. Now, when can we—"

The door swung open and Ned rushed in, dripping wet. "Mollie, there you are," he said, gasping for breath. "I'm so sorry about what happened. It's all my fault. I was heading down to tell the guys at the Travelift about your emergency when I tripped and fell in the water." He pulled a cell phone out of his pocket. "I tried to call, but I'm afraid this didn't survive."

"What were you doing making haul-out arrangements?" Nancy asked.

"The phone rang. You were in the back," Ned said as he wrung out his shirt.

"Are you okay?" I asked.

"I think so," he said. "Probably just a few bruises and scrapes."

Nancy reached under the counter and pulled out a rag. "Here, wipe yourself off," she said gruffly. "Then you should go upstairs and change out of those clothes."

As Ned tried to get water out of his ear, Nancy made a call to the Travelift crew. "Okay, they can haul you out in about a half hour. You're lucky. We only have one spot left in the boatyard." She handed me a form and a pen. "Fill this out."

"Can't this wait, Nancy?" I asked. "I really want to go back and give Scooter an update."

"It will just take a minute." She eyed Ned. "If this had been filled out before someone arranged for an emergency haul-out, you wouldn't be in this situation."

Ned threw the rag on the counter. "You and your organization, Nancy. I'm getting sick to death of it." He stormed out of the office, the screen door slamming behind him, leaving me wondering what had happened to the normally mild-mannered Ned.

* * *

"Are you sure those straps are strong enough to hold *Marjorie Jane*?" I asked. "She must weigh a ton."

"Eleven and three-quarters, to be exact," Scooter said.

"You're such a nerd."

My dorky husband smiled as he cleaned his glasses with a cloth. "You didn't seem to complain when we won fifty dollars at that pub trivia contest. And all because I knew that *Isotelus trilobite* is Ohio's official state fossil."

I shrugged. "Okay, so it comes in handy from time to time." I watched as the operator, who was sitting in a cab attached to the side of the large marine hoist, pulled on some levers. *Marjorie Jane* slowly rose out of the water, then dangled in the middle of a large metal frame. "But seriously, what would happen if the straps did break?"

Scooter ran his fingers through his hair. "I don't even want to think about it. We've had enough bad luck today." He looked around. "Where's Mrs. Moto?"

"Ben's got her. He'll meet us in the boatyard."

The operator reversed the Travelift, backing onto a concrete pad. He hopped out of the cab and grabbed a power washer. "This is going to take a while," he said. "See all these barnacles? When's the last time you cleaned the bottom?"

"We just bought her a few months ago. This will be the first time we've done it," Scooter said.

After quite a bit of blasting with water and scraping by hand, the operator stepped back and surveyed his work. "That'll have to do. Looks like you've got a lot of work ahead of you. Most of the bottom paint is gone, and these might be blisters here." He chuckled. "Reckon you'll be spending a long time in the boatyard."

Before he climbed back into the cab, I collared him. "Exactly what happened earlier with *The Codfather?*"

"Whaddya mean?"

"Norm pulled in front of us. We told his nephew that we had a leak and needed to get hauled out, but he acted like he couldn't care less. Didn't you hear us yelling at you that we had an emergency? Then right after that, Liam had a few words with you, maybe slipped you a little something, and next thing you know, they're getting hauled out and not us."

He pulled his arm away. "Listen, lady. I don't know what you're implying, but it was a scheduling snafu. Take it up with Nancy."

"Just let it go," Scooter said. "Come on, let's walk behind and make sure nothing happens." We watched as the Travelift slowly made its way down the road, *Marjorie Jane* swaying gently in the slings as the operator turned into the boatyard.

There were around twenty boats arranged in a U shape around a workshop in the center, all propped up with metal stands and wooden blocks. It looked precarious, to say the least. One stiff breeze coming through this place and I could imagine them all toppling over like dominoes.

My heart sank when I realized the Travelift was headed toward the only empty space in the yard, right between a catamaran named *Mana Kai* and my archenemy, *The Codfather*. After the operator and his assistant positioned *Marjorie Jane* in her spot and propped her up off the ground on jack stands, they unfastened the straps and left us to our own devices.

"Hey, you're that broad who believes in little green men, aren't you?" a nasally voice called out. I glanced up and saw Norm leaning over the side of his boat holding a beer can. "What's the name of your boat, *ET*?" The obnoxious man snickered at his own joke, took a big swig, then burped loudly. He pointed at Scooter. "Want one?" he asked, holding up his can.

"No, I'm good," Scooter said. "Besides, we've got a lot of work to do."

Norm guffawed. "You can say that again. *ET* doesn't look like she'll be flying off into outer space anytime soon."

"Her name isn't *ET*," I said indignantly. "It's *Marjorie Jane*. And she's a fine boat." No one was allowed to say disparaging things about our boat except me.

"How would you know? Women don't have any place on boats. They're bad luck." He added with a smirk, "Unless, of course, they're paying customers. But that's where I draw the line. Women certainly shouldn't be in the boatyard. They don't have a clue about how to fix anything on a boat."

"I have just as much right to be on this boat as my husband does. And I can fix anything that he can."

"Oh yeah? Are you going to be the one who paints the bottom?" he asked doubtfully.

"I am. It's my project."

Scooter's mouth fell open. I had been doing my best to avoid boat projects ever since we'd got this wreck. Now here I was volunteering to lead one. I stepped back and stared at *Marjorie Jane*. I had never seen her out of the water before. The bottom half looked massive. I hadn't painted anything since kindergarten, and that was with finger paints. How in the world was I going to manage this?

"Hah, I don't think you'll last two hours." Norm crushed

his empty beer can with one hand, then tossed it on the ground. "Make that two minutes."

"Well, I will. You'll see."

"Want to make a little wager?"

Scooter whispered in my ear, "That's enough, Mollie, you've made your point."

I put my fingers on his lips to shush him, then turned back to Norm. "Sure," I said. "If I paint this bottom, then you have to name your boat *ET*."

"You're on. And if you lose, you have to paint the bottom of my boat."

"Deal."

Norm grinned. "See those paint cans down there under my boat? You'll need those when you lose." He pulled his phone out of his pocket. "Guess I'll call Liam and tell him he can cross the bottom paint job off his list."

"That's one guy you don't want to make angry," a voice said behind us. I turned and saw Leilani struggling to carry a laundry bag with one hand.

"Here, let me help you with that," Scooter said. He took the bag from her. "Where to?"

"Right here," she said, pointing at the catamaran. "Looks like we're neighbors. Did I hear that right? You made a bet with Norm about bottom painting?"

I put my head in my hands. "I guess so. Sometimes I'm a little..."

"Impulsive?" Scooter suggested gently. He glanced at Leilani and smiled. "Sometimes it gets her in trouble, but it is one of her best qualities. It's probably why we have so much fun together."

I walked over and picked up a paint can. "These are heavy."

"Twenty-three pounds, to be exact," Scooter said. "The anti-fouling chemicals they add to the paint to keep stuff from growing on the bottom add about nine pounds. So a can of that is much heavier than your average house paint."

"You're just hoping that will come up in a trivia contest, aren't you?" I asked with a smile.

"Not only are they heavy, they're also expensive," Leilani said. "They're having a sale at Melvin's right now. You might want to get some before the price goes back up."

"Why don't I take this bag up onto your boat? It's going to be hard enough for you to climb up with that cast as it is," Scooter offered.

"Oh, you don't need to worry about that. I see my husband over there. He can take care of it." I looked over and saw a young man with dark hair carrying a briefcase. "He just got back from giving a lecture about sea turtle nesting patterns at the community college." She looked at him proudly. "Ken's a marine biologist. We met right after he finished his PhD." She waved at him with her good arm, then frowned. "I wonder what's going on."

Her husband had set his briefcase on the ground and was standing stiffly while a young man with dreadlocks gripped his shoulder and whispered something in his ear.

"Hey, isn't that one of the guys from last night?" I asked Scooter.

"Yeah, I think so."

"Do you know Darren?" Leilani asked.

"No, we haven't been formally introduced," I said.

"He's normally a nice guy. I'm not sure what's gotten into him," she said. She watched anxiously as Darren jabbed her husband in the chest. He gave Ken a mock salute, then walked toward the entrance to the boatyard. Ken clenched his fists, then caught sight of Leilani. He gave her a weak smile before picking up his briefcase and coming to join us.

"What was that about?" Leilani asked after giving him a kiss.

"Nothing," he said.

"It didn't look like nothing."

"Babe, don't worry—" Ken's phone beeped. I watched the color drain from his face as he read a text message. He shoved the phone back into his pocket. "It's nothing," he said with a note of finality.

But I wasn't so sure it was nothing, especially when I spied Darren standing by the workshop, holding his phone, watching Ken, and looking very pleased with himself.

CHAPTER 3
THE DATING GAME

MRS. MOTO PADDED ALONGSIDE ME as we made our way down the boardwalk at the marina. When we neared the stairs that led down to the beach, she stopped, crouched down, and slowly inched toward the top step.

"I bet you want to go and harass those seagulls, don't you?"

She gazed up at me and made a chirping noise.

"Okay, but don't stay too long. Otherwise, you'll miss out on all the bits of hamburgers and hot dogs that people 'accidentally' drop on the ground for you."

She meowed in agreement, then sneaked down the stairs. Both the calico and I looked forward to the potluck and barbecue that the marina hosted every Friday night. Ned and Nancy provided the meat, and everyone else brought a side dish or dessert to share. I walked toward the buffet table, occasionally pausing to chat with some of the friends we'd made since owning *Marjorie Jane*.

"Humph. Store-bought brownies again?" Nancy asked,

noticing the distinctive purple box from Penelope's Sugar Shack I was holding. She shook her head and gave me one of her patent-pending tsk-tsk sounds. "You have crumbs on your shirt, dear."

I looked down at my top and saw a chocolate chip precariously balanced on my collar. If there hadn't been any witnesses, I probably would have plucked it off and popped it into my mouth. No point wasting perfectly good chocolate.

Nancy interrupted my thoughts about how to discreetly rescue the chocolate morsel. "How many brownies did you eat on the way to the marina this time?"

"I don't know what you're talking about," I said, brushing the crumbs off my shirt and saying a silent farewell to the chocolate chip as it fell to the ground.

"Last week, Penelope told me you bought two dozen brownies. When I opened the box, there were only twenty inside. That means four were unaccounted for."

"Wow, you've got some impressive math skills, Nancy. Must come in handy when you're counting up all the quarters from the washing machines and dryers." I gave her an appraising look. "How do I know *you* didn't make off with the missing brownies? Everyone knows how much you love chocolate."

"Don't change the subject, dear," she said. As I started to place the box on the table, Nancy pointed at the bowls of pasta salad, coleslaw, and baked beans. "You know the rules. Only side dishes on this table. Desserts go over there. We wouldn't want cross-contamination, would we?"

"As much as I hate to say it, Nancy, I'm on the same page as you when it comes to this. Brownies and vegetables don't go together."

As I put the box on the appropriate table, Nancy said, "For someone who's always bragging about her homemade quadruple-chocolate brownies, you never seem to bring any."

"I just haven't had time to bake lately," I said. "I've been so busy with work since I've been promoted to investigative reporter."

"Ooh, did I hear that right? Are you really a reporter?" Leilani asked as she gingerly set a colorful straw tote bag down at the end of the table.

"It's not what you think, dear," Nancy said. "She doesn't work for a TV station or newspaper. It's with some strange organization. What's it called again, FLAKEOUT?"

I sighed. Although I had become used to people making fun of my career, sometimes their derision was hard to take. "No, it's FAROUT—the Federation for Alien Research, Outreach, and UFO Tracking."

Leilani's eyes lit up. "That sounds fascinating. What kinds of things do you investigate?"

Nancy rolled her eyes. "Why don't you two talk about that somewhere else? I need to get everything organized." She pointed at Leilani's bag. "I assume this is for the potluck?"

Leilani nodded and tried to unzip it with her bruised left hand. "Here, let me," Nancy said. She opened the bag, pulled out a large plastic container, and placed it next to the coleslaw. "How did you manage to carry this down here with just one arm? Why didn't that husband of yours help?" She put her hands on her hips. "I don't know what's with your generation. No sense of chivalry."

Leilani looked down at her cast. "He offered, but I told him I could manage." She pointed over in the direction of the barbecue. "Besides, he's busy helping Ned with the grill." She smiled. "Your hubby is such a sweetheart. I saw him doting on Mrs. Moto earlier. That's something he has in common with Ken—they're both animal lovers."

Nancy pursed her lips. "Well, if Ned knew what was good for him, he'd spend less time with mangy creatures like that cat and more time concentrating on the marina. He was ten minutes late getting the grill set up."

"Relax, Nancy. No one will mind. We're all here to have a

good time," I said. "Besides, it's not like there's a firm schedule for these types of things."

"Of course there is." She pulled a small notepad out of the pocket of her neatly pressed Bermuda shorts. "According to this, I'm five minutes behind getting the buffet table set up. Now shoo, and let me get on with it."

Leilani and I managed to keep from bursting out laughing until we were out of earshot. After we stopped giggling, she said, "Now, tell me all about your job."

"I investigate UFO sightings, alien encounters, that sort of thing. You know, we actually had a case of alien abduction here at the marina when we first bought *Marjorie Jane*."

Leilani's eyes lit up. "I heard about that. Wasn't that all part of the mur—"

I spied Scooter from the corner of my eye and interrupted before she could utter the word "murder." My husband gets a little squeamish when it comes to stuff like this. Even the mere mention of homicides, blood, or corpses can drive him headlong into a bag of chocolate.

"Yes, that's the one. Unfortunately, I wasn't able to prove definitively that the abduction took place. I'm also in charge of community outreach." I swallowed. "I actually have to give my first public lecture next week. I'm so nervous. I've never done anything like that before."

Leilani smiled. "You seem so confident to me. I'm sure you'll be great."

Scooter came up behind me and put his hands on my shoulders. "What will you be great at?" he asked.

"My talk next week."

"Of course you'll be great. You've been practicing for days. I only wish I didn't have that conference call scheduled so I could go."

"I wish you could come too," I said. "I could use the moral support."

"I'll go," Leilani offered.

"Perfect. Now you'll have a friendly face in the audience." Scooter pointed at a table. "Come over and join us. Penny is telling me stories about sailing in bad weather, and Alejandra seems to be...well...wishing she weren't the center of attention. She might need our help to change the topic of conversation."

We had become fond of Alejandra Lopez during our time in Coconut Cove. Not only was the young woman our favorite waitress at the Sailor's Corner Cafe but she had also been sharing family recipes with us and giving us cooking tips.

As we walked over to the table, Leilani told me about her job as a virtual assistant. Although the thought of answering emails, updating spreadsheets, and scheduling appointments didn't sound all that appealing, I did like the fact that she didn't have to change out of her pajamas to start work. All she needed was her laptop and an internet connection.

When we got to the table, I saw that Alejandra was surrounded by three young men—Darren was sitting to her right, Liam to her left, and Ben was standing behind her. I noticed that the wannabe pirate had taken my advice and traded in his "booty" T-shirt for one that featured two cute dolphins diving through the water. What girl could resist dolphins?

Liam was leaning back in his chair, his sunburned arms folded behind his head. "Maybe you could teach Ben a thing or two about manicures," he said to Alejandra. "Just look at all that grease on his hands."

"I work for a living, that's why they're greasy," Ben said gruffly, shoving his hands in his pockets.

Liam pulled out his wallet and waved a wad of cash at Ben smugly. "I work for a living too, and I make a lot more money than you do. You haven't changed at all since high school. Still scrounging around, trying to make ends meet." He glanced over at Alejandra, then back at Ben. "And you don't have a clue how to dress to impress the ladies."

Ben's shoulders slumped. He looked down at his shirt, then

walked to the other side of the table and sat next to Scooter.

Alejandra gave him a smile. "I think you look great, Ben. Did I ever tell you that dolphins are my favorite animal?"

Ben perked up, but before he could respond, Liam leaned in close to Alejandra. "Did you see my new car? How about you and I take her out for a spin after dinner and go for a moonlight stroll on the beach at Treasure Cove?"

She pulled back. "Sorry, I can't. I told Ned and Nancy I'd help them clean up after the barbecue."

"They don't need your help. Look at them." He pointed at Ned, who was taking hamburgers off the grill and placing them on a big platter that Nancy was holding. "They've got it all under control."

"Leave the girl alone," Darren said, pushing his dreadlocks off his face. "She's not interested." He pulled his chair closer to hers. "I'll stay and help you clean up."

Alejandra shrugged. "Sure, I guess. The more the merrier."

He beamed. "Great. Then you'll be done quicker, and afterward *we* can go out for a stroll."

"Hey, if she's going out with anyone, it'll be with me, not you," Liam said.

Alejandra placed her cup on the table. "Stop it! I'm not going out with any of you." She looked firmly at the squabbling duo. "It was bad enough having to put up with you two fighting over me in high school. Aren't you guys ever going to grow up?"

Darren pushed back his chair. He pointed angrily at Liam. "See what you did? We were having a perfectly friendly conversation until you got involved."

Liam rose and advanced toward Darren. "Want to see friendly? What do you say we head down to the beach and talk about this man to man?"

As the two of them lunged toward each other, Scooter pulled Darren back. Ben did the same with the other young man.

"Hey, what's going on here?" Norm strode over to the table. "What did I tell you about getting into fights, Liam? It's bad for business." He gestured at the far side of the patio. "I've got some potential customers lined up over there. What are they going to think if they see their charter boat captain punching some guy's lights out?"

"But—" Liam started to say.

"I don't want to hear your buts. Now, the hamburgers are done," Norm said. "I suggest you go over there, fix yourself a plate, and eat it as far away from here as possible."

Liam looked down at the ground and muttered something. "What was that?" Norm asked.

"Nothing," he spat out, and stormed over to the grill.

Norm turned to Darren. "And you. I should have known *you'd* be involved. You're as bad as your uncle."

"Leave my uncle out of this!"

"Tell that old man to head back to the Bahamas. Things were a lot more peaceful here when he wasn't around."

"Seriously, after all that he's been through, how can you say something like that?" Darren asked, his voice dripping with venom. He grabbed his soda can from the table. "I seem to have lost my appetite." He turned to Alejandra. "Sorry about what happened. I'll make it up to you later."

She nodded. Ben sat down in the chair next to her. "You okay?" he asked.

"I'm fine."

"You know how guys get when there's a pretty girl involved." He reached behind his head and tightened his ponytail. Then he stared at his hands. "Do you really mind the grease? I scrub them after work, but I just can't seem to get it off completely."

Alejandra gave him a gentle smile. "They're fine, Ben. You work hard. It's nothing to be ashamed of."

Ben brightened up. "Cool. Now that they're gone, what do you say to heading over to the Tipsy Pirate later?"

Alejandra shook her head. "Sorry, Ben. Like I said, I'm not really interested in dating anyone at this time. I've got too much going on with waitressing, my business classes, and trying to get my nail salon off the ground."

"How's that going?" I asked.

"Really well," she said, seeming relieved to be talking about something other than her love life. "I'm looking into the licensing requirements and checking out a few potential sites in town. It'll be a while yet before I can quit waitressing, but one of these days."

"You'll do it, sugar," Penny said. "You're determined, hardworking, and smart. Look at me. I'm only in my thirties and I run two businesses now—the sailing school and the boat brokerage. No reason you can't do the same. I bet in ten years' time you'll own half the town."

"Well, I'm not too sure about that. Norm seems to own half the town. I'm surprised he hasn't run for mayor yet."

"Thank goodness he hasn't," Penny said. "I'm not sure Coconut Cove could cope with his style of leadership."

* * *

"Here, kitty, kitty," I called out as we neared the boatyard. "I wonder where she got to," I said to Scooter. "She must be starving. She didn't stick around the patio long enough to get her usual handouts from people."

"Well, with all that commotion going on with the guys fighting, you really can't blame her. It's much more peaceful back here."

The place was deserted. Although a few people lived in the boatyard while they were working on their boats, like Ken and Leilani, Ben had told me that most of the boat owners were locals who went home each night.

We picked our way through the yard, walking around piles of wood, metal jack stands, toolboxes, and a couple of dinghies.

I saw lightning out of the corner of my eye. A few seconds later, a large clap of thunder startled me. As we neared the section where our boat, Norm's boat, and the Chois' boat were located, the overhead lights flickered, then went out.

"Looks like a power outage," I said.

I heard a crashing noise, followed by the sounds of someone in pain.

"Scooter, was that you?"

"Yes, I tripped over something."

I retraced my steps. "Are you okay?"

"I'm fine. Here, help me up," he said, holding out his hand.

"I'm not so sure you're fine. You're favoring your right leg."

"It's okay. I twisted my ankle a little bit. Just need to walk it off." I watched him hobble in the direction of our boat.

"I guess you won't be playing basketball with the guys this week," I said.

"Stop worrying. It's nothing." He glanced up at the sky. "Come on, let's find that cat and get out of here before it starts pouring."

I got a flashlight out of my purse and illuminated our path. When we got to *Marjorie Jane*, the light caught a pair of green eyes staring down at us from the deck. The feline yawned, then stretched her front paws in front of her lazily.

"Are you ready to go home?" I asked.

Scooter climbed partway up the ladder, wincing in pain, and lifted her down to me. "I'm just going to gather a few things off the boat. Why don't you get her ready to go?"

As I tried to hold on to Mrs. Moto while digging in my bag for her harness and leash, a lizard dashed in front of me. The cat squirmed and jumped out of my arms. I sighed as she ran under the boat in pursuit and then into the wooded area at the back of the boatyard.

"Why do you always have to chase things?" I yelled after her. "Just leave that poor lizard alone. It won't be nearly as tasty as one of the cans of Frisky Feline's gourmet delicacies I have waiting for you back at home. Just think, tasty morsels of fish in a savory cream sauce. Sure, it smells disgusting, but the label promises a rich, hearty taste you can't resist."

No response. Maybe I shouldn't have added in that part about how it stunk. I walked carefully toward the edge of the wooded area. I heard a rustling sound to my right. When I pointed my flashlight in that direction, I saw a large object covered in a blue tarp with an overturned paint can lying beside it. Mrs. Moto stood with her back arched next to it, hissing loudly.

"Did that lizard fight back?" I asked her.

She nudged the tarp with one of her paws and yowled.

"What is it, kitty?" I pulled back the tarp, expecting to see a lizard. Instead, I saw Darren, his dreadlocks covered in a mixture of blood and paint. It didn't look like he would be going on any moonlight strolls with a pretty girl on the beach ever again.

CHAPTER 4
THE MOST ANNOYING EYEBROWS EVER

"WHERE IS SHE?" I ASKED impatiently. "She said she would be here at nine and it's already nine thirty."

"Stop pacing, my little panda bear. She'll be here when she gets here. Why don't I make you another mocha while we wait?"

"Fine," I snapped. "I don't even know why she's coming, anyway. I never agreed to sell the cottage and move onto *Marjorie Jane*."

"I told you, I tried to cancel, but she didn't answer her phone, and for some reason it didn't go to voicemail." He ruffled my hair. "You look like you could use some extra chocolate in this one."

I nodded and passed my mug to him. "Sorry I bit your head off. I didn't sleep well. I kept having nightmares about finding Darren underneath that tarp. And if that wasn't bad enough, I also had dreams about cans of paint flying around trying to knock me off the boat."

"Flying paint cans?" Scooter asked as he turned the

espresso machine on.

I shuddered. "Like those flying monkeys from *The Wizard of Oz*. They always creeped me out when I was a child." I sat on one of the barstools at the kitchen counter.

"That does sound bad." Scooter foamed up some milk. "You want full-fat milk, right?"

"Is there any other kind?" I asked.

"Not according to Mrs. Moto. She turns up her nose when I try to give her skim," Scooter said. "We're lucky she can tolerate milk, unlike most cats. Can you imagine if we had to tell her no? We'd have to wear earplugs because she'd scream so much."

"Remember when we told her to stop sharpening her claws on the couch?" I asked.

Scooter sighed. "Yep. That's when she added the armchair to her list of feline-approved scratching posts."

I inhaled the smell of coffee and chocolate as Scooter placed my mug on the counter. But even the tantalizing aroma couldn't help me forget my nightmare. "At least the paint cans didn't have bushy eyebrows like Chief Dalton. I don't think I'd ever be able to sleep again if I had a dream about those. I wonder if there's some sort of class about how to read eyebrows. If he ever lost the power of speech, he could communicate solely with them, like some sort of sign language."

Scooter sat on the stool next to me. "He can't help it if his eyebrows resemble...what is it you always compare them to?"

"Caterpillars. Fuzzy caterpillars. I can't keep my eyes off them. They're mesmerizing, but not in a good way." I blew on my mocha to cool it down. "It wouldn't have been so bad if he hadn't kept asking the same questions over and over." I tried to imitate his gruff voice while raising my eyebrows. "What were you doing in the boatyard at that hour? Did you touch anything at the crime scene? Isn't this the third murder victim you've found in Coconut Cove?" I took a cautious sip from my mug. Nope, still too hot. "It's almost like he thinks I deliberately try to find dead bodies."

Scooter frowned. "Well, I don't think it's deliberate, but you do have a knack for it."

"Hang on a minute—"

The ringing of the doorbell interrupted my retort.

"What a charming little cottage," a voice rang out brightly as the door opened before either Scooter or I could answer it.

An overpowering smell of floral perfume wafted around the corner, followed by a woman who looked to be in her midthirties from a distance, but closer to her late forties up close.

"Panda, this is Suzanne. Suzanne, this is my wife, Mollie."

"Panda. That's adorable," she said. "The only pet name my husband calls me is...well...I probably shouldn't mention it in polite company." She giggled, then extended her hand. "Pleased to meet you," she said. "Your husband has been telling me all about you. Isn't that right, Scooter, darling?"

I was fascinated by her elaborate hairdo. Her auburn hair was piled on top of her head in a manner that could only be achieved with an endless supply of bobby pins and at least two cans of hairspray. She wore a formfitting sheath dress of white linen and teetered on impossibly high stiletto heels.

"Here you go, all my details," she said, handing me a business card. "What's that heavenly smell?"

"Do you mean my mocha?" I asked, although I wasn't sure how she could smell anything over her cloying scent.

"Mmm...yes. A skinny latte would be divine before we begin," she said.

"Don't look at me," I said. "Scooter is the resident barista."

"My, you're such a talented man, aren't you? A successful businessman, and you also make coffee. What else should I know about you?" she asked, squeezing his bicep.

Scooter glanced down at the hand on his arm. "Uh, sure. One latte coming right up," he said, escaping from her grasp.

Suzanne flitted around the kitchen while her beverage was being prepared, regaling me with stories about her real estate career and gossiping about her clients.

"Thank you, darling," she said when Scooter set a mug in front of her. She swirled her latte with a spoon, then took a tiny sip. "This isn't skim milk, is it?" She set the mug back down. "Never mind. Let's have a look around, shall we?" she said as she edged past me into the living room. "Now, I believe you said this was a two-bedroom, two-bath, didn't you?"

"One-and-a-half-bath," Scooter said.

"Hmm. Well, that's not ideal, but we'll find some way to spin it," she said breezily. "This is such a lovely space. So light and airy. I bet the view of the sunset over the water is just magnificent." She pulled a notebook out of her bag and jotted something down. "I think that will be a top selling point."

She perched delicately on the edge of the couch and fiddled with the bracelets around her wrist, then delicately stifled a yawn. "Can you believe the police came to our house to question my husband and me last night? They kept us up so late." She leaned forward and said dramatically, "You did hear about what happened at the marina, didn't you? Someone was murdered!"

"Here, why don't you finish this?" I said, handing Scooter my mug, knowing that talk of homicide would be upsetting to him. "The chocolate should help." He gulped it down in one swallow.

"Yes, we know," I said. "I was the one who actually found the body. Poor guy. He was so young."

"You found Darren? Simply ghastly! I can't imagine how I would have reacted if it were me. Fainted, I suppose. It was a good thing you had such a nice strong man there to help you."

Scooter coughed and gave me a look.

"Oh, I'm not the one who fainted. He did. He landed on the ground before I could catch him." Scooter's look turned into more of a glare. I was beginning to think he didn't want me to tell people about what had happened."

"I didn't faint," he said, giving me yet another pointed look. This one I was able to interpret easily. "I had just twisted my ankle. It went out on me, so I stumbled and fell down."

"That makes much more sense," Suzanne said, her faith in male courage and bravery in the face of dead bodies restored.

"Why did the police question you?" I asked.

"Oh, didn't I say? There was some silly fight at the marina earlier that evening, and for some reason, they thought my husband's nephew might have been involved."

"Liam?" She nodded. "So that means that Norm's your husband?"

"That's right. We're coming up on five years. It's a second marriage for both of us."

"So what do you know about Darren?" I asked.

Suzanne sighed. "Well, I know him a bit. He graduated from high school with Liam and my son, Xander. The three of them used to hang out. We would see Darren at school events, football games, that type of thing."

"Didn't Alejandra go to school with them too?"

"Oh yes. Her family moved to Coconut Cove at the start of high school. She's such a nice girl. She and Liam are really sweet on each other. Who knows, maybe wedding bells in the future?"

"Really? It didn't appear that way last night. She didn't seem to want anything to do with him, especially after that fight between the guys."

"Well, just between you and me, Liam can be a bit of a hothead. He was constantly getting into trouble at school. My son would have been a much better match for Alejandra. They went to prom together, you know. But after graduation, Xander decided to move in with his father back in Arizona and go to college out there. I keep hoping he'll come back to Coconut Cove and help Norm with his businesses. He's got such a good head on his shoulders. Liam's great at the grunt work, but what Norm really needs is someone who can take over when he retires." She sighed. "But all Xander can talk about is how much he loves it out west, so I guess I shouldn't get my hopes up."

Scooter showed her the rest of the house while I tidied up the kitchen. As I poured Suzanne's latte down the drain, I thought about what she had said about Liam's temper. Was it possible that jealousy over Alejandra had driven him to murder Darren?

"This is such a charming house," Suzanne said, interrupting my thoughts. "I love how you've decorated it, Mollie. The baskets with seashells on your nightstands are a cute touch. I'm sure I can get you guys a great price for it, assuming you're willing to move quickly." She set her purse on the counter. "Your delectable husband says you're going to move onto your sailboat. That sounds so romantic. Me, I couldn't do it, but you look like a woman with simpler tastes." She eyed me head to toe the way they do on those TV shows that promise to turn someone frumpy into someone fabulous.

"The only person thinking about moving onto the boat is Scooter. Not me. In fact, it was his idea to have you come see the cottage."

"Oh, don't be silly. I don't believe that for a second." Suzanne opened up the patio door and took in the views of the beach, then turned back to me. "Do you know Leilani Choi?"

"You mean Mrs. Diamond?"

Suzanne furrowed her brow. "Who?"

"Sorry, you mean the woman who broke her arm, don't you?"

"Yes, that's the one. You should talk to her. She and her husband sold their house last year and moved onto their catamaran. I bet she could give you lots of tips about downsizing, having garage sales, paring down what you need to a minimum, that sort of thing. She's a lovely young thing. A bit of a hippie, but a sweetheart. I don't think she owns too many clothes, either. Fashion isn't important to everyone, is it?"

"Why exactly is the market so hot?" Scooter asked, trying to change the subject before I said something he thought I might regret. I'm not sure I would have regretted it, but I'm certain he wouldn't have been pleased.

"Oh, you know, just snowbirds who come down here every year, then decide to sell their property up north and make it a full-time thing. Besides, Coconut Cove is a darling town. We've got lovely restaurants, bars, shops..." She reached over and whispered, "You might check that new boutique out, Mollie. They've got some gorgeous dresses in the window. Men like it when we ladies make an effort." Then in a louder voice she added, "And we're close enough to the big city to stock up on things. It's a wonder the town hasn't grown. It's ripe for development."

"But wouldn't that ruin its charm?" Scooter asked. "My uncle used to own this place, and one of the things he loved about Coconut Cove was the fact that it was a small town. If you let large developers come in, it won't be any different than any other place on the coast. Strip malls everywhere, heavy traffic, and no character. I'd hate to think that's what selling this place would bring to the area."

"See, Scooter, we shouldn't sell," I said enthusiastically. "We don't want that to happen here."

"No, no," Suzanne said in a reassuring tone. "We have strict zoning laws. Nothing like that will ever happen here. It's just that a few snowbirds will move down and splash their money around the town. It'll be good for everyone."

As she went to pick up her purse, her wrist jangled against the counter.

"Your bracelets are quite distinctive. That one in particular," I said, pointing at a heavy gold one laden with charms.

"Isn't it? Every time I make a really big sale, I treat myself to a new charm. See, I even have one of a sailboat. Business has been so good lately that I'll probably have to get another bracelet for my other wrist," she said with a laugh.

"Now, I'll let you two get on with the rest of your day. I'm going to run over to the office and type up all the agreements." She yawned. "Although a nap does sound tempting after all that police questioning."

"The chief does like to ask a lot of questions," I said. "I bet he asked where you and Norm were when Darren was murdered."

"Oh, he did."

"And where was that?"

Suzanne seemed annoyed. "At our office, dear. It's in that building right near Penelope's Sugar Shack. We were both there all night catching up on paperwork. You know how it is when you're a successful businessperson, don't you, Scooter, dear?"

As we walked Suzanne to the door, she told us that she'd send the photographer out the next day to take pictures of the cottage.

"Listen, Suzanne, I appreciate your coming out here, but Scooter and I have a lot to talk about before we move forward. *If* we move forward. So, no photographer," I said.

She winked at Scooter. "Everyone gets cold feet, but once you see that big, fat deposit in your bank account and move onto that cute sailboat of yours, you'll be glad you sold this place."

***

As the door to the Sailor's Corner Cafe swung open, I could smell the aroma of burgers and fries. It helped clear the stench of Suzanne's perfume out of my nostrils.

Alejandra waved to us as she scooted past with a tray full of ice cream sundaes. "*Hola.* Pick any table. I'll be with you in a sec."

We sat at a booth by the window looking out on Main Street. Scooter twisted around to read off the lunch specials from the board by the kitchen. "Okay, they've got minestrone soup, grilled ham and cheese sandwiches, and something called 'Ocean's Delight Stew.' Any of those sound good to you?"

I crinkled my nose. "Ocean's Delight? That sounds like the kind of cat food Mrs. Moto would eat. What do you suppose is in it?"

After Alejandra described what was in the stew, we both opted for the grilled cheese.

"What can I get you to drink?" she asked.

"Root beer for me," Scooter said.

"I'll have an iced tea, please," I said.

"Unsweetened, right?"

"Yes, I get enough sugar elsewhere in my life."

"You know, *chica*, if you live down here in the south long enough, you're going to have to start drinking sweet tea."

"That'll be right after I start eating tofu."

Alejandra smiled as she made off with our menus.

Scooter leaned forward. "Well, what did you think of Suzanne?"

"You're going to have to be a bit more specific. Her fashion sense? Her overuse of the word 'darling'? Her admiration of your biceps?"

Scooter flexed his arm. "Well, I do have nice biceps, but I was thinking more along the lines of her selling our house."

"I just don't get why you're so hot on selling the cottage? The one good thing about having her out this morning was that she pointed out all the great features it has, like the ocean view, how light and airy the rooms are, and how nicely I decorated the place. After hearing all that, why would you want to move onto a cramped sailboat?"

"Because—"

"And it has a washer and dryer. Did you know Leilani and

Ken have to do their laundry in coin-operated machines at the marina?"

"But—"

"And don't even get me started on what happens if you insert the wrong quarters."

Alejandra set our drinks down on the table.

"Can I say something?" Scooter asked after taking a sip of his root beer.

"Sure."

"Remember that article I showed you the other day in that sailing magazine? The one about that couple who sold everything to move aboard their boat, and how much they loved their new lifestyle?"

"You realize that's just propaganda, don't you?"

"No, it was a real story. You should talk to Leilani like Suzanne suggested. She's not a propaganda machine. She can tell you what it's really like. Besides, if we want to sail to the Caribbean or maybe even to the South Pacific, we're going to have to move aboard the boat one of these days."

"Whoa, big fella. One step at a time. The longest cruise we've done on *Marjorie Jane* was from our slip to the Travelift. And you know how well that went. Why don't we go slowly? First things first—we've got to fix up the boat. Then we can take her out for a day, maybe a weekend, and see what that's like. You don't have to jump into everything headfirst, you know."

Scooter smirked. "Isn't that like the pot calling the kettle black? Remember that time you signed up for skydiving lessons before you remembered you're scared of heights?"

"That was different."

"How exactly?"

Fortunately, Alejandra came by with our meals before I had to explain how jumping out of a plane could come in handy in the future.

While we ate our lunch, I looked out the window and

noticed Ben and Liam having an animated discussion across the street. Ben threw his hands up in the air and walked over to the cafe. He saw Alejandra through the window and waved. She nodded and gave him a lukewarm wave in return before going back to taking an order. Undeterred, he came inside and sat down next to me.

"Hey, what's new?" he said as he grabbed a fry off my plate.

"Daring move, Ben," Scooter said.

"Sorry, Mollie," Ben said sheepishly. "I haven't eaten all day."

Alejandra came over to top up my iced tea. "What can I get you, Ben?"

"How about coming to the Tipsy Pirate tomorrow to hear me play?"

"Uh, I can't. I've got to catch up with…" She stared out the window and chewed on her pen, then continued. "With Nancy. We're going to check out some new nail polishes that she ordered." She finished filling up my glass and placed it back in front of me. "Did you want anything to eat, Ben?"

Ben looked downcast. "Nah, I lost my appetite." Alejandra shrugged and bustled over to the kitchen.

"Is this the band you were telling me about?" Scooter asked.

"Yeah. It's me and some high school buddies. We call ourselves Eye Patches and Peg Legs."

"That's an interesting name," I said.

"Do you like it? I had to convince the other guys in the band to go along with it. We play all sorts of stuff, from Jimmy Buffet to Bob Marley. Why don't the two of you come?"

Scooter nodded. "Sure, we'll be there."

Ben smiled, slyly stole another fry, and scooted out of the restaurant.

"Poor Ben," I said. "He just doesn't seem to get a break. First, he was sweet on Penny, and now he's got a thing for

Alejandra. There's this girl in FAROUT who might be perfect for him. I think I heard her mention that she likes rum. That's a pirate drink, isn't it?"

"No matchmaking, Mollie. Just stay out of it."

Screams of laughter erupted in the back section of the restaurant. I glanced over and saw Penny surrounded by several young kids banging their spoons on the table. "Ice cream, ice cream, we all want ice cream!" Alejandra rushed over and grabbed spoons from some of the more rambunctious children. It didn't really help matters. They used their hands to beat on the table while they shouted, "Spoons, spoons, we all want spoons!" What they didn't realize was that you could eat ice cream just as easily with a fork, provided you gobbled it up quickly enough. Trust me, it can be done. If I were them, I would have gone back to chanting about ice cream rather than spoons.

"Look, there's Katy," I said.

Scooter laughed. "Can you picture the expression on Nancy's face if she were here and saw what a mess they've all made of the table? I can't imagine she'd approve."

"Well, Katy is her granddaughter. I'm sure she lets her get away with things no one else would be able to."

I walked over and tugged on one of Katy's braids. "What are you making such a fuss about?"

"Mollie, it's you! Guess what?"

"What?"

"No, you have to guess!"

"You won the lottery?"

"No, don't be silly. Guess again!"

"Your grandmother said you could have a kitten at her place?"

Katy giggled. "Of course not. Grandma doesn't like anything covered with fur, not even Grandpa. Once he let his beard grow for a few days, and she made him shave it off."

"Okay, then you have to tell me. I'm out of guesses."

Penny looked at Katy encouragingly. "Go on. Tell her."

"We won the regional competition! I took first place! Penny is treating us all to hot fudge sundaes as a reward!"

"That's fantastic, sweetheart. I'm sure everyone is so proud of you."

Katy held out her wrist. "Look what else I got—a candy bracelet."

"Oh, I'd love one of those," I said.

"You don't need one. You always wear your necklace with the little lighthouse," Katy said before proceeding to eat some of the candy beads.

I glanced over to Penny. "Sure you can handle this by yourself?"

"Well, it'll be worse for the parents when they pick them up, and they're all hyped-up on sugar."

I felt Scooter put his hands on my shoulders. "I paid the bill. We should probably get going and head over to Melvin's to pick up some supplies while the sale is still on." He rubbed his fingers on the back of my neck. "Hey, where's your necklace?"

I put my hands on my neck. "It's gone!"

***

After a fruitless search for my necklace at the cafe and many tears on my part, we reluctantly gave up and drove over to the marine store.

"Welcome to Melvin's Marine Emporium," Chad said chirpily. He adjusted the name tag on his blue vest, then held out his hand to Scooter. "Nice to see you back here, Mr. McGhie."

"I'm surprised you aren't on a first-name basis by now, considering my husband is in here practically every day," I said.

"That's what we like to see—satisfied return customers,"

Chad said with a big grin on his face. "Now, what can I help you with today, sir?"

Well, of course they were fond of return customers. The whole marine industry depended on repeat business. Everything on a boat broke down frequently, almost as if it had been engineered that way. And while you might pop into Melvin's for the sole purpose of getting a replacement fuse, you usually ended up walking out with a number of items all designed to help you lead a more nautical lifestyle—a holder for your fishing rod that doubled as a beer-can dispenser, a tote bag which could be converted into a bathing suit cover-up or beach hat, and a brass plaque reminding landlubbers not to flush anything down the head unless they'd eaten it first.

Despite the fact that he was still in high school, Chad had a flair for sales, talking customers into buying things they didn't really need. "Did you see the new multipurpose tool we just got in?" he asked Scooter. "Not only does it have a knife, scissors, screwdriver, bottle opener, and tweezers but it's also attached to a floating key chain in the shape of a dolphin. Buy two, and you get the third free."

Chad pointed at a colorful display case. Scooter's eyes lit up. He was in danger of thinking he needed three of them when even one would be overkill. And I don't think he had really thought through the fact that the tool itself was so heavy that there was no way the poor foam dolphin key chain could keep it afloat in the water. That's why I carried the credit cards in my purse and why he wasn't allowed to shop at Melvin's unsupervised anymore.

"Remember, we're just here to get supplies to paint the bottom, nothing else," I said.

"I know, but it can't hurt to look," he said over his shoulder as he went to check out the amazing, once-in-a-lifetime opportunity. He held one up to show me. "Don't you think these would make great Christmas presents?"

"You realize it's only February, don't you?"

"Yeah, but they're on sale now."

While Scooter was trying to decide whether his sister would prefer the blue one or the orange one, I glanced out the window and saw Chief Dalton standing outside talking with Officer Moore. Chad followed my gaze. "Did you hear what happened at the marina?" he asked.

I sighed. "Yes, we did. In fact—"

Chad gasped. "Did you find the body?" I nodded. "Wait a minute," he said. "Didn't you find both of the people who were murdered there a few months ago?"

I nodded again.

"So that makes—"

"Three bodies," I snapped. "Yes, I've found three bodies at the marina."

A couple looking at deck shoes turned and stared at me. Chad struggled with his desire to go over and cajole them into purchasing a few dozen pairs and his desire to know more of the gory details about the murder. Gore won out. He lowered his voice. "So what happened?"

"I'm not sure. I found him at the edge of the boatyard over by the wooded area. He had been covered by a tarp. There was an open can of bottom paint next to him, which had spilled everywhere." I checked to make sure Scooter wasn't in earshot. "From what the chief said yesterday, it appears as though someone hit him on the back of the head with the paint can."

Chad took a step backward. "I hope that paint wasn't bought here. It'd be awful if people associated Melvin's with murder. I'm not sure he could take it, especially after all the trouble he had with the previous store manager."

"I'm sure people don't blame Melvin for what happened before, and no one would think any less of him if the paint came from here."

"I hope you're right. It's bad enough that he has to deal

with the death of his nephew. Imagine how he'd feel if he knew the murder weapon had been purchased here," Chad said. He pointed at his name tag. "Something good did come out of the last manager getting fired. I got a promotion. You're looking at the new assistant store manager. After I graduate high school this year, I'm sure Melvin is going to promote me to store manager."

I smiled at his enthusiasm. I'm not sure I would have the temperament to deal with all the paperwork that went along with managing a store, let alone try to sell stuff to people, but I could see Chad reveling in it. He began telling me about his ideas for inventory management, but I steered the conversation back to the murder. "I didn't know Darren, but from what everyone says around town, he was a nice young man."

"He was always friendly when he came in," Chad said. "But he spent most of his time running Melvin's fishing charter outfit."

"I know that Coconut Cove is a popular tourist town, but is there really enough business to support two fishing charter companies? I saw Darren and Melvin get into an argument with Norm and Liam about it on Thursday night."

"Wasn't that Valentine's Day?" Chad asked. "Did Mr. McGhie give you a nice present?"

"He played it safe this year and got me chocolates."

Chad frowned. "I asked Tiffany to go out with me, but she said she had to work late at Penelope's that night. She always seems to have to work late." Chad reminded me of a younger version of Ben in a way—no luck with the ladies.

"What do you know about Norm and Liam?" I asked to distract him.

"They get a lot of foreign tourists. Liam likes it because he gets really good tips from them. He makes a big production out of filleting their fish when they get back in port, tossing knives between his hands. Then he drops their fish off at Chez Poisson and they cook it up for the tourists."

"I heard a rumor that there was some poaching going on. Do you think Liam could be involved in that? I heard him bragging about having a new car last night, and I'm not sure just getting good tips is enough to make those kinds of payments."

Chad looked around, then leaned toward me and whispered, "I overheard my dad and his buddies talking about the poaching that's going on."

"What exactly do the poachers do?" I asked.

"They take catch out of season, go after protected species, keep under-sized or over-sized fish." He shrugged. "My dad says it ruins it for the rest of us. Not to mention the environment."

"I'm impressed with your knowledge on the subject," I said.

Chad beamed. "My dad and his buddies are really angry that people are getting away with it. Everyone knows it's going on, but no one has been able to prove it yet."

Melvin stuck his head out of the office door. "Do you have those reports for me, Chad?" He looked at me and walked over. "Oh, I'm sorry, ma'am. I didn't mean to interrupt."

"Oh, it's no problem. Chad was just telling me about his promotion."

Melvin smiled fondly at Chad and patted him on the shoulder. "He's a hard worker. He deserved it." He stuck his hand out. "I'm Melvin Rolle, owner of this establishment."

"Mollie McGhie," I said. "I can't believe we've never met before."

"Well, I've been back in the Bahamas for the past several months," he said, his eyes welling up with tears. He took a handkerchief out of his pocket and dabbed them. "Sorry about that. I still get misty-eyed thinking about the passing of my Velma."

I squeezed his hand. "I'm so sorry about your loss. How long were you married for?"

"Forty-one years. I was a lucky man." He glanced around the store. "She's the reason for all this. She believed in me and my dreams." He dabbed at his eyes again. "As much as I miss her, I'm glad she doesn't have to deal with the loss of Darren. She was so fond of the boy. It would have broken her heart."

"When did you get back to Coconut Cove?" I asked.

"Last week. I decided it was time to come back and face things. The store needs someone looking after it full-time. Chad does a great job working after school and on the weekends along with a couple of other high school kids, but you really need someone managing it day to day." Chad looked crestfallen. "And this young man will be heading off to college next year. He's got a bright future in front of him."

"You must have a lot on your plate with the store and your fishing charter business," I said.

"We used to have four boats, but then...well, we just have the one now, and it's a struggle to keep that going." His voice choked up. "Now that my nephew is gone, I don't know what I'm going to do."

"Mr. Rolle," a deep voice said behind me. "Are you ready for some more questions?"

I didn't have to turn around to know whom that voice belonged to. I was all too familiar with the burly man behind it. "Chief Dalton, what a surprise to see you here," I said.

The chief raised his bushy eyebrows and scowled. "Well, it's not really a surprise to see you here, Mrs. McGhie. Whenever there's a body to be found and a murder to be investigated, you're right there in the thick of things." He turned to Melvin. "Sir, if I could have a minute of your time."

"How many questions can you possibly have?" Melvin said, raising his hands in the air. "I don't have time for this! Darren's parents are flying over from Nassau later today. We've got to organize everything for the funeral, and I've got to cancel the fishing charter I had scheduled for tomorrow."

"It won't take long. Just a couple more questions regarding your whereabouts last night."

"I told you everything already. I was home alone, watching TV, trying not to think too much about Velma." He turned to me. "It was our wedding anniversary yesterday. I watched *Roman Holiday* and made conch fritters with some pigeon peas and rice. I even made a pitcher of *switcha*." He smiled at the quizzical look on my face. "That's what we Bahamians call lemonade, except we make it with limes. That was how we celebrated every year."

"I love that movie, especially the part where Audrey Hepburn drives around the streets of Rome on a Vespa scooter."

"Velma liked that part too," Melvin said. He started sobbing.

The chief coughed. "Mrs. McGhie, you can talk about movies on your own time. Right now, I'm here to speak with Mr. Rolle."

"My own time? What are you talking about?" I said. "It's not like I work for you. But if I did, I would know better than to badger people." I pulled out a pack of tissues from my purse and handed it to Melvin, while the chief gazed on dispassionately. "You should be ashamed of the way you're treating him!"

The burly man's eyebrows twitched. "Fine. Why don't I come by your house later today, Mr. Rolle, and we can discuss matters then?" Melvin nodded. The chief turned to me. "And while I'm in the neighborhood, why don't I come by and have another chat with you?"

"That'd be delightful," I said with a touch of sarcasm. Okay, maybe more than just a touch. "I always look forward to our visits." I watched as he walked toward the door, praying he wouldn't turn back around to have another go at the older man.

"What did he mean by 'in the neighborhood'?" I asked

Melvin. "Wait a minute—you don't happen to live in the pink cottage on the beach, do you? We've never seen anyone there. I assumed it was vacant, maybe a rental property. We're right next door in the blue one."

He nodded. "Yes, the pink one's mine. Maybe I should rent it out. It doesn't feel the same without Velma there."

"Have you ever thought of selling?" I asked. "A real estate agent was out at our place. She's desperate to get us to list it."

"I bet that was Suzanne Thomas," he said bitterly. "If I were you, I'd stay clear of her and her husband. The police should be talking to them about Darren's death, not me."

"Do you think they had something to do with it?"

"I wouldn't put it past them," he said darkly. "They've destroyed businesses all over town. I don't think they'd bat an eye at killing someone to get what they want."

CHAPTER 5
MYSTERY INGREDIENT

AFTER ALL OF NANCY'S SNIDE comments about the fact that I rarely cooked, I decided to go all out and make a big Sunday lunch for Scooter and me. While I was in the kitchen mashing up some potatoes, my husband wrapped his arms around my waist and nuzzled my neck.

"I see sour cream, butter, bacon bits, and shredded cheese on the counter," he said. "Does that mean what I think it means?"

"How do twice-baked potatoes sound?"

"That sounds great," he said. "But what did I do to deserve them?"

"By not buying those ridiculous multipurpose tools yesterday. Your self-control was awe-inspiring."

"But that was just because you had the credit card in your purse," he said as he tried to peek in the oven.

"Hey, stay out of there."

"It smells good. What is it?"

"You'll see. It's a new recipe. There's a special ingredient in it that I think you're going to love. Why don't you go wait on the patio? I'll be out in a little bit. I just have to finish up in here." I handed him a bottle of salad dressing. "Here, take this with you."

"Salad?"

"It's good for you."

"All right, just make sure you put extra butter in those spuds to make up for it."

* * *

After reluctantly eating a bowl of salad, Scooter gobbled down everything on his plate in record time. "You've outdone yourself, my little panda bear. This chicken is delicious," he said. "There's something so familiar about the breading, but I can't put my finger on it."

"Well, if you can figure out the mystery ingredient, you can have dessert. I made brownies earlier."

Scooter's eyes lit up. "Well, I'd better have another piece in the interest of research."

I pointed at the cottage next to ours. It was painted a bright shade of pink with lilac trim and shutters. "I can't believe that's Melvin's place. Did your uncle ever mention him?"

"I guess he did say something about a Bahamian guy living next door, but I never put two and two together." Scooter took a sip of water. "You know, he bought this cottage from Alligator Chuck around fifteen years ago. Chuck's family originally owned all the cottages on this stretch of beach. I wonder if Melvin bought his cottage from him at the same time."

I turned and glanced at the purple cottage on the other side of us. "I wonder why he kept that one to live in. They're pretty much all the same inside, aren't they?"

"I think the layout is the same, but Chuck made improvements to the yellow cottage on the other side of his so that it'd have more appeal as a rental property."

"We hardly ever see him around here," I said. "He's probably too busy running his barbecue joint." I watched as Scooter finished off the rest of the chicken. "We haven't been there in a while. I wouldn't mind getting some ribs sometime this week. Besides, it's always fun to listen to him tell tourists his alligator-wrestling stories. It's amazing what they'll believe. Remember the one about the poodle?"

Scooter chuckled. "That was a good one." He leaned back in his chair and rubbed his now-extended belly. "But, to be honest, I'm too full to even think about ribs right now."

I looked at the plates on the table. "We really should have invited Melvin over to lunch. Poor guy, all on his own."

"You were talking to him quite a bit at the store," Scooter said. "He seemed really broken up."

"Of course he was. First, losing his wife, now his nephew. And then the chief started harassing him."

"Harassing seems like a strong way of putting it. He must have some reason for wanting to question Melvin."

"From what Melvin says, it's Norm and Suzanne he should be questioning. He practically accused them of killing Darren."

Scooter took his glasses off and rubbed his eyes. "Maybe I shouldn't tell you this, but..."

"Tell me what?" When he didn't reply right away, I added, "Don't forget that brownies are at stake here."

Scooter smiled. "Okay, but don't turn this into some sort of dark conspiracy that you need to investigate."

"Me? Never."

"Well, Suzanne called to arrange for the photographer to come out, and then she went on about how Darren was involved in all this poaching activity everyone's been talking about."

"Darren? Everyone I talk to says it's Liam. Haven't you heard about that flashy car of his?"

He shrugged. "I have, but it's none of our business. Right?"

"I'd better clear the table," I said, stacking the plates and utensils.

"Right?" Scooter asked as I walked inside. I came back out with a notebook and pen.

"Okay, time to make a list."

Scooter sighed. "Don't you have enough lists already?"

I opened up the notebook to a blank page. "Okay, the first person I need to speak with is Norm. There's obviously no love lost between him and Melvin. Maybe Norm killed Darren in order to drive Melvin out of business? Melvin is already having to cancel fishing charters because he doesn't have anyone to captain the boat."

I underlined Norm's name, then wrote Suzanne's next to it. "I'll also have to talk to his wife, but I'm afraid that's going to be a tricky conversation."

"Why? You think she'll be evasive?"

"Well, that goes without saying. But what I'm really concerned about is that she'll try to turn the conversation into a discussion about my fashion sense, or lack of one. Plus, that perfume she wears is quite overpowering."

"Maybe I should have gotten you a bottle for Valentine's Day," Scooter said with a smile.

I wrinkled my nose. "No, you did just fine. You can never go wrong with chocolate." I tapped my pen on the table. "Okay, next on the list is Liam. He's an interesting suspect. I can think of two motives as to why he would have killed Darren. The first is the same as Norm—to drive Melvin out of business. The second is jealousy. He wanted Darren out of the picture so he could have Alejandra all to himself."

Scooter scoffed. "Jealousy? Who would kill someone because of love? If a relationship doesn't work out, you move on."

"My, how logical you are, Mr. Spock."

"Is he the pointy-eared guy?"

"You know he is. I love how you pretend not to know anything about any of the sci-fi shows I watch, yet you always happen to sit next to me when I have them on and pester me with a million questions. Admit it, you're a sci-fi geek too."

"The only reason I watch those shows is because you hide the remote from me."

"Speaking of hiding things, do you remember that conversation between Darren and Ken in the boatyard the other day? I wonder what they were talking about. It almost seemed like Ken was scared of Darren." I made a note on my list. "That will be easy. I'll go talk with Leilani about downsizing and then slip a few questions into the conversation about Ken."

"So you are seriously thinking about moving onto the boat!" Scooter said triumphantly.

"Calm down. It's just a ruse. I have no interest in selling this cottage."

Scooter grabbed my notebook from me and put it on the other side of the table. "Okay, enough of that. Let's have dessert."

"But you haven't guessed the secret ingredient yet."

"Oh, come on, I'll never figure it out. It's probably some exotic ingredient. Or a fancy French thing I can't pronounce. In any event, it was delicious. I did eat every last bite." He got a puzzled look on his face. "Hey, wait a minute. *I* ate every last bite. That never happens. Mrs. Moto is always at my feet demanding handouts. I haven't seen her in a while. Where is she?"

"That's a very good question." As we walked into the house, I heard a rustling noise in the hallway and went to investigate. "Scooter, come here. I think I solved the mystery of the disappearing cat."

I pointed at a box on the floor. Mrs. Moto had her head inside of it and was trying to knock it off. Scooter picked her up, pulled the box off, and handed her to me.

"Listen, little kitty, this is my Cap'n Crunch cereal." He stroked the calico's head. "You have very good taste." She meowed in agreement, then tapped the box with her paw. "Yes, it's empty," Scooter said. "We'll have to get some more. Wait a minute, is this—"

"Yep, you guessed it. That's the secret ingredient—I used Cap'n Crunch in the breading on the chicken."

* * *

The Tipsy Pirate was a favorite hangout among both locals and tourists. Visitors to the area loved to have their picture taken with the wooden statue of Coconut Carl, a pirate who'd plied the local waters and had been known for his love of plunder and women, but most of all for his love of rum.

Legend had it that he'd once donned a dress and put a coconut underneath in an attempt to disguise himself as a pregnant woman and evade capture. However, he was more than a little tipsy at the time and forgot to shave off his mustache and beard, which made his story a little less believable.

It was considered good luck to rub Coconut Carl's belly while drinking a shot of rum. Tourists gobbled it up, while the residents politely hid their laughs. After all, they knew the legend was good for the local economy.

Despite differing views on the Tipsy Pirate's kitschy mascot, everyone agreed that happy hour there was the place to be. The owners had converted an abandoned fish-processing plant into the local watering hole. A large wooden deck extended out the back over the water. The inside was decorated with fishing rods and lures hanging from the rafters, mounted fish on the walls, and a long bar made out of two old wooden rowboats.

"Thanks for the ride," Melvin said to us. "After I got home from church, I just wanted to crawl back in bed and try to forget everything that had happened. I'm sure glad you came over and convinced me to get out of the house and do something tonight." He waved at a couple of older men sitting in the corner. "I'm going to go catch up with my pals for a few minutes."

"It's really crowded tonight," I said, glancing around to see if there were any empty tables. "We might have to sit up at the bar, and you know I hate that. Why do they have to make the barstools so high? I can barely climb up on them with my short legs."

"Your little legs are in luck," Scooter said. "Leilani is waving us over. Looks like they have some empty seats."

"Perfect," I said. "I can ask her and Ken about Darren."

Scooter shook his head. "You mean downsizing, right?"

"Darren, downsizing—same thing. They both begin with D."

"Here, sit next to me," Leilani said, patting a seat between her and Alejandra. "We girls can catch up, while the guys get us some drinks."

"I thought you weren't going to come tonight," I said to Alejandra.

"I wasn't, but then I felt bad about making that thing up about looking at nail polish with Nancy. I decided I really should come out and support Ben and Liam. They've been working so hard getting their band together." She toyed with her coaster. "As annoying as they can both be at times, they're still my friends."

A young woman wearing a tie-dyed tank top and purple leggings walked on stage and picked up the microphone. "Hello, everyone, and welcome to the Tipsy Pirate," she said. "I hope you're all having a good time. We're Eye Patches and Peg Legs, and we're delighted to be here this afternoon. So kick back, grab another drink, and we'll play our first set soon."

"What can I get everyone?" Scooter asked. He pointed at me. "Gin and tonic, right, my little panda bear?" I nodded. Leilani and Alejandra both asked for rum and cokes. Ken rose.

"I'll come with you and help carry the drinks back."

Alejandra giggled. "Panda bear? I thought he used to call you his little sweet potato?"

I sighed. Scooter always had the most ridiculous pet names for me. He rarely called me Mollie, and when he did it usually meant he had something serious to say, or he was in trouble.

"He started using panda bear after we won a trivia pub game. He was the only person who knew the Chinese call them giant bear cats. Scooter thought it was cute because my mom gave me panda bear pajamas for Christmas, and he claims that I'm always sneaking around like a cat investigating things."

"I think it's cute too," Alejandra said.

"Well, I guess it's better than having someone refer to you as a root vegetable."

I watched as Ben and Liam walked up to the stage. There didn't seem to be any of the tension I had seen the previous night. Ben got his guitar out of its case while Liam sat behind a drum set. A third guy picked up a bass. After conferring for a few minutes with the band, the woman sat down on a barstool at the front of the stage.

"She's got a great voice," Leilani said. "We heard her last week."

"Did you know she lives in a van?" Alejandra asked as Ken passed us our drinks. "I can't imagine living in such a small space."

"Living on a boat can't be much different," I said, squeezing a lime into my drink.

Alejandra considered that. "I guess you're right. Either way, you have to downsize." I tried to ask about my other D topic, but before I could utter Darren's name, she shushed me when the band began to play. She was right—the young woman had a great voice, and the band was surprisingly good.

While they took a break between sets, Alejandra told us some more about van living. Then she turned to Leilani. "I have to ask. Why in the world did you move onto your boat?"

She thought about it for a minute. "A lot of reasons, really. We wanted to lead a simpler life and not get caught up in that whole competing-with-the-Joneses mentality. You know, having a new car, a big house, expensive clothes. When I look at my parents, sure, they have lots of nice things, but I'm not convinced those things make them happy. They actually encouraged us to go simple now, while we're young."

"Did you have a house before you got the boat?" Alejandra asked.

"Yes, a two-bedroom townhouse."

"You must have had to get rid of a lot of stuff," Alejandra said.

Leilani smiled. "Oh yes. Anything you want to know about selling your stuff online and at yard sales, I can fill you in. But at least we didn't have thirty, forty years of stuff to get rid of." She turned to me. "Do you know Louise?"

"Sure, I take sailing lessons with her."

"Well, she and her husband sold their place when they retired. It was so hard for her to get rid of everything. She told me that when she looked through a box of presents her kids had made for her over the years, she broke down in tears. In the end, she couldn't bear to part with everything, so they got a storage unit. She figures after they've been cruising for a while, if she doesn't miss what they've put in storage, then she can get rid of it. But if things don't work out, and they decide to move back on land, she'll still have her prized possessions."

"Sounds sensible," I said.

"Do you think that's what you'll do?" Leilani asked me.

"Huh?"

"When you sell your cottage."

"What, when did this happen?" Alejandra asked.

"It hasn't. It's just another one of Scooter's crazy ideas, like buying a boat. It's never going to happen."

"Well, you did buy a boat," Alejandra pointed out.

"Okay, it's like the time he wanted to...wait, we ended up doing that." I put my head in my hands.

"Would it be so bad?" Leilani asked. "What is it about living on a boat that puts you off? Is it getting rid of your stuff?"

"No, it's not that so much. We did a bit of downsizing before we moved to Coconut Cove. Sure, there's some things I can't imagine living without, like my collection of boots, but it's more the thought of living in such a small, cramped space. For example, I made a nice lunch today, and there were dishes everywhere. I can't imagine making a meal like that in the tiny galley that *Marjorie Jane* has."

"Maybe you need a bigger boat," Alejandra suggested with a smile.

"Don't you dare let Scooter hear you say that," I said.

"To be fair, it does take some getting used to," Leilani said. "But it is possible to live in a relatively small space."

The band started playing again before I had a chance to change the subject away from downsizing and toward the murder investigation. While the singer paused to take a drink of water, the doors to the bar swung open.

"I told you not to trust Liam with the accounts," a shrill voice rang out. I watched as Suzanne stood in the entrance, jabbing her finger in Norm's chest. "He failed algebra in high school. Did you really think he would know the difference between an asset and a liability?"

Norm brushed her hand away. She continued, oblivious to the fact that the room had gone silent and everyone was watching her. "The real liability here is Liam. I really think I should call Xander and persuade him to move back here and help you with the business."

"For the last time, Xander is your son, not mine. Liam is going to be the one who inherits, not Xander."

Suzanne's jaw dropped as she watched him storm off to the bar. Then she looked around the room, her eyes lighting on the band. She waved at the singer, the gold charms on her bracelet flashing in the overhead light. "Can you sing something by Jimmy Buffett, dear?"

After the band resumed playing, she joined Norm at a table next to the one where Melvin was sitting with his buddies. Suzanne waved a waitress over, then whispered something to her husband. Norm scowled and pushed his chair away from hers, bumping into Melvin.

"Oh, I think this is going to get ugly," I muttered.

"What's that?" Alejandra asked.

I pointed at Melvin, who had risen to his feet and was towering over Norm. I couldn't hear what he was saying over the noise of the band, but his meaning seemed quite clear by the way he slammed his fist down on the table.

As the singer belted out the last of the lyrics to "Cheeseburger in Paradise," Norm stood and lunged at Melvin. By the time she got to the final note, the entire audience was staring at the fight breaking out, not at her. Once the music stopped, Melvin's voice could be clearly heard.

"I know it was you, Norm. You killed Darren. And if you think you're going to get away with it, you've got another thing coming. You strut around town like you're the top dog here, but you're nothing but a liar and a cheat. We all know what your nephew really gets up to when he's out on one of your boats. You can be sure that the fish and wildlife warden is going to hear about that!"

Norm threw a punch, landing it on Melvin's right cheek. Melvin staggered backward, his face flushed and his hands balled into fists. Before he could strike, two of Melvin's buddies pulled him away. Suzanne grabbed Norm's arm.

"It's not worth it, darling. Let it go." She added in a stage whisper that everyone could still hear. "This kind of thing won't look good if you want to become mayor."

Norm pulled his arm away. "Fine, let's go."

As they walked toward the door, Melvin yelled out, "And don't think I don't know about your role in that property deal, either. You and your wife are both going to end up in jail."

* * *

Everyone at our table was dumbstruck after watching the drama between Norm and Melvin unfold. Leilani attempted to lighten the mood by telling us about what it was like to grow up in Hawaii, which was fascinating. Scooter tried to impress us with some random trivia about the Aloha State, which was a tad boring. And Alejandra told us the secret to making a great tamale, which made me wonder what we were going to have for dinner.

Finally, we all decided to call it a night. While Scooter went over to see if Melvin wanted a ride back, I took a detour to pay a visit to the statue of Coconut Carl. I waited my turn while a couple of young guys downed shots of rum and rubbed Carl's belly. From the way they were watching a group of attractive young women seated at the bar, I was pretty sure they were trying to enlist Carl's help in successfully chatting them up.

It was times like this that made me so glad I was married. The thought of having to ever dive back into the dating scene made me shudder.

When it was my turn, I put my hand on the pirate's stomach and whispered in his ear. "Coconut Carl, here's the thing. I've got to give a speech at the FAROUT meeting this week, and I'm scared to death. I hate speaking in public. What if they boo me off the stage? What if I forget what I'm supposed to say?"

"Ahem, are you almost through?" I turned and saw a tourist holding up his phone. "I want to get a picture of my wife." A woman stood next to him, grinning from ear to ear and holding two shot glasses in her hands.

"I'll just be a minute," I said. I turned back to Carl. "So, do we have a deal? I'll rub your tummy, and you'll help me out with the speech. I don't really like rum, but I figure that part is just an old wives' tale, right?" I looked Carl in the eye and rubbed my hand on his midsection three times in a clockwise direction. I stepped back. "He's all yours."

As I was about to join Scooter at the car, I saw Ben and Liam standing on the deck, engrossed in conversation. I decided it wouldn't hurt to pop outside and have a quick look at the view over the water. And if I happened to overhear anything that could shed some light on the murder investigation, well, that would just be a bonus.

I leaned over the railing and watched fish searching for the morsels of food that people tossed into the water for them. The guys were so caught up in what they were discussing that they didn't notice me.

"Come on, tell me the truth, man," Ben said. "Did you get Darren involved in poaching?"

"I don't know what you're talking about," Liam said.

"There's no way you can afford that car on what you make, even with tips. And I heard you bragging about how much your new watch cost you." Ben took a sip of beer. "Everyone knows what you're up to. Darren couldn't exactly keep a secret. It's only a matter of time before you're caught."

"Sounds like someone who's jealous. Look at you, Ben. You live on a boat that's a wreck, you don't even own a car, and you bought your watch at the dollar store. No wonder you can't get a girl." Liam lowered his voice. "If you want to change all that, I can help you out. But if I do, you can't go around telling everyone about it."

"Like you helped Darren out? No way, man. I don't worship you the way he did in high school. He would have done anything you told him to. I bet you tried the same spiel on him, and he fell for it, hook, line, and sinker. And see what happened. It cost him his life."

Liam drained his glass. "I didn't have anything to do with

that," he said coldly. He stared off into the distance, drumming his fingers on the railing. "Tell you what, Ben. Why don't we forget what you said? You're just upset about Darren. We all are." He punched Ben's arm playfully. "Come on, let's get another beer before our next set."

CHAPTER 6
OOMPA-LOOMPAS VS. SMURFS

"I WOULDN'T DO THAT IF I were you." I glanced up and saw Ben leaning over the side of Ken and Leilani's boat, *Mana Kai*.

I had learned that the name of their boat was Hawaiian for "Spirit of the Ocean," which was a lot prettier than boring old *Marjorie Jane*. They'd also told me that if you reversed the words you got *kaimana*, which could be translated as "diamond." I thought that was quite fitting, considering that I used to refer to the young couple as Mr. and Mrs. Diamond, on account of her diamond necklace.

"You wouldn't do what?" I asked Ben. He pointed behind me. "No, I didn't mean you, I meant him." I turned and saw Scooter grinning as he snapped a picture of me with his phone.

"Tell me you didn't just do that," I demanded. "I look ridiculous in this getup!" I tugged at the white plastic head-to-toe protective suit I was wearing. Well, it had used to be white. Now it was covered in a blue dust that had blown all over me while I was sanding the paint off *Marjorie Jane*'s bottom.

I removed my safety goggles and gloves, then pushed back the hood. "We've talked about this before, Scooter. You're only allowed to take pictures of me when my hair looks good, I don't have spinach caught in my teeth, and I'm wearing something that doesn't make my rear end seem enormous. This hardly qualifies."

I wiped the sweat off my forehead and pushed my frizzy hair behind my ears. Ben and Scooter both chuckled. "What's so funny?"

"It's just that you look like a..." Ben was consumed with laughter before he could finish his thought.

"Like a what?" I demanded.

"A Smurf," Scooter said. He took one look at my face and quickly added, "An *adorable* Smurf." He snapped another photo and smiled as he gazed at the screen. "A really adorable Smurf."

"Give me that," I said, seizing the phone. "Ugh. That is not a good look."

Scooter pointed across the boatyard at a couple who were sanding the bottom of their boat. "It could be worse. If *Marjorie Jane* had reddish-orange bottom paint like that one, you would look like some sort of demented Oompa-Loompa. Although given your love of *Charlie and the Chocolate Factory*, I imagine you'd rather be one of those than a Smurf."

While I was pondering which version of the movie was better—the original with Gene Wilder or the remake with Johnny Depp—my husband grabbed the phone back from me and stuck it in his pocket.

"Are you sure you don't want me to take over sanding?" he offered. "It's hard work."

Part of me desperately wanted to shout out, *Yes! Save me from this torture that's turning me into a small blue creature who lives in a tiny mushroom-shaped house!* Sanding was hard work.

My arms were killing me, it was insanely hot outside, and we'd already mentioned that I wasn't going to win any fashion awards wearing my Smurf suit. But I was determined to stick it out and win the bet with Norm.

"No, I've got it," I said. "You keep working on trying to sort out the cause of the leak."

Ben leaned over the side of *Mana Kai* again. "Hey, did you know Mrs. Moto is aboard the Chois' boat?"

"Yeah. They've got air conditioning, and Leilani offered to let her stay there while we're working on our boat. I don't want her running around the boatyard when I'm sanding and Scooter has all the floorboards torn out of *Marjorie Jane*. I'm worried she'll end up getting stuck some place we can't get her out of. Hope that's okay with you."

"Fine by me. She's good company while I'm working." He smiled. "Well, maybe except when she bats screws off the chart table, and I have to get on my hands and knees to pick them up."

"Yes, I know that game well," I said.

As I was readjusting the hood of my Smurf suit, Liam pulled up in his flashy new car, the stereo blaring. He got out and stepped back to admire his baby. Then he glanced up at Ben. "Practice later this week at my place?"

"Sure thing," Ben replied. "Text me the details. How's your head today?"

"I'm fine. Norm's the one with the hangover. That's why I'm here and he's not."

"He and Melvin really got into it, didn't they?" I asked.

"It's always been like that between the two of them," Ben said. He looked at his red-haired friend. "You and Darren always used to be at odds too," he said with a frown.

"We were never as bad as the old guys," Liam said. "Sure, Darren and I had our differences, but we were still buddies." He bit his lip. "Well, enough about that. I've got to get some work done."

Before walking over to his uncle's boat, he examined the progress I had made with *Marjorie Jane*'s hull. "You're tougher than I thought," he said grudgingly. "You might just give my uncle a run for his money."

A black SUV pulled up behind Liam's car, blasting its horn. Ken leaned out the window. "Hey, move your car! The spot by my boat is for my car, not yours. Unless you and your uncle want to buy this part of the boatyard too, just like you're trying to buy up half the town?"

"Take it easy, man," Liam said soothingly. "I'll move, don't worry. You've probably got enough on your mind as it is, don't you? I don't want to add to your troubles."

"What's that supposed to mean?" Ken asked.

"Oh, nothing," he said. "Hey, did you hear that? Sounds like your phone is beeping, Ken. I heard you've been getting interesting texts lately."

Ken pulled out his phone and looked at the screen. "There's nothing on here."

"My mistake. Although you might want to check your old messages. Maybe someone sent you something important that you really should deal with, if you know what I mean."

Ken gave him an icy stare. "I have no idea what you're talking about. Now, get your car out of my spot."

Liam held his hands up. "Sure, no problem."

After the guys got their cars situated, I nudged Scooter. "Why don't you go over there and have a chat with Liam? See if you can find out more about these texts he was talking about. I'll do the same with Ken."

"You're kidding, right?"

"I never kid. This is important. It could be related to what happened between Ken and Darren the night of the murder. I remember Ken reading a text on his phone, and it seemed like Darren had sent it to him." Scooter appeared unconvinced. "Pretty please?"

He smiled. "Fine. I'll go have a chat with him. Not because

you asked, but because he's wearing a shirt with my college basketball team's logo on it. I want to see what he thought about the game. Besides, I could use a break."

While Scooter talked about sports and texting with Liam, I approached Ken. "What was that about?" I asked.

"I don't know. I think he's just playing mind games," he said. "He's one of those guys who never grew up. Here, do you mind holding this?" he asked, handing me his briefcase. He pulled a cardboard box out of the back of his vehicle, carried it over to his boat, and set it on the ground by the ladder. "Articles for my research on sea turtle habitat encroachment," he said.

"That looks like a lot of reading. I guess you have to do a lot of that if you have a PhD. You must always have your head in a book."

"Well, I do read a lot of academic journals and research papers, but I also spend a lot of my time doing fieldwork outdoors."

"Do you ever get a chance to relax?"

"Sure. I like to watch movies."

"We do too. What was the last one you saw?"

"Hmm…that's a good question." He glanced down at the box on the ground. "Oh, I saw one on Friday. One of those action, shoot-'em-up flicks."

"That's right. You and Leilani came back to your boat after the barbecue," I said. "I'm surprised neither of you heard anything when Darren was attacked."

"I wish we had," he said ruefully. "Maybe I could have stopped the attack." He shook his head. "No, we had the AC running full blast, and the volume on the TV was up really loud. We couldn't hear a thing happening outside."

"Leilani was watching the movie too?"

"No, she doesn't like that sort of thing," he said. "Rom-coms are more her cup of tea. She was in the aft cabin working." He picked up the box. "I've got to go through this."

"And I guess I've got to get back to sanding *Marjorie Jane*'s bottom," I said reluctantly.

"Listen, if you're interested in the work we do with sea turtles, how about if you take a break this afternoon, and come with me out to the sanctuary? I told Penny I'd show her around, and it'd be great to have you along as well."

I watched as Scooter walked over to us. I wondered if he had obtained any useful information from his conversation with Liam. "Hey, we're going to see turtles this afternoon," I said as I tried to read his face for clues.

"You should come too," Ken said.

"I wish I could, but I've got a conference call this afternoon."

We all turned as Mrs. Moto started meowing on the deck of *Mana Kai*.

"Sorry, Mrs. Moto," Ken said with a chuckle. "No animals allowed. At least, no furry animals."

She batted a screw off the deck, then gracefully bounded down the ladder onto the ground to investigate. "Come on, kitty. You shouldn't be down here," Scooter said. Before he could grab her, she darted across the boatyard toward the wooded area.

"She must have seen another lizard," I said. "I'd better go get her."

"How about if I pick you and Penny up by the marina entrance at two?" Ken asked.

"Sounds good," I said over my shoulder as I chased after the calico.

After acquiring some new scratches from poking between prickly bushes, I spotted my little lizard hunter—smack-dab where Darren's body had been. She apparently didn't believe the police tape cordoning off the murder scene applied to her.

I crouched down and called out softly, "Here, kitty, kitty. Why don't you be a good girl, and come out from there? If I have to go back there to get you, the chief will be furious."

Instead of rushing into my arms, she stared at a small glittery object a couple of feet outside the cordoned-off area. She crouched down, wiggled her rear end, and made a trilling sound. After pouncing on the object and toying with her "prey" for a few minutes, she swatted it toward me. I picked it up and brushed the dirt off, uncovering a small gold charm in the shape of a sailboat.

There was one person I knew in town who sported a charm bracelet—Suzanne. She had made a point of telling me that she wouldn't be caught dead in the boatyard, so how could her charm have ended up here? Could she have been here the night of the murder? Then I brushed that thought aside. Suzanne hoisting a heavy paint can and bashing Darren in the head while wearing those high heels of hers—I just couldn't picture it.

* * *

"Are you ready, ladies?" Ken asked, leaning out the window of his vehicle. "Hop in. Next stop—the Gulf Coast Turtle Sanctuary."

As we drove up the coast, we passed through towns that all looked the same—strip malls, gated retirement communities, chain hotels and restaurants, people driving golf carts on the sidewalks, and bumper-to-bumper traffic. "This is what I'm afraid Coconut Cove is going to turn into if developers have their way," Ken said. "It'll become just another generic-looking town with no character. Places like the Tipsy Pirate and Alligator Chuck's BBQ Joint will be replaced by fast food chains."

While I'd been known to patronize the occasional drive-through for a cheeseburger and chocolate shake, I agreed with Ken's assessment. One of the reasons I liked our newly adopted home was that it was a small community with unique spots that added to its charm.

After about an hour of fighting traffic, I spotted a large sign with two smiling sea turtles. "Here we are," Ken said as he pulled into a gravel parking lot.

As we entered the visitors' center, an elderly woman greeted us. "Hello, Dr. Choi. We haven't seen you here in ages." She patted his hand. "You should have told me that you were coming today. I would have baked you some of those oatmeal cookies you're so fond of."

Ken rubbed his stomach. "That's why I didn't tell you, Mabel. I've been putting on weight ever since you began volunteering here."

"You're too young to be worrying about that sort of thing," she said. "Now, who are these two lovely young ladies you brought with you?"

"This is Penny," Ken said, pointing at the blonde Texas transplant. "She's a boat broker at the Palm Tree Marina, and she also runs the sailing school."

"Oh my. That must keep you busy," the older woman said. "My son has been talking about getting a boat."

"That would be fun, Mabel," Ken said. "He could take you and your husband out on day sails."

"No, not me," she said, clutching her chest. "I'm scared to death of the water."

Penny handed Mabel a business card. "If I can be of help to your son in looking for a boat, tell him to give me a call."

"Are those new?" I asked.

"Yes. Aren't they cute?" she said, passing me one as well.

"It's very pink," I said. I shouldn't have been surprised, considering that was Penny's favorite color. It found its way into every aspect of her life from her clothes to her sailboat, fittingly named *Pretty in Pink*.

"I know. Don't you just love it?" Penny beamed. "Did you see the starfish logo in the corner?"

Mabel placed the card on the front desk. "I'll be sure to give this to him. It must be an interesting job, selling boats.

Kind of like a car salesman, I imagine."

Penny stiffened. "It's nothing like selling cars."

"Well, you have to admit that it's a little bit like it," Ken said. "You show people boats, try to find one that suits their lifestyle and budget, take them out for test drives, and do all the paperwork."

"The paperwork is the worst part of the job," Penny said. "It's something the previous owner, Captain Dan, didn't take seriously. Did you know I had a woman call up screaming the other day about how he had messed up the paperwork for a boat he sold her? She hasn't been able to get insurance for it or register it. I've been trying to help her, even though the sale happened before my time."

"There are just some people who are always trying to cheat the system," Ken said. "People who think rules and regulations apply to everyone but themselves."

Mabel turned to me. "Now, what about you, dear? What do you do?"

After I explained to her about my work with FAROUT, she smiled politely. "Investigating aliens. That sounds...um...interesting."

Based on her reaction, I decided she probably wouldn't be interested in signing up for our mailing list.

"Well, ladies, why don't I show you the exhibits in the visitors' center, and then we can go outside to the saltwater lagoon, and you can meet our resident sea turtles?"

"Oh, Dr. Choi. Don't forget to check your office before you leave. You have some mail back there."

"How long did it take you to get your doctorate?" Penny asked.

"It's a long process," he said, trying to usher us into the next room.

"He's such an impressive young man, isn't he?" Mabel gushed. "Imagine all the studying he had to do to become a doctor."

Ken looked impatient. "We should get going."

Mabel grabbed his arm. "My grandson is working on his PhD in marine biology too," she said proudly. "I'd love for him to meet you one day. Imagine...two doctors in the same room. He'd be so inspired by the work you're doing here at the sanctuary. Maybe when he comes to visit this summer, you can give him a tour."

"Sure," Ken said. He tried to pull his arm away from Mabel.

"Summer seems like a bad time of year to visit," I said. "It gets way too hot here."

"You're not from these parts?" Mabel asked.

"No, we moved here from Cleveland."

"Oh, that's where you got your degree, isn't it, Dr. Choi?"

Ken muttered something under his breath.

"What was that, dear?" Mabel asked. Before he could answer, the phone rang, and she walked over to the desk to pick it up while Ken hurried us into the display area.

* * *

After learning about the dangers of toxic algae bloom in the local waterways, that seahorses develop in a kangaroo-like pouch on the male of the species, and how oysters purify water, we left the air-conditioned building to explore the rest of the sanctuary.

"Make sure you put some sunscreen on," Ken said, handing us each a water bottle. "Even though it's winter, the sun is still strong."

"That's a good idea." I pulled a bottle out of my purse and slathered it on before offering it to the others. "I'm trying to take better care of my skin. I don't want to end up with a bad sunburn like Liam has. I guess that comes with the territory when you're a redhead like he is."

Ken pointed at a large pool behind the visitors' center. "We pump in water from the ocean. You'll see all sorts of creatures in here, including sharks, game fish, and, of course, sea turtles. Come on, let's head over to that pavilion, where you can get a better view."

Once we were situated in the shade, Ken told us about the sanctuary's mission. "We aren't able to release these guys back into the wild. That one over there is a loggerhead." He smiled. "His name is Donatello. We ran a contest. You should have seen how excited the kid was whose name we picked. He came out here with his family for a naming ceremony. Mabel baked a huge cake in the shape of a turtle."

He leaned over the railing and sighed. "It's a sad story, really. Donatello was hit by a boat, and the damage resulted in buoyancy issues. Fortunately, he can spend the rest of his natural life here with us."

"It's great that places like this exist," Penny said.

"I just wish we could do more," Ken said. "We're reliant on grant money and donations. In fact, we're hosting a cocktail party here next week to try to raise money to protect nesting grounds."

Ken warmed up to his subject, telling us how population growth and urban development were putting turtle habitats at risk. "If we don't act now, we're in danger of losing these magnificent creatures forever."

He took us on a short walk down to the beach to show us where the turtles nested. "Female turtles come ashore after mating to lay their eggs, usually during the warmest months of the year. They return to the same beach each time they're ready to nest, often just a few hundred feet away from their last nesting grounds. Did you know that the beach by your house is also a popular spot, Mollie?"

"I've seen signs there telling visitors not to disturb turtles and their nests. There was even one warning that it's illegal to shine lights on the beach at night."

"Yes, that's because artificial lights can keep females from nesting and disorient hatchlings. The Florida Turtle Trust helped to fund the signs. We're trying to do more work in the area but keep running into roadblocks from some of the local business owners. They think it will hurt tourism if we block off access to the beach."

Penny frowned. "I would think that would actually be a tourist draw."

"Potentially, but there's a fine line between ecotourism and creating more damage and putting the turtles in jeopardy. We're hoping to set aside land up there as a protected wildlife sanctuary, but some powerful people want to build a big resort there instead."

"Really? Do you know who's involved in that? Suzanne Thomas came by our cottage and said we could get a lot of money for it. She didn't mention anything about a resort, though."

Ken frowned. "I hope I can persuade you and Scooter not to sell. Especially not to any buyers Suzanne puts forward. She's all about how much commission she can make, not what's in your best interests."

"You don't have to worry about persuading me," I said. "I don't want to sell. It's Scooter you have to talk to. Maybe you'll have more luck than me."

As we walked back into the visitors' center, Mabel called out, "Don't forget about your mail."

While we waited, I examined a display of brochures by the front door. Ken came up behind me holding a stack of mail. He opened up a large manila envelope and chewed his lip as he read the enclosed document. Some photos fluttered onto the ground. I started to pick them up, but he swiped them from me and shoved them back into the envelope. Despite the fact that we were back inside the air-conditioned building, he was perspiring.

"Everything okay, Ken?" I asked.

He glanced at me sharply. "Everything's fine. It's just a bill." He shoved the papers back into the envelope, then pointed at the brochures. "Go ahead and take those if you want," he said with a smile that didn't quite reach his eyes. "There's some good information in that one about the turtles you just saw, and that one has details about how you can contribute to the Gulf Coast Turtle Sanctuary."

While Ken went over and said goodbye to Mabel, I shoved the pamphlets in my purse and wondered what exactly had been in that envelope. Sure, no one liked to get bills, but they didn't usually cause you to break out in a nervous sweat. Nor did they generally come with photos attached.

CHAPTER 7
SUGAR CRAVINGS

"DO YOU MIND DROPPING ME off here?" I asked Ken as we approached Penelope's Sugar Shack. The lavender brick building with its bright purple awning had become a favorite haunt of mine since we moved to Coconut Cove. "I'm not sure why, but all that talk about turtles has given me a serious sugar craving."

"When don't you have a sugar craving?" Penny asked.

I ignored her. "I'm thinking of picking up a pie for dessert, but I'll walk back to the marina with it and burn off some calories as a preventative measure."

"Are you sure?" Ken asked. "I don't mind waiting for you."

"No, it's fine. It's not a long walk."

"I'll tell you what," Penny said. "I'll join you. I have a serious craving for one of Penelope's flax and chia seed carob almond bars. They're so good for you."

"But how do they taste?" I asked.

"Delicious."

"As delicious as that tofu you tried to pass off as potato

salad at one of the marina potlucks?" I asked as I got out of the car.

"Before you knew what was in it, you said you liked it."

"I was just being polite. I could detect that something wasn't quite right," I said with a smile.

Penny chuckled. "One of these days, we're going to do a blind taste test. I bet you'll end up picking dishes made with tofu over ones made with mayonnaise."

"Sure, right after I give up sugar. And that'll only be because my taste buds will feel betrayed and decide to punish me with soy products."

She held her hands up. "I give up." While she went inside in search of her healthy treats, I examined the unhealthy ones on display in the window. My taste buds seemed adamant that I should get some red velvet cupcakes in addition to a pie. Who was I to argue with them?

As I opened the front door, I spied a fresh-faced teenager behind the counter. "When did you begin working here, Tiffany?" I asked.

"After the holidays. I needed a part-time job, and I really didn't want to go back to Melvin's. Chad was constantly asking me out, and I was running out of ways to say no without hurting his feelings. Then Penelope said she needed some help, so here I am." She straightened her purple polka-dot apron, then asked, "What can I get for you?"

"How about two of those?" I said, pointing at the cupcakes in the window. "And do you have any chocolate pies left?"

"No, sorry. Someone just bought the last one. But I've got a pecan pie left. Want to give that a try? It's almost as good as chocolate."

"I suppose," I said. While Tiffany went into the back to get the pie, I turned to Penny. "Why are you empty-handed?"

"They ran out," she said. "See, that's how popular they are. They sell out by noon."

Tiffany came back with a purple box, then packed up my

cupcakes. As she was ringing up my order, the door burst open. Suzanne barged in, followed by Norm. The stench of her floral perfume trailed after her, overpowering the smell of freshly baked pastries.

"Tiffany, we're running late. Can you grab my catering order?"

"Sure thing, ma'am, just as soon as I ring Mollie up here."

"I'm sure she can wait, can't you, dear? We're in a rush." She pushed me aside and waved at the back of the store. I had to step back quickly before her bracelets made contact with my face and left their mark. Some of her charms had really sharp edges. "Now be a dear, pop in the back, and get my order."

Tiffany apologized to me before going into the back room. Norm leaned up against the display counter and checked his phone.

"Why are you standing there like that?" Suzanne demanded. "Go help Tiffany. After all, that's why you're here—to carry everything."

"I don't know why you had to have this meeting in the first place," Norm protested. "The last thing we need is a bunch of people running around the office. I've got work to do."

"The meeting isn't for me, it's for you. You're the one who wanted to impress these overseas investors."

Norm shook his head and went back to reading texts.

Suzanne plucked the phone out of his hand. "If Xander were here, he could have hosted the event with me. He looks so nice when he's dressed up in a suit. He'd be so charming that they'd be fighting each other to be the first to give us a check."

She tucked his phone in her purse, then waved dramatically toward the back. "Be a good boy, and go help Tiffany."

After he slunk away, Suzanne turned to me. "Now, what time should I come by the cottage tomorrow?"

"Why would you come by?"

"To sign the paperwork, of course. I'll also bring the photographer with me."

"Suzanne, I don't seem to have been able to get my point across clearly before, but let me try again. I have no intention of selling our cottage."

"That's not what your husband says."

"That's because he has this ludicrous dream of living on a boat."

"Oh, is that what you're worried about?" she asked. She put her arm around my shoulders. "Of course you're not going to live on a boat. That sounds dreadful. You'd never catch me on one."

"I live on a boat," Penny said.

"You poor thing." Suzanne pulled a card out of her purse. "Here, give me a call, and we can set up some viewings and get you off that boat in no time."

Penny pulled out a card from her bag and handed it to Suzanne. "And here are my details so that I can show you some boats."

Suzanne fingered the pink card dubiously, then turned back to me. "There's a darling condo that you absolutely have to see. I just know you're going to love it." She pulled out her phone. "Let me just put this in my calendar. I'll come by the cottage at nine. Then once we're finished there, I'll take you to view the condo."

Before I could tell her exactly what I thought of her plan, Tiffany and Norm came out laden with boxes.

"Penny, be a dear, and get the door for these two," she said as she punched a number into her phone. "See you at nine," she said breezily as she followed after them.

When Tiffany came back in, she shook her head. "I'm so sorry about that. It's just that it can be hard to say no to her, and she spends a lot of money here on catering."

Penny chuckled. "Don't worry about it. Mollie knows how

hard it is to say no, don't you? After all, you just agreed to see a condo tomorrow."

"I don't know how Norm puts up with her," I said.

"I do," Penny said. "They're a match made in heaven. They're both bossy and push people around."

"My mom says she remembers when they first started seeing each other," Tiffany said. "No one thought it would last, but Suzanne told my mom that every woman needed a man on her arm. Norm was apparently the best catch in Coconut Cove at the time."

"I'd rather be single than be with a guy like him," Penny said. "I've been burned in the past by men like that."

"What else did your mom say?" I asked.

"That Suzanne felt that Norm needed someone to push him to take more business risks. Suzanne told my mom that behind every successful man is a more successful woman."

"Well, maybe it paid off. She's certainly strong willed, and she sure does seem successful," I said. "Just look at those clothes, all those rings, and her bracelets. She's wearing more money on her than our cottage is worth."

"Maybe it's all an illusion," Penny said. "For some people, appearances are more important than reality. For all we know, they could be up to their ears in debt. Maybe some of those gems she wears are fakes."

"You may have a point. Hmm...maybe they're not as rich as they act like they are," I said.

"Your husband seems successful," Tiffany said as she wiped down the counters.

"He does all right," I said. "But he'd never go around bragging about it or telling everyone how much he's worth."

"That's what I like about the two of you," Penny said. "You're both so unpretentious and down to earth."

"Well, that's how we were raised. Be grateful for what you have, and don't rub people's faces in it. Luck comes and goes. You never know when yours might run out." Tiffany handed me my change, and I picked up my box and my bag of cupcakes. "Come on, we'd better get going before I starve to death and eat a piece on my way back to the marina."

"Is that what you're having for dinner?" Penny asked.

"Well, as tempting as that sounds, we're having real food before our dessert. Scooter's in charge. I think he's planning on a Thai recipe."

"Didn't a Thai restaurant just open up in town?"

"Precisely."

* * *

After meeting up with Scooter and Mrs. Moto at the marina and stopping to get takeout, we had a nice meal back at the cottage—pad thai and spring rolls for the humans and liver pâté from a can for the feline. Over dessert, I filled Scooter in on our visit to the turtle sanctuary.

"Mabel, the volunteer there, reminded me of your aunt Ethel. She was fawning over Ken, going on and on about how smart he was and the fact that he's a doctor. Ken looked like he wanted to die. He was so embarrassed."

"But I don't have a doctorate."

"No, but your aunt is always bragging about what a great basketball player you were in college. It's all she ever talks about."

Scooter's face reddened. "That's sweet, but I wasn't that good."

"See, that's what I love about you. You're so self-effacing. Penny and I were talking about that earlier."

"You know I hate it when you talk about me," he said.

"Oh, it really wasn't so much about you as it was about Suzanne and Norm. I guess they have a reputation in town for flaunting their wealth and bragging about how successful they are. You never do that."

"Well, first of all, we're not rich. And second of all, I wouldn't say I was successful. Remember all those issues I had with my last company? You never know when something is going to go south."

I pushed my dessert plate toward him. "Go on, why don't you finish this? You look like you could use it."

After polishing off the piece of pie, he said, "Let's talk about something more cheerful. Tell me more about Mabel. She sounds interesting."

"She seems to enjoy her volunteer work," I said. "I don't really know that much more about her."

"You know, we should do some volunteering."

"Uh, you realize that I already do volunteer work, don't you?"

"You mean with FAROUT? I thought you didn't like it when I referred to that as volunteer work."

"I don't. It's a real job."

"But you don't get paid."

"That's not the point. It's important work. What I'm talking about are all the hours of my life I spend fixing up *Marjorie Jane*. I should get a medal or something for that. She's a lost cause. That's got to be considered charitable work."

"I have to say, I have been impressed with how hard you've been working on her. You might even win this bet you have with Norm. Liam said the same thing."

"Hey, you never did tell me about your conversation with him. What did you find out about what's going on between him and Ken?"

"I didn't ask him about that. We ended up talking about the game on Friday night. I never did end up getting to see it because of...what you found."

"You mean Darren's body?" Scooter blanched. I squeezed his hand. "I'm sorry. I shouldn't have said that out loud. Maybe we should develop some sort of code when we talk about murder investigations." Scooter started to look faint. At least he was sitting in a chair this time. If he passed out, hopefully he would slump over the table and not on the floor.

"Want me to get you some more pie?"

"Please."

"Why don't you tell me about the basketball game?" I said, hoping to distract him while I served him another slice.

After he gave me a play-by-play recap and scraped the last bit of pecans off his plate, his color improved.

"Hmm...it sounds like Liam gave you a really detailed account of the game," I said.

"I guess that means he has an alibi," Scooter said. "The game was on when the you-know-what happened."

I sighed. "I don't know. I really thought he might have done it, especially after that conversation I overheard him having with Ben at the Tipsy Pirate."

"You never told me about that," Scooter said.

"Sure I did."

"Nope. But that's probably because you were eavesdropping, and you knew I would give you a hard time about it."

"I wasn't eavesdropping. I just happened to be standing nearby when they were talking about poaching fish. It sounded like Liam was involved in it, and he got Darren messed up in it too."

Scooter raised his eyebrows. "Uh-huh."

"No, you're the one who always forgets to tell me things. I bet you bought a powerboat and you've forgotten to tell me about it."

Scooter grinned. "Trust me, after what happened when I bought *Marjorie Jane* for you, I'd never buy another boat without talking to you about it first."

"Speaking of boats, I want to show you Penny's new business card." I walked over to the counter and looked through my purse. "Huh, it's not here, and neither is my wallet."

"Where do you think it is?"

I shrugged. "Maybe I left it at Penelope's, or it fell out of my purse on the way back to the marina." I slung my purse over my shoulder and gave Scooter a quick kiss on the forehead. "I'm going to retrace my steps and see if I can find it. That means you're on dish duty," I said quickly over my shoulder as I dashed out the door.

* * *

As I drove past the bakery, I noticed that the lights were off, and the sign on the door said Closed. I parked the car in their lot and began retracing my steps back toward the marina. I halted in my tracks when I reached Suzanne and Norm's office and reviewed the listings displayed on the large window extending from the corner of the building to the entryway. Wow, property really was going for a pretty penny in Coconut Cove.

After reading the details for a condo in town and admiring the large pool that residents had access to, I noticed a picture of a very familiar-looking cottage next to it. I peered through the window and spotted Suzanne sitting at a desk with her back to me, tapping on a keyboard with one hand while holding a phone up to her ear with the other.

When I knocked on the glass to try to get her attention, she turned and gave me a wave before looking back at her computer. I pushed the office door open and marched up to her desk.

"What's the meaning of that?" I demanded, pointing at the window.

She glanced up at me, held up her phone, and motioned for me to sit on a chair. Instead, I strode over to the window and tore the advertisement down. When I turned it over, I realized I had ripped the wrong one off the glass—this was the condo. The views from the balcony overlooking the pool really were nice.

I moved over to the file cabinets running along the wall, where office supplies were stacked. I took some tape and reattached the condo ad to the window, but not before noting that it had a large spa tub in the master bath. I do love a good soak in a big tub. Then I pulled the one featuring our cottage down and slammed it on Suzanne's desk.

"Care to explain this?"

"Just a sec," she said to the person on the other end of the phone. "Mollie, have a seat. I'll be with you as soon as I can."

"Tell them you'll call back," I said forcefully. "I want to talk about this now."

Suzanne frowned, then ended her call.

"Now, what's all this fuss about, dear?"

I pointed at the picture of my cottage.

"Oh, that." She clucked her tongue. "You're right. It isn't a great picture, but it's the best I could do with my phone. When the photographer comes out tomorrow, he'll get much better shots. This one is just a temporary one."

"Suzanne—"

"No, don't say another word. I take full responsibility for not having the photographer come out earlier."

"But—"

She wagged a finger. "Really, it's my fault. Now, you look like you could use a cup of coffee." She pushed back her chair and walked over to the back of the room where there was a small seating area. She picked up an insulated coffee carafe and poured some into a china cup. "How do you take it?"

"I don't really want any—"

"Let me see if I can guess." She looked at me thoughtfully. "You seem like a gal who takes two sugars and plenty of cream. Am I right?"

"Actually—"

"Of course I'm right." I shook my head as she fussed with the coffee. "You know what would go nicely with this? One of the chocolate tarts we have left over from our client event tonight. How does that sound?"

"No, I couldn't..." I started to refuse, but I had given

Scooter most of my piece of pecan pie. "Oh, what the heck. Why not?"

"You just have a seat over here," Suzanne said. "I'll go grab them from the kitchen."

As I sank into the comfy chair, she set the box down in front of me. "French provincial?" I asked, pointing at the white coffee table.

"Why, yes, it is." She gave me an appraising look. "I'm surprised you recognized the style."

"My mom is really into interior design." In an effort to distract Suzanne from the crumbs I'd brushed off my shirt, which had landed on the Persian rug, I pointed at a lamp. "Tiffany?"

"Right again. That's Norm's side of the office," she said. "I had a hard time convincing him that it would add a touch of class to his desk."

The shared office space was a study in contrasts. Suzanne's side was feminine. The furniture was white, the rugs were pastel, and there were needlepoint cushions on the pale blue velvet-upholstered couch in the seating area. Norm's side was full of dark wood, leather seats, and a variety of taxidermy specimens adorning the walls.

"I don't know how he works like that," Suzanne said, waving her hands dramatically. "His desk is tucked back against that wall, and he can't see out the window." She poured some more coffee into my cup. "Now, if my Xander were working here, we'd reconfigure the whole space, maybe knock out that wall there, and—"

"Suzanne, can I interrupt you for a second?" Before she could refuse, I quickly added, "We really need to talk about the cottage." I walked over and picked up the advertisement from her desk, crumpled it up, and tossed it in the garbage can. Or rather, next to the garbage can. I really need to work on my aim.

"When—I mean if—we ever decide to sell, we'll let you

know. Right now, the cottage isn't on the market."

"You're being a tad dramatic, don't you think, dear? I promise you, we'll get better pictures." She picked the paper off the ground and smoothed it out on her desk. "We'll make sure to get a shot that shows off those lovely flower beds."

I tried to snatch the paper back and ended up knocking some files onto the ground. I bent down and was shoving the pages that had fallen out back into the folders when I noticed a document labeled "Coconut Cove Tropical Resort."

"Here, give me those," Suzanne said. As she placed them on her desk, her charm bracelet caught my eye. How could I have forgotten Mrs. Moto's discovery earlier today?

I walked back to the seating area and picked my purse up off the coffee table. I pulled the gold charm out and held it up. "Does this look familiar?"

She rushed over. "Oh, you found it! I've been searching for that. Where was it?"

"In the boatyard."

"The boatyard? That doesn't make sense. I never set foot in there." She clutched the charm in her hand. "Thank you so much for bringing it back. I'm so lucky you found it."

"Actually, it wasn't me who found it. Mrs. Moto did."

"I don't think I know her. Is she new to the area?"

"No, she's lived here for a while at the marina."

"Another one of those people who lives on a boat, like your friend Penny. I should have a word with her. I just got a new listing she might be interested in."

"I think she might have a hard time getting a mortgage."

"Oh, bad credit?"

"No, she's a cat."

"A cat?" After she considered this for a moment, she asked, "Is she one of those pets who had a rich owner who left her everything in the will?" She chewed on her lip. "I might just know the perfect place for a well-to-do feline."

"She's happy where she is," I said. "Now, getting back to

the charm—Mrs. Moto found it near the murder scene."

Suzanne gasped. "What a grisly thing to find." She dropped the charm on her desk, opened up a drawer, pulled out a disinfectant wipe, and scrubbed her fingers. "Well, I'm just glad it's back safe and sound with me and out of that nasty, dirty boatyard."

"How do you think it ended up there?"

She picked up the charm with a tissue, being careful to avoid touching it directly, and placed it on top of a notepad. "I'll have to take that into the jewelry shop tomorrow and have them clean it properly and reattach it to my bracelet," she said, ignoring my question.

I bit my lip. I was beginning to have second thoughts about giving the charm back to Suzanne. Even though it wasn't exactly found at the murder scene, Mrs. Moto did find it nearby. Perhaps I should have reported the discovery to the authorities.

"Uh, Suzanne, do you think maybe we should tell the police chief about the charm?"

"Why would they be interested in a silly little charm?"

"Well, because of where it was found."

"Don't you think you're overreacting, dear?" Suzanne said. "I'm sure there's a simple explanation."

"Like..."

She shrugged. "Maybe it fell off in the car, Norm put it in his pocket to give back to me later, and then it fell out of his pocket when he was working on the boat." She fussed with her bracelets. "Why are you so interested, anyway? It's not like we had anything to do with that poor young man's death. Besides, we were both here in the office the night of the murder."

"Well, if it wasn't one of you, who do you think did it?"

She leaned forward in her chair and lowered her voice. "I hate to speak ill of the dead, but apparently Darren was poaching fish. That sort of thing angers a lot of people."

"Do you really think anyone would murder someone for poaching fish? That seems a bit extreme."

"What's this about murder?" Norm asked darkly, standing in the entryway.

"Oh, Mollie and I were just talking about what happened to Darren. Such a sweet young boy." She gave Norm a warning look. "I was telling her how we were both here working late the evening he was killed."

Norm put his hand on the back of his wife's chair and glared at me. "What business is it of yours what we were doing? Do you think aliens were involved? Maybe one of them beamed down and killed Darren because he was going to tell everyone he had been abducted." He gave a humorless laugh.

Suzanne reached up and tugged on his arm. "Norm's just kidding. Isn't that right, darling?" she said.

"Sure, I was just kidding," he said. He walked around to the other side of his wife's desk, picked up the charm, and stared at it thoughtfully. As he set it back down, he grabbed the file folders. "What are these doing here? How many times have I told you to keep these locked up?" He walked over to a file cabinet, placed the folders inside, and shut the drawer.

I picked up my purse and made my way to the exit. As I opened the door, Suzanne took my arm. "Don't mind him. It's just the stress of everything. I'll see you tomorrow morning," she said as she gently pushed me outside. "And don't worry yourself into a tizzy about my charm."

"But—"

"Tell you what, why don't I tell the chief about it? Will that make you feel better?"

Before I could respond, she stepped back inside, shut the door, and flipped the sign in the window over to the Closed side.

I walked toward my car overwhelmed by questions. Was it really plausible that Norm had dropped Suzanne's charm in the boatyard? What exactly was the Coconut Cove Tropical

Resort, and why had Norm locked the files up? And more importantly, did Mrs. Moto think she was going to inherit a fortune from us when we died?

CHAPTER 8
THE CASE OF THE MISSING COLLAR

BEN LOOKED UP FROM SANDING the teak rails on *Mana Kai*. "Taking a break again, Mollie? Wasn't your last one five minutes ago?"

"No, it wasn't. It was..." Okay, just between you and me, it was five minutes ago, but I wasn't going to admit that to Ben. "I'm not actually on a break. I'm...uh...oh, never mind."

"Calculating how much paint you'll need to cover the bottom?" Ben offered helpfully.

I gave him a thumbs-up. "Yes, that's it."

"And how much paint do you think you'll need?" he asked.

"Um...I'm not sure yet. I think I'll need to do some more calculations while I have some water. Math problems are always so dehydrating." I plucked a bottle out of a cooler, closed the lid, and sat on it. "Want one?" I asked. "Looks like you're on a break too."

"Yeah, why not? I've been at it for a couple of hours."

I watched as Ben climbed down the ladder attached to the Chois' boat, holding on with one hand while balancing a large toolbox in the other. He lost his balance when his foot slipped on one of the rungs.

"Oh no," he said, looking at the hammers, screwdrivers, and wrenches scattered on the ground.

"Are you okay?" I asked. "You could have broken your arm like Leilani did."

"I'm fine." He put everything back in the toolbox with some help from me, then wiped dust off his tattered shorts. "Do me a favor. Don't tell Nancy what happened. She'll have a fit."

"She has fits all the time," I said. "What's so special about this?"

"We're supposed to hand things down to someone else or use a bucket with a rope attached to it to lower stuff down. 'Two hands on the ladder,' she always says."

"Don't worry, your secret is safe with me. Although, as much as I hate to say it, Nancy probably has a point."

Ben raised his hands in the air. "You're right. It won't happen again. I really don't want to lose this job."

He walked around *Marjorie Jane*'s hull and inspected my work. "How come you and Scooter don't pay the boatyard to take care of your projects?"

"Well, Scooter wants us to do everything ourselves. That way we'll know the systems inside and out."

Ben nodded. "Makes sense. Of course, things end up taking twice as long or more when you're doing them for the first time. I can see how Scooter would think it's an exciting challenge doing all this, but what about you? You don't seem like you're enjoying it."

I laughed. "There are times when I've thought a root canal sounded like a much more pleasant way to spend the day. But I don't want to spend a penny more on this boat than we have to. She's costing us a fortune as it is." I brushed my hand along the keel, noting areas that needed more sanding. "Plus, there's the matter of that bet I have with Norm. I would love to see the look on his face when he has to name his boat *ET*."

"I think there are a lot of people who'd pay to see that," Ben said. "By the time you're finished with this, you're going to be a pro, Mollie. Maybe you should get a job working at the boatyard too."

"I probably should," I said. "At least that way I'd get paid to be tortured instead of paying the marina for the privilege of having our boat here to work on it."

"Are you seriously thinking of getting a real job?" Ben asked.

I scowled. "Why does everyone think my work with FAROUT isn't a real job?"

"Hey, I get it," Ben said. "When I'm not working here, I'm practicing my guitar. I consider it my real job. The boatyard is just what pays the bills." He started strumming an air guitar. "One of these days, I'm going to make it big."

"I admire the fact that you can get up there in public and perform." I unzipped my Smurf suit in an attempt to cool down. "I would get such stage fright."

"You? That surprises me. You seem like you'd be a natural at it."

"Well, we'll find out soon enough. I have to give a speech tonight at a FAROUT meeting." I shaded my eyes and looked up at the sun. I wasn't sure how much longer I could stand to work outside in this heat. I kept reminding myself that I should be grateful I was doing this in winter. Things would be even worse during the summer. Hopefully, we'd be done working on this boat by then.

Ben gulped down the rest of his water. "Is your bottle empty? Give it to me, and I'll toss these in the recycling bin. Then I should probably get back to work. Break time's over."

While I debated whether I should continue sanding or go practice my speech, I noticed that Scooter had left his cell phone on a work table next to the Chois' boat. At last, my opportunity to erase those horrible Smurf photos he'd taken of me. I went over, picked it up, and tapped the screen. For some reason, his phone was unlocked. Not that it was ever hard to crack his passwords. His one for the computer was always the name of his current favorite cereal, and the PIN for his phone was my birthday.

I tapped on the album icon and scrolled through the photos. When had Scooter taken all these pictures of turtles? When had he even had a chance to go to the turtle sanctuary? And what were all these ones of the beach about? I was always the one who took those kinds of shots when we were out for a stroll. Not one single Smurf picture. Had he already deleted them?

His phone beeped, and a text flashed up on the screen.

I've got proof. If you don't do what I say, everyone will know what you did.

Proof of what? What did Scooter do? Who would send him something like this?

"No problem. I'll just head to the house and call you from there. We can walk through the contract then," a familiar voice said behind me.

I turned and saw Scooter holding a phone up to his ear. Then I looked back at the phone in my hand.

He ended his call, walked over, and gave me a quick kiss on the cheek. "Listen, panda, I've got to head back to the cottage for a while. Problems with that deal I'm working on. How about if I bring some fish-and-chips by for lunch?" The phone in his hand rang. "Oh, gotta get this. See you later," he said, dashing off toward the car.

If Scooter was talking on his phone, then whose phone was this? Did he have two phones?

I reread the text and noticed that it had come from Liam. Why would Liam text my husband? They barely knew each other. When I checked the other texts, there was a series of similar threats, but from Darren, not Liam.

As I puzzled over this, Ken pulled up in his vehicle. He

leaned out the window and shouted up at Ben, who was back working on the teak rails. "Hey, have you seen my phone anywhere?"

"No, man. Sorry, I haven't," Ben said.

"Is this it?" I asked, holding up the phone. "I found it on the work table."

"That's it! Thanks, Mollie. Got to go. Class starts in thirty minutes."

As he pulled away, I wondered why Liam was threatening him, and Darren before that. What was Ken mixed up in?

* * *

After sanding the bottom for a couple of hours and elevating my Smurfiness to a new level, I took another break. Okay, okay, I'd only been sanding for thirty minutes, but it had felt like hours. Was this bet with Norm really worth it?

The answer to my question came in the form of a conversation I overheard between Liam and his uncle. The redheaded young man was on his phone, leaning against his car. "I'm telling you, at the rate this chick is going, you'd better plan on changing the name of your boat. On the plus side, *ET* is only two letters, so it won't cost as much to get the vinyl decal printed up."

By the way in which he held the phone away from his ear, I guessed that he was getting chewed out. "Relax. I was just kidding." He listened for a moment. "You want me to do what? Oh, come on, it's just a stupid bet." After another pause, he interjected, "Hey, just wait a minute. I did everything you asked—"

My back was getting stiff from crouching under *Marjorie Jane*. I thought about coming out from underneath the boat, but I didn't want to be seen, especially when the conversation was getting so interesting.

"No way. I'm not going to. I've been asking around town

about her, and—just let me finish, will you? Anyway, apparently she's really nosy, always asking questions and getting involved in things that aren't her business. The last thing we want to do is give her a reason to poke around in our affairs."

Norm must not have liked his answer because Liam held the phone away from his ear again. I could hear his uncle's voice, but I couldn't make out what he was saying. I did my best imitation of a limbo dancer and crept under *Marjorie Jane* to get closer. I lay on the ground, grateful for once that I had a protective suit on. The dirt and grime on the tarp underneath the boat was disgusting.

From my new listening post, I could make out about every other word that Norm said. "Paint...send message...scare...crazy...broad...Yoda...fish..." He also mixed in a lot of swear words, which I won't repeat here. And yes, it sure did sound like he said "Yoda." Of course, if Scooter were here, he would have said that perhaps I've watched the *Star Wars* movies one too many times and that Norm probably said something like "you shoulda," and I misheard it.

Liam ended the call after assuring his uncle that he would take care of the matter. I was beginning to worry that I might be the matter in question. I was shimmying backward when a cloud of dust swirled around me, causing me to cough loudly.

"Mollie, what are you doing under there?" Liam asked.

"Uh, just checking the...um..." I tried to remember what could be on the bottom of the boat that I would be looking at. Scooter had given me a book on sailboats for Christmas. Granted, it wasn't one of his best gift-giving ideas, but at least it had been better than presenting me with another *actual* sailboat. One was enough. The book itself was really dry—I hadn't made it past the first chapter—but it did make a handy coaster on my nightstand. It had a diagram on the back cover showing the different parts of a sailboat. I chewed on my lip while I tried to remember what was underneath the boat.

"Checking the what?" Liam asked.

"Um...the running rigging," I said, hoping I had guessed right.

"Do you mean the thru-hulls? Or maybe the sacrificial zinc?" Liam asked.

I climbed out from underneath the boat. I tried to visualize the back of the book again, but drew a blank. I didn't have a clue what a sacrificial zinc was, but thru-hulls sounded vaguely familiar. "Um, yeah, the thru-hulls. That's what I said."

"No, you said 'running rigging.'" He pointed upward. "Those are the lines you use with your sails."

"Don't be silly. I know that. Everyone knows that." I made a mental note to do a bit more studying up on sailboats going forward.

Liam looked at me with a bemused expression on his face while he tapped his phone against his leg.

"Hey, can I borrow your phone?" I asked.

"My phone? Why?"

"I need to call Scooter. You don't mind, do you? I left mine at home."

He handed me his phone reluctantly.

"Let me guess," I said. "Is the password 'YODA' by any chance?"

"What?" He snatched the phone back. "Give me that." After punching in a few numbers, he handed it back.

I clicked the text icon and scrolled through his past messages. Sure enough, there was the one he'd sent to Ken. There was also a very naughty one to a female friend. Then I saw an interesting series of old messages from Darren.

Found a sweet fishing spot
They're biting! Gonna be a good haul!
Crap! Patrol boat!
Dumped overboard b4 they boarded

"I thought you were making a call?" Liam said.

"No, I said I was going to text him," I said, quickly closing the incriminating texts. "You might want to get your hearing checked. I said 'thru-hulls' before, and you heard 'running rigging.' A minute ago, I said 'text' and you heard 'call.'" I pointed at my ears. "Do you go to a lot of loud concerts? That can destroy your hearing."

"Can you just hurry up?"

I looked at Liam's sunburned arms. "You probably should start wearing sunscreen more often too." I punched in Scooter's number and reminded him to get extra tartar sauce when he picked up our fish-and-chips.

Liam seemed confused. "But you just called him, not texted him."

I tapped my ears. "Really, go see the doctor. I said I was going to call him. Why would I text him? What if he texted back after I gave you back your phone?"

The young guy looked like he needed to sit down and take a few minutes to process everything.

"Hey, speaking of Scooter, he said you guys chatted about the game the other day."

He nodded and rubbed his temples.

"So that's your alibi for the night Darren was murdered, right? Watching a game? Watching it all by yourself?"

He looked at me sharply. "You ask a lot of questions, don't you?"

"It's called making conversation. So you said you watched the game at home, right? Where's that?"

"I'm staying with my uncle and Suzanne."

"Oh yeah, that's right. But you're a young guy. How come you don't have your own place?" I pointed over at his car. "If you can afford that, I bet you could afford a nice apartment. In fact, I bet Suzanne could fix you up with a sweet one."

"Believe me, she's tried," he said. "She keeps saying how cramped it is at their house, and goes on and on about the fact that her precious son doesn't have any place to stay when he comes to visit because I'm there. Not that he would ever come to visit. He can barely stand that witch either."

"She told me that she wants Xander to come back and take over your uncle's business."

"He's welcome to it."

"Really? I thought you liked working for him."

"No way! The man's a tyrant. Always telling me what to do and giving me the crap jobs. He doesn't want to get his hands dirty, but he doesn't mind if I do."

I carefully considered my next question. While I knew that Liam was mixed up in something, I wasn't sure if it was just poaching or if it was something more deadly. I felt safe enough talking to him in the middle of the day in a crowded boatyard, but the snippets of his conversation with Norm were causing knots in my stomach.

"So, what do you mean by getting your hands dirty?" I asked tentatively.

He clenched his fists and stared at me. "Working on boat projects. Cleaning fish. That kind of thing."

I laughed nervously. "I know exactly what you mean. Just look at me. I'm covered in dirt and paint dust and who knows what else. I guess I get stuck with the dirty jobs too."

Liam's posture relaxed. "Yeah, how come Scooter isn't helping you?"

"Good question. I'll be sure to ask him." I put my goggles back on, secured my Smurf suit, and got back to sanding. While *Marjorie Jane*'s old blue paint slowly came off, I thought about what other "dirty jobs" Liam was involved in. I was pretty sure there was more to it than just gutting fish and fixing Norm's boat.

* * *

"I want to thank all of you for coming to the first in a series of lectures on alien abduction," I said. "Tonight, I'm going to talk to you about the checklist we use to identify individuals who may have—"

"Ahem. Mrs. McGhie?" I turned and saw Chief Dalton standing in the doorway.

"May I interrupt your..." He stroked his chin. "Your *performance* for a minute?"

I had given up on sanding the boat and had escaped to the air-conditioned lounge at the marina to rehearse. I felt my face grow warm. Rehearsing in front of a cat was one thing, but having the chief overhear me was another.

"Uh, sure. I was just practicing my speech for the FAROUT meeting tonight."

The burly man raised one of his bushy eyebrows. "FAROUT? Is that the little club you belong to? We had something like that when I was a boy. The meetings took place in our tree house. There was even a secret handshake."

My face grew warmer, but this time it was due to anger, not embarrassment. I was tired of everyone mocking what I did. "It isn't a *club*. It's a nonprofit organization. We even have an accountant."

He raised his other eyebrow. "Oh, an accountant," he said dryly.

"Listen, if it wasn't for the work we do, your phone would be ringing off the hook."

"Is that right?"

"If people want to report alien activities, they can call the FAROUT hotline. We take their calls seriously. When they contact the police, they just get mocked."

"No one in our department would mock anyone, no matter why they were calling," the chief said.

"Are you sure about that?" I asked. "When's the last time anyone reported an alien abduction or UFO sighting?"

The chief scratched his head. "Well, I'm not sure. I don't recall seeing anything like that in the monthly reports."

"That's because people are too afraid to contact you. Either you'll make fun of them, or worse, you'll bully them."

"Hey, hang on there, Mrs. McGhie. We certainly don't bully people."

"Oh yeah? How do you explain your treatment of Melvin Rolle the other day? The man is grieving. First, he lost his wife, then his nephew, and all you could do was grill him as though he was a suspect."

Chief Dalton furrowed his brow. "How would you know if he's a suspect or not? That kind of information is confidential."

"Because he's not on my suspect list, that's why!"

Both his eyebrows shot up. "Your suspect list?"

I pulled out my notebook, opened it, and held it up to him. "See, there it is. Now why don't you have a seat, and I'll take you through it."

The chief smiled. "Why not? I could use a break. This should be entertaining."

As he was lowering himself onto one of the armchairs, Mrs. Moto growled.

"That's her spot," I said. "Come on, Chief, you know the rules when it comes to cats. They get first dibs on all the comfortable spots. You can tell which ones they like by all the hair they leave behind." I pointed at the couch. "Why don't you sit there instead?"

While he eyed Mrs. Moto warily, I sat on a chair opposite him.

"Well, first on the list are Ken and Leilani Choi. They were on their catamaran when the murder took place. He told me that they had the AC running, and the TV was blaring, and that they couldn't hear anything that took place outside over all that noise."

I tapped my pen on my notebook. "On the face of it, their alibi seems solid. They can both vouch for each other. Of course, Leilani couldn't have done it with her broken arm. I would think you would need two hands to lift the paint can up in the air and hit someone on the head with it. But there's something about Ken that makes me wonder."

"Such as?" the chief asked.

"Well, on the day of the murder, I saw him and Darren arguing in the boatyard. Then this morning, I saw a number of texts on Ken's phone threatening to expose him as a fraud. Most of them were from Darren, but there was also one that Liam had sent."

"Dr. Choi showed them to you?"

"Well, not exactly." There went those eyebrows again. "Look, it was an accident. I thought it was Scooter's phone when I picked it up. But then there were all these pictures of turtles. Totally not what I expected."

"What were you expecting?"

"Smurf photos."

"Smurfs?"

"You know, the little blue people."

"Are they any relation to the little green men that you're so fond of?"

I sighed. "Can we just get back to the topic at hand?"

"Why not?" he said. "Let me try to recap. You took Dr. Choi's phone without his permission. You looked at his pictures and you read his texts, again without his permission."

"You're forgetting the most important thing here."

"No Smurfs?"

I threw my hands up in the air. "No, the threatening texts!"

Mrs. Moto jumped onto the back of the couch and sniffed the side of the chief's face. She pressed her paw on his cheek and meowed loudly before bounding back to her chair.

"See, she's trying to tell you to pay attention." I flipped over a page in my notebook. "Let's just continue, shall we?"

"By all means."

"We should probably talk about the other texts."

"Wait, there were more on Dr. Choi's phone?"

"No, Liam's phone."

"Did you accidentally borrow his too?"

"No, he loaned it to me. He was standing right there when I read the texts."

The chief furrowed his brow. "He knew you were reading his texts?"

"No, of course not. I think he would have been really embarrassed if he knew I saw the one he sent to a girl named Fiona."

"So this is about what, sexting?"

"No, this is about poaching. Pay attention."

"I'm trying, but this conversation is starting to remind me of one of those telenovelas. You know, those Spanish-language soap operas with the overly dramatic, convoluted plots."

"You don't strike me as the kind of guy who watches soap operas."

"I don't. My ex was into them. Is there a point here?"

"Liam and Darren were taking fish illegally. I know that's not your department's responsibility, but you should touch base with the Fish and Wildlife people about it."

"Noted."

"Ready to go on?"

"Sure. This is almost better than TV, even soap operas."

"Next up are Norm and Suzanne Thomas. They're another one of those husband-wife alibis. Suzanne told me that both of them were working in their office the night of the murder."

"I heard that you've listed your cottage with Mrs. Thomas."

"What? Where did you hear that?"

"I'm the chief of police. I hear everything."

"Well, did you hear about all the fights?" I leaned forward in my chair. "Melvin and Norm appear to have a long-standing feud. They nearly got into blows on Valentine's Day, and then they really got into it at the Tipsy Pirate on Sunday night."

The chief perked up. "Hmm. Go on."

I took a deep breath and continued. "And, of course, getting back to Norm's nephew, Liam, he isn't much better. He got into a fight with Darren on the night of the barbecue over Alejandra Lopez. He claims he was watching a basketball game on TV that night, but I'm not sure if he has anyone to back up his alibi."

I scrawled a few notes down on things I wanted to follow up on. I noticed that Chief Dalton had his arms folded over his chest. "How do you keep track of all this, Chief? Don't you have a notebook or anything?"

The chief tapped the side of his head. "It's all here. Carry on. This is most enlightening."

I leaned back in my chair. "Maybe it's your turn to enlighten me. Did Suzanne talk to you about her charm?"

"It would be inappropriate for me to comment on whether a woman is charming or not. Especially a married one."

"No, I meant the charm that fell off her bracelet."

"I have no idea what you're talking about."

"Didn't she call you about it?" The burly man shook his head. "We found it in the boatyard near the murder scene. I recognized it from Suzanne's charm bracelet. I considered telling you about it, but it wasn't in the cordoned-off area, and when I returned it to Suzanne, she said it wasn't any big deal. She thought maybe her husband had dropped it. But she did say she'd tell you about it."

The chief got a small notebook out of his pocket and scribbled something down. "You said 'we found the charm.' Who was with you?"

"Mrs. Moto. She's actually the one who found it. I just returned it to Suzanne."

"Mrs. Moto found it?"

"Yes, she's a very clever cat."

The calico began purring loudly. The chief watched as she kneaded the cushion.

"She also appears to be a cat in need of a collar and license," he said.

I looked at Mrs. Moto's neck and put my head in my hands. "I can't believe she's managed to lose another one." She rolled onto her back. I walked over, sat on the armrest, and rubbed her belly. "She doesn't like wearing a collar. They're too constrictive."

"If she's going to be an outdoor cat, she's going to have to learn to wear one," he said sternly. "My two Yorkies manage to wear their collars without complaining."

"Maybe we just haven't found the right one yet. She's very particular about what they look like."

The chief arched one of his bushy eyebrows. "Well, I suggest you find one that she'll wear, or keep her indoors." He looked at his watch. "Before I go, what exactly did this charm look like?"

After I described it and answered a few more questions about where it was found, he walked toward the door. He put his hand on the doorknob, then looked back at me. "Mrs. McGhie, can I offer you a piece of advice?"

I nodded reluctantly. When someone asks you if they can offer advice, it's usually not something you want to hear.

"If you really want to be an investigator"—he held his hand up—"and I'm not saying you should pursue that line of work, then you need to be objective. I noticed there were people you didn't have on your suspect list. Now, maybe that's because they're friends of yours or because you think they're too nice to have committed a crime, but you can't rule people out for those reasons."

"Friends of mine? Like who? Do you mean Ben and Penny?"

"I don't mean anyone in particular," he said. "But we can rule them out anyway. They were both playing Mexican dominoes late into the night with a group of people."

I breathed a sigh of relief. It had never occurred to me that they would be involved, but it was good to hear that the police wouldn't be harassing them with questions.

As if he could read my mind, the chief added, "I would also caution you not to characterize the questioning of individuals as *harassment*. There are things you aren't aware of, information you're not privy to."

"Well, you could be a little nicer about how you ask questions," I said.

The chief rubbed his face with his hands. "Maybe you should just stick to this alien stuff. You actually have people in Coconut Cove convinced it's real."

My eyes lit up. "Really? Like who?"

"Well, my ex-wife for one. She reads your newsletters."

"Is she the one who does paintings of fairies?"

He rolled his eyes. "Yep, that's her." He pointed at Mrs. Moto. "Don't forget that collar."

After he left, I sat on the couch and considered what he had said. Was it possible I wasn't as objective in this investigation as I had thought I was? Were there other people I should have on my suspect list?

CHAPTER 9
STAGE FRIGHT

"WELL, HERE GOES NOTHING," I said as I pulled into the parking lot of the community center. "I really wish I hadn't had those cookies before we left. I feel like I'm going to throw up."

"Don't be nervous. You're going to do great," Leilani said, unfastening her seat belt. As we walked toward the building, she added, "I heard about how you handled Norm when he was making fun of you for believing in aliens. You weren't a shrinking violet. You put him in his place."

"But that was in the heat of the moment. There were only a few people there. There are over fifty people signed up for this event." I gulped. "Fifty!"

I pivoted and began walking back to the car. Leilani grabbed my arm. "Wrong way, Mollie. Take a deep breath. You can do this." She steered me toward the entrance while I tried not to hyperventilate.

A young man with spiky orange hair and an alarming number of facial piercings greeted us at the door. He was wearing a bright green T-shirt with a picture of a spaceship beaming a human aboard and the words "Pick Me" printed underneath. I had purchased a shirt just like it at the FAROUT convention last year for Scooter, but for some reason he never wore it.

"Are you here for the talk?" he asked.

"We are," Leilani said. She nudged me. "Well, actually, I'm here for the talk. This lady here is your speaker."

"You're Mollie?" he asked. "I'm Simon." He took my hand and shook it vigorously. "I'm so honored to meet you! I read your recent article in the newsletter about the alien abduction case at that marina in Coconut Cove. Whatever happened to the victim?"

"Oh, it's a long story," I said. "Suffice it to say, other issues came up."

"I want to hear more about that," Simon said. "I hope you're going to cover it in your lecture."

Those cookies were making their presence seriously known in my stomach. "Do you mind if we go inside? I'd like to freshen up before we start."

I pushed the door open and darted for the ladies' room. When I came back out, a small crowd had gathered around the registration desk. Simon was handing out FAROUT brochures and answering questions. He waved me over.

"Can I get you a cup of coffee or tea before we begin?" he asked. "One of the volunteers also brought some chocolate macaroons. I can get you a couple of those too."

Fortunately, I'm not fond of coconut, so it was easy to pass on the macaroons, which my upset tummy thanked me for. I took my cup of coffee and made my way to the front of the room, nodding nervously at the people sitting in folding chairs. I put my purse on the table next to the lectern and pulled out my key chain. I stroked the tiny Wookiee doll attached to it for good luck, just in case rubbing Coconut Carl's belly hadn't been enough to help me get through the evening.

"Everyone, take your seats, please," Simon said. "It gives me great pleasure to introduce our speaker tonight, Mollie

McGhie, who's going to talk about alien abduction. Mollie is not only an investigative reporter for FAROUT but also lives on a sailboat and has plans to sail around the world with her husband. Maybe they'll even explore the Bermuda Triangle." Several people oohed and aahed. Simon smiled at me. "I'm sure she'll be happy to answer questions about their planned voyage at the end of her talk."

Leilani smiled at me from the front row and gave me a thumbs-up sign. I narrowed my eyes. Did Scooter have her on his payroll? Was she the one spreading rumors about Scooter and me circumnavigating the globe on our boat?

Fortunately, thoughts about *Marjorie Jane* sinking in the Bermuda Triangle distracted me from speaking to a large crowd. After explaining the signs that indicated that someone had been abducted, giving evasive answers to questions about sailing, and blushing at the loud applause at the end, I joined Simon and Leilani at the refreshment table.

"You did a fantastic job," Leilani said. She fished a tea bag out of her cup and tossed it in the trash. "I didn't realize that sleepwalking and bruises were signs that you had been abducted."

"Sounds like we've got another convert." Simon handed her a membership form. "You should join FAROUT."

"I'll think about it. Right now, I belong to a lot of organizations, mostly to do with sea life conservation. I don't know if I can commit to another one just now."

"Ooh…sea life conservation. My girlfriend's really into that. She leads scuba diving tours and does underwater photography in her spare time. How did you get into it?"

"It's kind of the same for me. My husband got me into it. He's a marine biologist. He works at the Gulf Coast Turtle Sanctuary, and he's an adjunct professor at the community college." Leilani took a sip of her tea and smiled. "Some friends set us up on a blind date. I thought he was really smart and cute, and the next thing you know, I started volunteering at the same organization. I really enjoyed working with the nesting habitat project with him, and in no time at all, we got married."

"How long were you dating before you got engaged?" I asked, wishing they had something to eat other than macaroons. Maybe I could convince Leilani to grab a bite to eat before we headed back to the marina.

Leilani blushed. "Only six months. It was love at first sight. My parents objected to us getting married so quickly. They said we didn't have time to really get to know one another, but they were wrong. I couldn't be happier."

"Did they warm up to him after that?" I asked.

"Oh yes, especially once they found out he had a doctorate. They were very impressed by that."

"Same for me and my girlfriend—love at first sight," Simon said. "So what other organizations do you guys belong to? Maybe we're all part of the same ones."

"Well, there's the Florida Turtle Trust, the Waterways Protection Society, and the Coastal Environment Action Group."

"The Coastal Environment Action Group?" Simon frowned. "Aren't they the ones who were responsible for sabotaging those boats in the Florida Keys last year?"

"Why did they do that?" I asked.

"There was a group of fishermen who were taking lobster out of season. They had already been investigated and fined by the authorities, but apparently that wasn't good enough. These people are really hard-core. The-ends-justify-the-means type of group. They'll do anything to send a message."

Leilani shook her head. "That was all hyped up by the press. It's run by a group of scientists who wouldn't hurt a fly. In fact, they'd go out of their way to save a fly. Well, maybe not a fly, but dolphins and whales and that sort of thing."

Simon pursed his lips. "Well, that's not what my girlfriend says, but—"

My stomach growled loudly, interrupting his thought. "Leilani, do you mind if we get going? I'm starving. I really need to get something to eat."

Leilani shrugged and mumbled goodbye to Simon. As we walked out the door, I remembered that I had left my purse by the lectern. Simon intercepted me as I went up front to get it. "How much do you know about your friend and her husband?" he whispered. "No matter what she says, the people who run the Coastal Environment Action Group are into some scary stuff. I'd be careful if I were you."

Leilani called out, "Are you ready, Mollie? It's starting to rain outside." I pulled the car keys out of my bag and looked at my lucky Wookiee charm. I knew many members of FAROUT were prone to conspiracy theories. Maybe Simon was reading more into the group Ken belonged to than there really was. Or maybe Leilani and Ken were mixed up in something more serious.

* * *

I chowed down on a cheeseburger, fries, and a chocolate shake on our way back to the marina. Leilani swore she wasn't hungry after eating macaroons at the FAROUT meeting, but I did notice that she helped herself to a number of my fries.

"So, what did you think of Simon?" I asked, hoping to maneuver the conversation toward the topic of the Coastal Environment Action Group.

"Nice guy," she said, pilfering another fry. "Although I can't say I liked all those piercings he had on his face. Looks painful."

"It was quite a coincidence that his girlfriend and Ken have so much in common. Maybe you'll run into her and Simon at some conservation meetings in the future."

Leilani angled the air-conditioning vent toward her. "Maybe. Although Ken hasn't been going to as many of those lately as he used to."

"Does that have anything to do with the sabotage Simon was talking about?"

Leilani frowned. "Like I said before, that's just someone trying to stir things up. Look, he cares about poaching and its effect on sea life populations, but he would never stoop to something like that. He's an environmentalist, not an ecoterrorist."

I stopped at an intersection and reached down to grab a fry, only to find that Leilani was holding the bag in her hand.

She popped one in her mouth, then stared at me earnestly. "Ken focuses more on educating the public about the dangers of big companies and developers. Their whole focus is on making money. They don't care what damage they do to the environment. They'll say or do anything to get around zoning laws and regulations, including trying to tarnish the reputation of people like my husband." She crumpled up the french fry container and shoved it into the paper bag forcefully.

As we neared the entrance to the marina, I saw Liam standing on the corner having a heated discussion with a woman. He was leaning forward and jabbing his finger in the air repeatedly. She put her hands on his chest and pushed him backward, then ran across the street, her flowery dress flapping in the breeze behind her.

Liam stared at her retreating back, his face contorted with rage. She tried to open her car but dropped the keys on the pavement. She leaned against the car and put her head in her hands. Liam crossed the street, picked up her keys, and handed them to her. She looked at him tenderly as he wiped away a tear on her face.

"What was that about?" I asked as the light changed. I made a right turn into the marina parking lot and pulled into a spot.

"I don't know," Leilani said. "I think that was Fiona Anderson. She and her husband live in the Tropical Breeze condos."

"She's married?" I adjusted the rearview mirror to have a better look. Liam was holding the door open as she got into the car. "They seem kind of cozy."

Leilani twisted in her seat to have a look. "Maybe there's an innocent explanation."

"Or maybe he's a bit of a player. Did you notice how he was all over Alejandra at the marina potluck?"

Leilani grinned. "He didn't have much luck, did he?" She grabbed her purse and the paper bag with her good arm. "Thanks for the ride. The FAROUT meeting was really interesting."

"So, do you think you're going to join?"

"I'll think about it," she replied. "Maybe when things calm down at work. I picked up a new client this week. He's really demanding, and I've got a huge database project to complete over the next few weeks." She opened the car door. "Hey, Ben should be done with the teak tomorrow. You'll have to stop by and have a look. He's done a great job."

"Will do. I have to be out here anyway. Lots more work to do on the bottom."

I watched as she tossed the bag into the trash, then made her way down the path toward the boatyard. As I backed out of my parking spot a horn sounded. I slammed on the brakes. I glanced in the rearview mirror and saw a dark SUV zip past me toward the back of the parking lot.

After my heart stopped racing, I continued reversing, making sure to keep an eye out behind me. As I put the car into forward, I looked behind me again. Someone wearing a dark hooded top got out of the vehicle and pushed through the brush that separated the parking lot from the boatyard.

I couldn't imagine ever being in such a hurry that I'd walk through there at night. Not only would you get scraped by the thorny bushes, but you could never be sure if a snake or rabid raccoon were lying in wait. Any sensible person would take the well-lit path instead. Unless, of course, you didn't want to be seen. Was that how the murderer had sneaked into the boatyard the night of Darren's death?

CHAPTER 10
HOW NOT TO CLIMB A LADDER

I DECIDED TO GO TO the boatyard early while Scooter slept in. He had been tossing and turning all night, worrying about the latest deal his company was doing. After taking a quick shower, brushing my teeth, and running a comb through my hair, I gave him a kiss on the forehead. He mumbled something that sounded like "more Cap'n Crunch"—probably a reference to the fact that we were still out of his favorite cereal.

Mrs. Moto lifted her head and blinked slowly at me, in that way that felines do to let you know you've been deemed worthy of being allowed to be part of their lives, as long as you keep their litter box clean and food bowl topped up.

She meowed softly, which I took to mean that I should pick up more cat food at the grocery store along with Scooter's box of crunchy nuggets. I scratched her on the head as she nestled back into the crook of her second-favorite human's arm. Of course, I was her number one human. That just went without saying.

Since Scooter wasn't up to make me my morning coffee, I

swung by Penelope's. I chose a couple of *pains au chocolat* fresh out of the oven to go with my cinnamon spice mocha. While I waited for my coffee, I noticed a large poster advertising the upcoming annual Coconut Cove Boating Festival. It promised all sorts of exciting activities—sailboat races, concerts, a parade, and a pet-costume competition.

Hmm...I wondered if I could get Mrs. Moto to wear a Sherlock Holmes outfit. Or maybe dress her up as Miss Marple. No, that would probably be a mistake. Miss Marple was always knitting something. I could just imagine the mischief she would get into if one of the props were a ball of yarn. Who was I kidding? We couldn't even get her to keep a collar on. Wearing an adorable detective-themed costume was never going to fly.

Next to the poster was a sign-up form for a cake contest that would be taking place during the festival. I scrawled my name down. I was confident that my fudge chocolate cake was going to win first prize. Then I noticed who was on the panel of judges—Nancy. Knowing her, she'd probably accuse me of trying to poison someone with my home baking.

The sun was just coming up by the time I parked next to *Marjorie Jane*. I decided to sit in the cockpit and watch the sunrise while having my breakfast. I clutched my coffee cup and pastry bag in one hand and slowly climbed up the ladder, holding on with my other hand. When I neared the top, I reached up to grab the railing on deck in order to hoist myself up the final stretch.

Instead of feeling something metal as expected, my fingers encountered a damp and slightly squishy object. I jerked my hand back, then started to fall backward. I quickly seized the ladder with my other hand, causing my cup and pastries to plummet to the ground.

I cautiously peeked over the side of the deck to see what the dampness and squishiness were all about. Three tree frogs stood stock-still staring at me before making their escape via some overhanging branches. I breathed a sigh of relief. Tree frogs were a far better outcome than some of the other scenarios that had played through my head.

Unfortunately, my early morning wildlife encounter had resulted in a tragedy. I gazed down at my coffee cup sitting in a puddle of cinnamon-chocolaty goodness. This was not a great start to the morning. On the plus side, the *pains au chocolat* had come through unscathed, but they definitely needed caffeine to accompany them.

After tossing the empty cup in the trash, I trudged back up the rungs. This time I had learned my lesson—two hands for the ladder. I didn't have a pail and rope to hoist my pastry bag up as Ben had suggested, so I did the next best thing and tucked the bag inside my shirt. Sure, it looked a little strange, but the boatyard was deserted at this hour of the morning.

I decided to hunt in *Marjorie Jane*'s galley for the jar of instant coffee that we had left on board for emergency purposes. If this didn't qualify as an emergency, then I didn't know what did.

The search proved to be a monumental challenge. In his quest to discover the source of our water leak, Scooter had removed all the floorboards, exposing the bilge, in order to gain access to the various hoses, fittings, and tanks that lay underneath. I had studied the sailing book Scooter had given me the previous night, so I now knew the bilge was the compartment below the waterline. Water could collect in this area, something both Scooter and I were now very familiar with. That's why a functioning bilge pump was so important. You wanted to get water out from inside the boat before it sank her.

Scooter had laid down some narrow pieces of lumber over the cavities at the bottom of the boat. I felt like I was walking the plank as I made my way across the cabin. One wrong move and I would fall into the bilge, likely twisting an ankle in the process. The experience reminded me of one of Ben's T-shirts, the one that read "Walk the Plank, Ye Scurvy Dog." I didn't have scurvy, but I was seriously suffering from a case of caffeine withdrawal.

Balancing on a board running the length of the galley, I finally found the instant coffee in the farthest cupboard. It was sitting behind a tub of dehydrated acai berries and a container of turmeric, both left over from one of Scooter's short-lived health kicks. I think that particular one had lasted thirty-eight minutes.

I got the kettle out, put it under the faucet, and turned the water on. Nothing. Then it hit me—our water tanks were empty. I should have realized this earlier. Why would we have water in the tanks if Scooter had the whole system torn up? The lack of coffee was really impacting my ability to think clearly.

I cautiously made my way across the plank and sat on the couch. I pulled out one of my pastries and took a few bites. The flaky crust and gooey chocolate filling gave me the energy I needed to figure out a solution to my problem. There was a water tap between our boat and *Mana Kai*. I could fill the kettle up there and presto, coffee would be served.

When I sat at the edge of the deck and prepared to twist my body around in order to climb down the ladder, I realized there was a problem. How would I keep both hands on the ladder and carry the kettle down? I remembered Ben's suggestion to pass things down to another person on the ground, but the boatyard was still deserted.

I looked at the kettle. It really wasn't a nice kettle. We had picked it up in a secondhand store, and it was beginning to show its age. So I dropped it overboard. I watched as it bounced off *Marjorie Jane*'s hull, chipping some of her red paint off, then struck the ladder and landed in the puddle of coffee at the bottom that I had never bothered to clean up.

I was beginning to think this was the worst plan I had ever come up with, but then I remembered the time I had tried to teach sign language to raccoons. Boy, had that ever been a disaster.

After washing the kettle off and filling it up with water, I faced my next hurdle—how to get the darn thing back up. It was too big to tuck inside my shirt. My throwing ability wasn't the best and would likely result in more paint being chipped off the boat and water ending up everywhere. I decided to take Ben's advice and hoist it up.

I searched around our boat for a rope to tie to the handle. All I found were a few toy mice that Mrs. Moto had batted off the deck, sandpaper, a chisel, and a large pile of rags. I poked under the stained and smelly scraps of cloth and discovered not one but two cat collars. So that's where she had been hiding them.

This whole enterprise was getting ridiculous. It now dawned on me why they referred to having your boat out of the water propped up on jack stands in the boatyard as being "on the hard." Just trying to make one simple cup of coffee was hard work for sure.

I remembered that Liam had tossed some ropes over the side of his uncle's boat. Surely they wouldn't mind if I borrowed one. I walked around the stern of *The Codfather* and stopped dead in my tracks. I looked on in horror at the scene in front of me—Suzanne, lying on the ground, her legs and arms twisted unnaturally beneath her.

After leaning up against the side of the boat for a moment, struggling to breathe normally, I forced myself to go over and check her pulse. But as I got closer, it was clear that I wouldn't find one.

As I collapsed on the ground in shock, I felt one of her stiletto heels under me. For some reason, all I could think about was how its robin's-egg-blue color matched the pencil skirt she was wearing. As I picked it up, the breeze caught a scrap of green paper and blew it across the boatyard. I spotted the other shoe by the bow of Norm's boat. I'm not sure why, but I felt compelled to take that one as well.

My eyes focused on the matching shoe, I tripped over the metal ladder on the ground next to Suzanne. That's when I noticed the message spray-painted on *The Codfather*'s keel: You've Been Warned, Now You'll Pay.

* * *

The chief found me huddled on the steps of the boatyard workshop. I was shivering despite sitting in the warm sunlight. While finding dead bodies was always unnerving, Suzanne's death had really shaken me. I wondered if it was because she had fallen off the ladder, something that I'd almost done earlier that morning.

"Mrs. McGhie, are you okay?" he asked gently. I think even he realized how upset I was. He held out his hand and helped me up. "I understand you were the one who found Mrs. Thomas. Are you up to answering a few questions?"

"I think so," I said. I reached up to touch my necklace, something I always did when I was feeling stressed or anxious. My eyes welled up when I realized it wasn't hanging around my neck. "I can't believe I lost it," I said, tears dripping down my face.

"Lost what?" The chief searched in his pocket, pulled out a crumpled-up napkin, and handed it to me.

"Thanks." I blew my nose. "The necklace Scooter gave me. I think of it as my good-luck charm, but I lost it a few days ago, around the time I found Darren's body. Do you think there's a correlation? Am I jinxed?"

"No, you're not. Besides, there's no such thing as luck, good or bad."

"Of course there is," I said. "You don't think it's bad luck that I've found *four* bodies now?"

"I'd say it's unfortunate. But it isn't because you're jinxed or because you lost your necklace. You just always happen to be in the wrong place at the wrong time." He reached in his other pocket and handed me another napkin. "What time did you find Mrs. Thomas?"

"About a half hour ago, I think," I said. "Although it could be longer than that. I'm not really sure." I chewed my lip. "It seemed like her body had been there for a while. I took a seminar at the FAROUT convention last year. It was given by a medical examiner. He told us that you can estimate how long someone has been dead by—"

"You don't need to worry about that," the chief said. "Our coroner will determine the time of death."

"But it was before I got to the boatyard, right? I'd hate to think she was lying there dying, and I didn't hear her screaming out in pain."

"Why do you think she screamed?"

"Well, you saw the body and the way she was lying on the ground. She must have been on *The Codfather*'s ladder when she fell off. Landing like that would be incredibly painful. She could have been lying there for hours in agony." I took a deep breath. "I guess we can only hope she was struck unconscious when she hit the ground."

"So, just to be clear, did you or didn't you hear anyone screaming?"

"No, I didn't hear anything. The place was deserted." I glanced over toward where I had found Suzanne. *Marjorie Jane* was right next to *The Codfather*. I should have been able to hear something from there. Next to our boat was *Mana Kai*. "Have you spoken to Ken and Leilani yet? They live on their boat. Maybe they heard something."

"Officer Moore is talking with them now."

"Now that I think about it, they probably didn't. Darren was murdered not too far from their boat, and they didn't hear a peep then."

The chief gazed over at the three boats. "Strange to think people actually live here."

"Strange is right," I said. "The idea of living on a boat is weird enough, but living on one here? That's crazy. Not to mention dangerous." I looked at the placard on the side of the workshop listing the boatyard's rules and regulations. "I hate to say this, but Nancy is right. Going up and down ladders here is dangerous. I almost fell off ours this morning. I can only imagine what would have happened if it hadn't been tied on. When I had that nasty tree frog encounter and let go of the boat, the ladder could have tipped backward. I could have been lying on the ground like Suzanne."

"So you think it was an accident?"

I glanced at him quizzically. "You don't?"

"I didn't say that."

"Oh my gosh! I just remembered something. The ladder next to Suzanne had some rope attached at the top. It had been tied on." I chewed on my lip while I thought through the implications. "That means that either the rope frayed naturally—although it's pretty unlikely that it happened at the same time on both sides—or someone deliberately untied it or cut it. Maybe they even pushed the ladder when she was on it."

"Hmm."

"That's all you can say—hmm?"

The chief shrugged. "Why exactly were you over by *The Codfather*?"

"I was making a cup of coffee."

The chief raised his eyebrows. "Coffee?"

"It's a long story." I sighed. "I could really use a cup right about now."

"We're almost through here. So, you were making coffee over by *The Codfather*, and..."

"No, I was looking for a rope."

"I've never heard of making coffee with rope. Sounds interesting."

Officer Moore walked over from questioning the Chois, saving me from explaining the whole kettle fiasco. She whispered something in the chief's ear and handed him a piece of green paper.

"All right, just a few more questions, Mrs. McGhie. Did you touch anything over by where you found the body?"

"I touched Suzanne to see if she had a pulse."

"Other than that."

I shook my head. "Nothing."

"Are you sure?"

"Positive."

"You said you were looking for some rope. You didn't pick any up?"

"No, I completely forgot about rope and coffee when I saw Suzanne."

"Let me try phrasing this another way. Did you pick anything up and remove it from the scene?"

"Of course not."

The chief stared at me. I stared back without saying a word. I was convinced I was going to win the stare-down competition, but then he raised both of his bushy eyebrows. I couldn't help but look up at them twitching above his eyes like fuzzy caterpillars making their way across a tree branch, just like the tree frogs had done earlier.

The minute I broke eye contact, he took a step toward me. "I'll ask one more time," he said, enunciating every word. "Did you touch anything, accidentally *borrow* it, put it in your purse or your pocket, and completely *forget* about it?"

His breath smelled like coffee, which caught me off guard. I had figured him for a sweet tea drinker. "Do you know where I can get a cup of coffee around here?" I asked. "I don't want to have to drive all the way back to Penelope's."

"Just answer the question."

"No, I didn't touch, borrow, stash away, or forget to tell you about anything. Are we done?"

"Just one last question. What do you think the message 'You've Been Warned, Now You'll Pay' means?"

I scratched my head. "It could refer to just about anything or anyone. Warning Liam off about poaching. Warning Norm and Suzanne about this property deal they're supposedly mixed up in, or..."

"Or what?" the chief asked.

"Or maybe someone could have left it because they were angry about Norm trying to drive other fishing charter businesses out of operation."

"Someone like whom?"

I took a deep breath. "Someone like Melvin."

* * *

Officer Moore had asked me to wait for her at the patio in case there were any follow-up questions. There was no way I was going to survive a minute longer without some form of caffeine. But here was the conundrum—there was bound to be a Coke or possibly even an iced coffee for sale at the marina office, but could I face dealing with Nancy before I had had any caffeine?

I'd have to try to sneak in, creep stealthily toward the coolers in the back, open them quietly, nab a couple of cans, and get back outside before she spotted me. The sticking point was how to pay for them without talking to Nancy. Perhaps I could tuck some money in between the beer and milk for her to find later.

My plan fell completely apart when Nancy yanked open the door, causing me to fall headfirst into the office, knocking down a display of fishing lures in the process.

As I tried to pick them up without slicing my fingers with the barbs, Nancy barked, "What were you doing skulking outside?"

Rather than tell her about my ingenious caffeine-procurement plan, I said, "Sorry, I was just preoccupied thinking about Suzanne's tragic death."

Nancy put her hands on her mouth, speechless for once.

Ned stepped out from behind the counter, holding a bucket full of cleaning supplies. "Did you say Suzanne was dead?"

I nodded while sorting the purple lures from the ones with orange spots.

"What are you doing on the floor?" Nancy asked, her power of speech restored.

I stood and placed the lures into color-coded piles on the counter. "Just picking these up."

"Humph. Those ones go over there," she said, pointing at the ones with long green streamers. "And those other ones go over there."

"Nancy, can you forget about the lures for a minute? I want to hear what happened to Suzanne," Ned said.

After I told them about finding her body at the bottom of Norm's boat, my theory about the ladder being deliberately untied, and the message the killer had left behind, they both peppered me with questions.

"Do you think the two murders are connected?" Ned asked.

"Hmm. That is a good question." I pondered the connection between Suzanne's and Darren's deaths while I hung the lures on the display stand. "I can think of people who might have wanted one of them dead but not the other."

Nancy handed me a lure. "Like who?"

"Well, Norm might have killed Darren to drive Melvin out of business, but he wouldn't have killed his own wife." Nancy and Ned exchanged glances. I looked back and forth at them. "Or would he?"

Ned shifted the bucket of cleaning supplies from one hand to the other. "Well, I did hear Norm complain about how much money Suzanne kept spending on furniture for their office. He said she married him for his money and was bleeding him dry."

"Interesting turn of phrase, considering she's the one who ended up covered in blood."

Nancy pursed her lips. "I can't say I like the man, but killing your own wife..."

"Sometimes a woman can be insensitive and stick her nose into things where it doesn't belong," Ned said.

She gave him a sharp look. "Well, sometimes a woman can just be trying to help, and her husband is too pigheaded to realize it."

"I've got a question for you guys," I said, trying to defuse the situation. "What was Suzanne doing there, anyway? She told me she would never set foot on a boat, let alone one on the hard." I thought about her robin's-egg-blue stilettos and skirt. "And she certainly wasn't dressed for climbing up a ladder and onto a grimy boat."

"That's a good point," Ned said. "She always was dressed to the nines."

Nancy pointed at the lures. "You need to redo that section, Mollie."

"What, aren't these organized enough for you?" Ned asked.

"Things can always be better organized." She glanced at the bucket Ned was holding. "And cleaned properly."

When he didn't respond, she turned back to me. "What were you doing in the boatyard at that time in the morning? I didn't think you were such an early bird."

"I couldn't sleep, so I decided to work on sanding the bottom before it got too hot."

"I doubt if you'll get any more work done on it for a while now," Nancy said. "The police will barricade it off while the investigation is under way."

"But it didn't happen by *Marjorie Jane*. It happened on *The Codfather*."

Nancy shrugged. "They're both right next to each other. What were you doing over by Norm's boat, anyway?"

"Trying to get a cup of coffee." Before Nancy could ask any follow-up questions, I said, "It's a complicated story. I don't want to go into it now. And it's been a really long morning, and I still haven't had a single cup of hot, liquid caffeine."

"You know we got a new coffee maker in the lounge, don't you?" Ned asked.

"That's the best news I've had all morning."

"Come on, I'll show you where it is."

Nancy frowned. "Why would you need to show her where it is? She isn't blind. I'm sure she'll have no problem finding it." She pointed at the pile of papers on the counter. "I need you to work on this after you're finished cleaning up over there."

Ned placed the bucket on the counter right on top of the papers. "Do it yourself. I'm on break. Come on, Mollie. Let's go have some coffee."

Nancy scowled. She moved the bucket to the side and shook off imaginary dust from the top sheet of paper. As we walked out the door, she said, "Don't forget to put some money in the donation jar next to the machine. Both of you."

* * *

"What's going on with the two of you?" I asked as I filled up our cups. Ned stirred sugar into his, then motioned over to the sofa. I leaned back against the cushions and took a sip from my cup. There wasn't any milk in the fridge, but I didn't care. Even black, this was the best coffee I'd ever had.

"Let me ask you a question, Mollie. Would you ever take something that was important to Scooter, that he had spent days organizing, and completely undo all the work he had put into it?"

"Well, he's pretty disorganized with laundry. He always leaves his dirty socks on the floor, and I end up having to put them in the hamper. Does that count?"

"Wow, that's brave. If I ever did that, Nancy would kill me." He smiled. "But that really wasn't what I was talking about."

"So tell me. Maybe I can help."

"I don't know if anyone can help," Ned said, wringing his hands together.

"Well, maybe I can't help, but I can listen. It might make you feel better to get it off your chest."

"You know how I like old movies?" I nodded. "I've been collecting DVDs for years and keep them in plastic storage tubs in the spare bedroom. Nancy started complaining about how much space they were taking up. Then our son suggested I transfer them to the computer. It sounded like a good idea. Nancy would be happy that there was more room, and I could play them directly from my laptop."

"That is a good idea. I've heard that lots of people who live on boats do the same thing."

"Right. Same reason that e-readers are so popular. Cruisers can't afford to carry lots of books, considering how many spare parts they need to stow on board."

"How does Nancy figure into all this?"

"I spent a long time separating them into different piles based on the type of movie they were—westerns, comedies, thrillers, epics, that sort of thing. I even had a stack dedicated to films featuring Peter Lorre."

I smiled, remembering how Ned had been the one to name our cat after Peter Lorre's detective character in his *Mr. Moto* films. Only he hadn't realized at first that it was a she, not a he, which was why she was now known as Mrs. Moto. Her black markings in the shape of eyeglasses and the fact that her breed had Japanese origins had reminded Ned of the lead character in the movies.

Ned took another sip of his coffee. "I had it all planned out. I put the discs in groups to make it easier to save them in separate folders on my computer. That way, if I was in the mood for a World War II movie, for example, I would be able to go straight to that folder and find one easily."

"Sounds like a great system. So what happened?"

"Nancy's what happened. She got a bee in her bonnet that I wasn't doing it right. She said my approach didn't make sense. I told her I had it set up just the way I wanted. Then one day when I was out, she decided to reorganize everything alphabetically. When I came back and saw what she had done, I was furious."

"Maybe she was just trying to help," I said tentatively.

"That's what she said. But I didn't ask her to help, and I certainly didn't want her help." He walked over to the window and stared outside.

While he collected his thoughts, I refilled our coffee, stirring extra sugar into his. After a few moments, he sat back down.

"Thanks," he said when I handed him his cup. "I'm sorry to dump this all on you."

"Don't worry about it. Sometimes you need to get things off your chest."

"When it comes to running the marina, her organizational skills are great, second to none," he said. "She enjoys doing all the paperwork, managing suppliers, and overseeing the staff. I'm happy she takes care of all that. Believe me, I don't want to be in charge of making arrangements for the garbage dumpsters to be emptied. But when it comes to *my* movies, I wanted to be the one in charge of that."

"Have you tried talking to her about it?"

"Lots of times, but she can't or won't admit to what she did."

"I have a feeling that kind of thing doesn't come easily to Nancy."

Ned smiled. "You're probably right."

"I can kind of relate to how she feels. I hate admitting when I'm wrong." I leaned forward and patted his hand. "You guys will work through it."

"You're right, we will. When I think about couples like Norm and Suzanne, I'm grateful that we've got a solid marriage at the core."

"Do you think he could have killed her?"

Ned hesitated, then said, "I can't say for sure."

"What can you say?"

"He has a temper." He shrugged. "Although everyone around town already knows that. But..."

"But what?"

"I saw him put a guy in a choke hold once. We're not talking an ordinary fistfight that sometimes happens when guys have had too much to drink. This fellow was standing outside the Tipsy Pirate having a smoke, and Norm grabbed him from behind, totally unprovoked. I saw him say something to him before letting him go, and then he laughed when the guy collapsed on the ground."

"That's awful!"

Ned chewed on his lip. "The worst part about it was that I was across the street and should have rushed over to stop it, but I just froze. By the time I came to my senses and went over to help, Norm had already taken off."

"Did you mention it to the police?"

"I did, but the guy didn't want to press charges, so nothing came of it."

Ned looked at me grimly. "So yeah, could I see Norm murdering someone? Sure. But his own wife? That I'm not so sure about."

CHAPTER 11
FUN WITH MARKERS

OKAY, SO REMEMBER WHEN I'D told Chief Dalton that I didn't touch anything at the crime scene, or accidentally borrow it, stash it away, and forget about it? Well, that wasn't exactly the truth. But it wasn't a lie either. I actually did forget. You would have, too, if you'd been confronted with a dead body. Finding Suzanne had really thrown me for a loop. It wasn't until later that I remembered the incident with the shoe. Of course, the chief didn't see it that way.

"What do you mean, you forgot?" The burly man leaned forward across his desk. "You picked up a shoe and went in search of another one. You just spent five minutes describing the exact shade of blue it was..." I waited while he referred to his notebook. "Here it is—robin's-egg blue. And you went on in excruciating detail about what type of skirt she was wearing..." He made another check. "A pencil cut skirt. Why would anyone name a style of clothing after a writing implement?"

"Can I go now?"

"No. Back to the shoe. You held it in your hand just

minutes before I questioned you, and you *forgot* about it?"

"But I dropped it."

"So when you drop things, you no longer remember them?"

He made a show of dropping a pen on the floor. He bent down and picked it up, then removed the cap in a dramatic fashion. "Good thing I remembered I was holding this just a second ago," he said. "It's one of my favorites."

He jotted down a few notes on a piece of paper while I tried to make myself comfortable on the hard wooden chair in front of his desk. I don't think the townspeople would object if he spent a little bit of our tax money on some cushions.

He raised his head and caught me squirming. "Officer Moore is going to be back in a few minutes with some photos of the crime scene. I'll want you to review them, so you can point out where the evidence was *originally* before you contaminated the crime scene."

While he was scribbling things down—probably specifications for a more uncomfortable chair for visitors to sit on—I looked around his office. There was a stack of file folders on one side of the desk next to a coffee cup crammed full of markers. Maybe he spent his spare time coloring in drawings of jail cells and squad cars.

I watched as he pulled a green marker and an orange one out. After debating between the two, he jammed the orange one back. Good choice—green was much easier on the eyes. Next, he underlined something on his notepad.

"What does green stand for?"

"Things to follow up on," he said without looking up.

"Like the message spray-painted on Norm's boat," I suggested. The chief ignored me and selected a pink marker.

"Okay, since you're not exactly in a talkative mood, how about if I make an educated guess? It has to do with the suspects in the two murders." I pulled the cup closer to me and selected a dignified marker, a fine-tipped black one. I got my notebook out of my bag and opened it up to a list of names.

The chief looked pointedly at the black marker.

"Do you mind if I use this one?" I asked.

"I do." He pulled open the top drawer of his desk and handed me a run-of-the-mill ballpoint pen. He pointed at the container of markers. I replaced the black one, then examined the pen in my hand.

"You don't happen to have a blue one I could use instead of this one, do you?"

"Does this look like Walmart?" He glanced at his watch and muttered something about Officer Moore taking a long time.

I put a star next to a couple of names on my list. The pen left annoying globs of ink on the page. "Okay, why don't we start with people who had motive to kill both Darren and Suzanne? Now, that's the tricky part of this investigation, isn't it? Who would want to murder both of them? Melvin wouldn't have killed Darren—he's his own flesh and blood—and one would think Norm wouldn't have murdered Suzanne—she's his wife. Rather, she was his wife."

I noticed the chief had paused his scribbling. I took that as a sign to continue. "But what about Liam? He and Darren got into a fight over Alejandra at the marina barbecue. He could have killed Darren in a jealous rage." I tapped my pen on my notebook. "Did you know that Scooter doesn't think anyone would kill just for love? But I happen to know for a fact that it's the number one cause of spousal homicide."

"And how do you know that?"

"I read an article on it. A *scholarly* article."

The chief smirked. "You do realize that what you read in the *National Enquirer* isn't exactly written by academics."

I slammed my pen down on his desk. "I'll have you know that I read it in *Extraterrestrial Studies Quarterly*, which is a highly regarded, peer-reviewed journal."

Chief Dalton plucked a purple marker out of the container and went back to his notepad.

"Although there did seem to be some issues between Suzanne and Liam."

I watched as the chief's eyebrows twitched slightly. He was definitely listening. "Suzanne went on and on about her son and how much better he would be as a successor to Norm. She didn't exactly think Liam had a lot going for him in the intellectual department. Maybe he got tired of her attitude?"

Both of his eyebrows shot up on his forehead. He quickly scribbled something down.

"Of course, Norm had his share of enemies. Maybe someone killed his wife to send a message to him."

"You do realize that the murders might not be related," the chief said. He tore off the colorful pages from the pad and stuck them in a file folder.

"I guess," I said. "But what are the chances that two murders happened within days of each other, in a small town, and they aren't related?"

The door to the chief's office opened, and Officer Moore poked her head in. "Do you have a sec, chief?"

"Sure." The burly man rose. As he walked around the desk, he pointed at the markers. "Don't touch anything while I'm gone."

I held out for a minute, but there was this one pen that looked like it might be a nice shade of robin's-egg blue. I couldn't help myself. As I reached across the chief's desk, my foot got caught in my purse strap and I stumbled, knocking the markers to the floor along with the file folders.

Fortunately, the coffee cup didn't break. I set it back on the desk, scooped up the markers, and replaced them in the container. The file folders were a different matter. They had scattered across the room, sending the papers flying out of them into a jumbled mess. I sat on the floor and attempted to sort everything back into the right folder.

Nancy would have had a field day here. I'm sure she could have organized the documents in no time, probably developing a new and improved filing system in the process. I, on the other hand, was struggling to determine whether all the expense reports belonged together or were meant to be placed in separate folders based on date.

As I started to collate the papers, I found an evidence bag stuck between two autopsy reports. Inside was a piece of lined pale-green paper that looked like it had been ripped out of a notebook. The top corner was missing, and there were dark stains scattered on the page. But what really caught my eye was the message, written in block letters.

If you want to get it back, meet me on The Codfather *at 9:00 PM. Bring $5,000 in small bills. Wait for me in the main cabin. Come alone. Don't even think about going to the police. If you do, I'll know about it and then I'll destroy you.*

While I tried to process what I had just read, the door opened. "What's going on here?" the chief demanded. "I thought I told you not to touch anything."

"It was an accident. These fell off your desk, and I was just picking them up."

"Give those to me," he barked. He grabbed the folders and papers, but I held on to the evidence bag.

"Do you want to tell me about this?" I asked.

"I most certainly do not."

"I've seen this before."

"Don't tell me you touched that, too, at the crime scene."

"I wasn't actually sure it was found there, but now you've confirmed it." He snatched the bag from my hand. "But I did recognize the paper. It's an interesting shade of green. I saw what must have been the corner of the page get blown away by the wind."

"So you didn't touch this?" he asked, placing the bag on the center of his desk.

"The shoes, yes. The paper, no." I leaned forward to have another look. "What do you think the message means? What did they have on Suzanne that she was willing to pay five thousand dollars for?"

Officer Moore knocked on the door. "I've got those photos ready."

"Great. Why don't you get set up in the conference room, and I'll bring Mrs. McGhie down there in a minute?"

I picked my purse up off the floor and edged toward the door.

"I'm not finished with you yet," the chief said.

While he paced back and forth behind his desk, I could hear Officer Moore in the hallway telling someone that they found an empty spray-paint can, but that there weren't any prints on it or on anything else at the scene. This was turning out to be a very productive visit to the police station. First, learning about the message the killer had sent Suzanne, and now the spray paint. And, as a bonus, when I'd picked up Suzanne's autopsy report, I'd noticed that the time of death had been between nine and ten in the evening.

"Are you listening to me?" The chief had stopped pacing and was staring at me.

"Uh, yeah." I tiptoed over to his desk and set the ballpoint pen he had lent me down. "There you go."

He threw his hands up in the air. "Fine. Let's just go look at those photos and be done with it."

* * *

After I had finished reviewing the photographs and explaining in excruciating detail exactly where Suzanne's shoes had been originally, I sat on a bench in the police station lobby and gave Scooter a call. He had left a few messages checking to see if I was all right. I reassured him that I had recovered from the shock of finding Suzanne's body and told him about the new leads I was going to follow up on.

Before he could try to dissuade me from investigating the two murders further and possibly putting myself in danger, I changed the subject and asked what he wanted to do about dinner. Apparently, he and Mrs. Moto had something special planned, provided I agreed to swing by the grocery store and pick up some Cap'n Crunch and half a dozen cans of Frisky Feline Ocean's Delight.

After he promised that cereal and cat food weren't involved in his secret recipe, I ended the call. As I walked down the steps from the police station, I ran into Melvin. He looked terrible. His face was gaunt, he had dark circles under his eyes, and his hands were shaking as they gripped the metal railing on the stairs. When he reached the top step, he stumbled. I rushed over to take his arm.

"Are you okay?" I asked. I pushed the door open, ushered him inside, and held his arm while he slumped on the bench.

"What is with these people?" he demanded angrily. "All I want to do is bury that boy in peace. I was at the funeral parlor with his parents making arrangements when the police chief summoned me here to answer more questions. How many more questions could they have of me? It's their job to figure out what happened and bring his murderer to justice, not mine!"

"Maybe it's not about Darren. Maybe it's about Suzanne," I said.

He cocked his head at me. "Suzanne? Why would the police want to talk to me about her?"

"You haven't heard? She was killed yesterday in the boatyard."

"Killed? How?"

"Someone untied the ladder from Norm's boat. Then when Suzanne was climbing up it, they pushed it, and she fell to her death."

"Are you saying it's murder?"

"Looks like it."

Melvin frowned. "No, I hadn't heard. It's no secret that Norm and I don't get along, but I'd never wish that on him. I know what it's like to lose your wife." He slapped his hands on his thighs. "No, this can't be about Suzanne. I didn't even know about it."

"I think it must have happened sometime between nine and ten. I'm sure you have a good alibi for then."

He rubbed his eyes. "Sure, sure. I was at the Tipsy Pirate then. You can ask anyone." He had a determined look on his face. "I don't have anything to worry about."

"I'm sure you don't."

"The person who should be worried is Norm. And not just about Suzanne. He killed my Darren. And now he's going to pay. He can grieve for his wife from prison."

"So you're sure he did it?"

"Of course he did." Melvin shook his head. "Not that going to jail is enough for what he did to that fine young man. And it sure won't keep me from going out of business."

"I didn't realize things were so bad."

"We were operating on a knife-edge with the charter business. Stealing customers from us was bad enough, but now he's been spreading rumors about how my boat isn't seaworthy. People are scared to charter with us."

"What about the marine store? Is that doing poorly as well?"

"No, it's doing okay. But to tell you the truth, I just don't have the energy to manage it anymore. I'm tired. Maybe I should just sell the store, retire early, move back to the Bahamas, and live out my final days there. I don't have any fight left in me anymore."

While I tried to console him, Officer Moore came out into the hallway. "Mr. Rolle, we're ready for you now."

He got to his feet slowly and squeezed my arm. "You won't tell anyone what I said, will you? I was just letting off a little steam."

As I watched him follow Officer Moore, I wondered if maybe he'd had a little fight left in him after all. Perhaps enough to have killed Suzanne as retribution for Darren's death.

* * *

After the police station, I went to the marina. Scooter had texted me to say that one of us needed to go to the office to deal with some paperwork. Nancy had updated the rules and regulations and was requiring all boat owners to review the changes and initial their acceptance. And since I was already in town, I had drawn the short straw.

"It's right here," she said, pointing at the printout on the counter. "Section 7.2(a). Only American quarters can be used in the washing machines and dryers. Anyone found using a non-American coin will be responsible for paying a fifty-dollar fine and the cost of labor to fix the machine." She handed me a pen. "Initial right there."

"Are you serious, Nancy? Is this because Leilani accidentally put a Bahamian quarter in the washer?"

"Do you know how long it took Ned to get it out?" She didn't wait for my answer. "Three hours! That's three hours he could have spent repairing the dinghy dock." While I considered the potential ramifications of not playing along with her rules and regulations game, Nancy glared at a fly on the counter. She raised the swatter in the air and smacked it down right next to my hand.

"Hey, there wasn't even a fly there," I said. "It had already flown away."

"They're everywhere, dear. The sooner you put your John Hancock on that piece of paper, the sooner you can get out of here. You don't want to get caught in the cross-fire, do you?" she asked as she took aim at another fly.

I scribbled my initials and stepped back quickly, bumping into Ned. "I'm sorry. Here, let me help you pick those up." I bent down and scooped up the screws that had fallen out of his hand.

"Thanks, Mollie," he said. He glanced over at the counter. "I see she's got you in here too."

I shrugged. "It's fine. I wash my clothes at home. No need to use the machines here, so it really doesn't apply to me."

"Are you finished yet, Ned?" Nancy asked as she stapled some papers together. He walked out of the office like he didn't hear her, swinging his toolbox. I guessed he wasn't quite ready to make up.

Nancy slammed down the stapler. "I don't know what's gotten into him. You make one little change, and he totally overreacts." She picked up the flyswatter and began decimating the insect population again, one smack at a time.

While I was debating whether to buy a regular iced coffee or a vanilla-flavored one, the door swung open, and Nancy's grandkids—Katy and her younger brother, Sam—ran in.

"Grandma, tell Katy not to touch my race cars," Sam said.

"What's this about, children?" Nancy asked, tousling their hair.

"They're my cars, not hers!" the little boy said.

"They were in my way," Katy said.

Sam leaned against his grandmother and sniffled. "She took apart my race track, and she hid my cars."

"I didn't hide them. I just put them away." Katy put her arm around her little brother. "I was just trying to help. Mama would have been mad if she came home and found them on the dining room table like that."

"See, Sam? Katy was just trying to help," Nancy said. "Now, why don't the two of you make up? Katy, say you're sorry for touching Sam's cars without his permission, and then you can each pick out a candy bar."

While I walked up to the counter with my iced coffee, I noticed Nancy looking thoughtfully at the two kids as they selected their treats.

***

By the time I left the office, it was a little after five o'clock. It's amazing how quickly the day goes by when you find a dead body, and there's a murder investigation going on. I spotted Leilani over at one of the patio tables typing away on her laptop with one hand. Her day had probably been more productive than mine.

"Did you hear about Suzanne?" I asked, pulling up a chair next to her. "It was just awful finding her body like that."

I set my purse on the table. Leilani looked up with a start. "Oh, hey there, Mollie," she said, removing a pair of headphones from her ears. "Did you say something?"

"Oh, I was just talking about the latest body in the boatyard."

She grimaced. "Wasn't that awful?" She wrapped the cord around her headphones and tucked them in her bag. "Sorry, I didn't hear you. I've been listening to an audiobook. I can't wait to find out whodunit."

"I've never really gotten into audiobooks. I like mine the old-fashioned way."

"Oh, they're fantastic. I listen to them all the time when I'm working. It helps the time pass faster, especially when it's a boring task, like updating spreadsheets or working on boat projects. I always turn the volume way up so I can't hear what's going on around me. The fewer distractions I have, the more focused I can be."

"I should probably leave you be so you can work."

"No, stay. I'm done for the day. Have you heard anything more about what happened?"

I told her about finding Suzanne and what Ned had said about Norm's temper. I also told her about the note in the evidence bag, leaving out the part about the markers and papers flying everywhere.

"But if Norm killed his wife, why would he have sent her a

note asking her to meet him at the boat? Couldn't he have just asked her to meet him?" Leilani asked.

"That might have been the only way he could have gotten her there. She would never have stepped foot in the boatyard unless she thought that was the only way she could get back what had been taken from her."

"So it was a diversion?"

"Maybe. Same thing with the message that was spray-painted on his boat. It was designed to throw suspicion off him." I opened up my iced coffee and took a sip. "I'm still surprised that you and Ken didn't hear anything. It happened between nine and ten."

"Hmm...between nine and ten? Ken wasn't there at the time. He was at a Florida Turtle Trust meeting. He didn't get back until eleven. And you and I were at the FAROUT meeting. You really were great, by the way."

"Thanks," I said. "I dropped you off around eight thirty, eight forty-five, didn't I?"

"Around then."

"What did you do after that?"

"Headed straight back to our boat." She tapped her ears. "Then I listened to my audiobook while I caught up on email."

"So you didn't hear anything?"

Leilani frowned. "No, I didn't. It's scary to think all that was happening just a few feet away from where I was sitting." She held up her broken arm. "At least I'm not a suspect. Of course, it's not like I had any reason to kill Suzanne. Besides, there's no way I could have pushed a ladder over with just one arm."

"Not to mention your other wrist," I said. "Is it getting any better?"

"A little bit. At least I can do some one-handed typing. Otherwise, I'd be so far behind with work it wouldn't even be funny."

"I'm impressed with how well you manage with just one arm."

"You learn to adapt, don't you?" She pointed at the teenage girl walking across the patio. "Tiffany's here, and it looks like she brought pie." Leilani closed her laptop. "Come on, we should probably get going."

"Going where?" I asked.

"Nancy's, of course. I love these girls' get-togethers of hers—wine, appetizers, dessert, and doing our nails." She stared at her hands, one in a cast and the other still bruised from her fall. "Of course, I think I'll just be sticking to my toes this time."

"Uh, I wasn't invited."

"Oh, I just assumed that's why you were here," she stammered.

"Don't worry about it. I'm not exactly one of Nancy's favorite people. She hates that Mrs. Moto runs around the marina, and I made a stink about one of the regulations a few weeks ago. Besides, I don't paint my fingers or my toes."

Tiffany came over to the table and set the pastry box down. "It's blueberry," she said. "I'm excited to do my fingernails in our school colors for the basketball game this weekend. It was so nice of Nancy to invite me. Probably because I babysit her grandkids."

"Ah, to be back in high school—those were the days," Leilani said. "What I wouldn't give to not have to worry about working for a living. It'll be nice to chill out this evening, especially with all the commotion in the boatyard."

"I haven't been back there since this morning," I said.

"The place is still crawling with cops. They've got the area around your boat and Norm's completely cordoned off. I was so relieved when they decided we would still be able to access our boat. Guess you're off the hook for a while on painting the bottom."

"I'd almost be happier to be sanding than have to deal with

Chief Dalton and his questions." I inched my chair away from the pastry box. The smell of blueberries was tempting me to crash Nancy's party just so I could have a slice of pie.

"I think we lucked out," Leilani said. "Officer Moore questioned us. She's a lot more pleasant to deal with."

Tiffany slid forward in her chair. "Who do you think did it? Everyone's talking about it around town. It's scary to think there's not only one murderer out there on the loose but possibly two."

"That's what makes it tricky—was it the same person?" I thought about the charm that Mrs. Moto had found. "One possibility is that Suzanne killed Darren. Then someone killed her as retribution."

"No, it couldn't have been Suzanne," Tiffany said. "I saw her working in her office that night."

"You did?"

"Well, promise you won't tell anyone, especially my parents," she said.

"I don't think we can make that promise until we hear what you have to say first," Leilani said. "Murder is a serious matter."

Tiffany took a deep breath. "Okay. I was at the park across from her office that night with my boyfriend. My parents don't like him, and they told me I'm not allowed to see him anymore." She made a face. "They keep telling me I should date someone like Chad."

Leilani and I exchanged glances.

"But it's not like anything happened," Tiffany said quickly. "We were just talking."

"Then you don't have anything to worry about," Leilani said. "I think you need to tell your parents and the police what you saw. It could be important."

She reluctantly agreed. While she texted someone—presumably her boyfriend to tell him the cat was out of the bag—Leilani asked me who the prime suspect was.

"I don't know if I have a prime suspect, but I'm leaning toward Liam," I said. "He's the only person I can think of who would have wanted to kill both of them."

"After what you've told me, I can see why he might be responsible for Darren's death," Leilani said. "But Suzanne?"

"There was a lot of animosity on Suzanne's part toward Liam. She resented the fact that Norm was working so closely with him instead of with her son, Xander."

Tiffany looked up from her phone. "I remember Xander," she said. "He used to play on the basketball team with my cousin. I was in elementary school at the time, but we still went to all the games. My dad's the coach. It's kind of weird now that I'm in high school. He knows all the guys in school and makes a point of telling me who I should and shouldn't date."

After describing how he had embarrassed her at the previous week's game, she added, "I heard Darren and Melvin arguing at halftime a couple of weeks back."

"They were at one of the high school games?" I asked.

"Coconut Cove is a small town," Leilani said. "Lots of people go to the games to cheer the team on even if they don't have kids in high school. We do sometimes too."

"The town I grew up in was a lot bigger," I said. "What were they arguing about?"

"Darren's uncle was furious at him because he had caught him poaching. He told him that it could cost him his business and fishing licenses."

"How did Darren react?" I asked.

"He seemed pretty upset, especially after Melvin threatened to call his parents and tell them."

Leilani glanced at her watch. "We should probably get going, Tiffany. Nancy doesn't like it when anyone's late." She looked at me. "You sure you don't want to come? I'm sure Nancy wouldn't mind."

"Thanks, but I'm good. Scooter is making dinner tonight.

I'd better scoot off myself."

On the drive home, I thought about what Tiffany had said. As much as I liked Melvin, doubts were creeping into my mind. Could he have killed his own nephew to cover up the poaching activity and protect his fishing charter business?

CHAPTER 12
ANOTHER MYSTERY INGREDIENT

"I'M BACK!" I MANAGED TO close the door with my foot while balancing the grocery bags in my hands. Mrs. Moto ran into the hall, rubbed against my legs, and purred loudly. "All right, I see you. Let me get these into the kitchen, and then I'll say hello properly."

Scooter plucked the bags out of my arms and set them on the counter. "I'd better make sure this doesn't burn," he said as he dashed back to the stove and looked inside a steaming pot.

"It smells delicious. What is it?"

"You'll have to guess."

"Give me a clue."

He removed a wooden spoon from a ceramic holder and gave his concoction a few stirs. "Hey, no peeking," he said as he covered the pot.

"Come on, just one tiny clue."

"What's it worth to you?" I gave him a peck on the cheek. "That works. Okay, are you ready for your clue?" He did a drum roll on the stove. "It doesn't involve cereal."

"Wow, that really narrows it down."

While he continued to stir our mystery dinner, I filled my husband in on my chat with the chief and my discussions with Melvin, Leilani, and Tiffany. We did have a bit of a digression when he disputed my characterization of my meeting with Chief Dalton as an "interrogation." He was of the opinion that the use of colored markers negated any potential intimidation factor. Then things naturally devolved into a debate about which of the fruit-scented ones that we'd had as kids smelled the best. I voted for orange; Scooter opted for cherry.

"I'm sorry Nancy didn't invite you to her shindig," Scooter said as he put canned goods away in the cupboards.

"I'm not. Why would I want to spend time with that grouchy old lady? Although there was blueberry pie. Which reminds me, did you make dessert?"

"No. I figured we could use a break from all that sugar."

"Really," I said, holding up two boxes of Cap'n Crunch. "Should I return these to the store? I still have the receipt."

"Give me those," he said, grabbing them from me.

Mrs. Moto jumped on the counter and supervised while I pulled out half a dozen cans of Frisky Feline Ocean's Delight. She sniffed at each one, and when she was satisfied I had bought the right brand, she hopped down on the floor and rolled over on her back.

"How am I supposed to put these bags away if you're in the way?"

"She doesn't want you to put them away," Scooter said. "Look." He took one of the reusable tote bags, opened it up, and set it on the floor. Mrs. Moto jumped into it, causing it to slide across the tiles. "See, it's a new toy." We watched for a few minutes as she darted in and out of the bag, then batted her toy mouse inside and wrestled with it.

"I think dinner is almost done. Why don't we eat at the kitchen counter so we can watch the floor show?"

I got out plates and napkins while Scooter dished up chicken with a dark brown sauce served over rice and accompanied by a black bean, cilantro, and mango salad.

I leaned over my plate and inhaled the fragrant odor. "This smells great. Better than any scented marker."

"Take a bite, and tell me what you think."

I sampled a piece of the chicken. "Oh, this is so good." I took another bite. "It tastes so familiar, but I can't put my finger on it."

"Keep eating. Maybe you'll figure it out." He pulled a bottle of Corona beer out of the fridge. "Want one? I think there might even be a lime around here to go with it."

While we sipped our beer and ate our chicken—and yes, I had seconds—Scooter told me about a video he had seen of a couple sailing in the Bahamas. "They were anchored off Staniel Cay. Isn't that where Melvin said his family was from? It'd be fun to take *Marjorie Jane* over there one day. Ned was telling me that some of the boats at the marina go down there every year. They call themselves the Coconut Cove Crew. Wouldn't that be a blast?"

"That sounds like a long way off," I said. "I'm not even sure when we'll be able to get back to working on the boat."

"I hope the chief wraps up the investigation soon."

"Well, if he stopped playing with markers and took me more seriously, he might stand a better chance."

* * *

After dinner, the three of us walked down to the beach. "We really have to do something about getting her a new collar that she'll actually keep on for more than two minutes," I said. We watched Mrs. Moto tap a crab on its back tentatively before retreating to a safe distance.

I breathed in the salt air and enjoyed the cooling breeze coming off the water. "It's so peaceful here. Why would you ever want to sell the cottage? Just think—could you have made a meal like that on board the boat?"

"Maybe you have a point," he conceded. "Hey, you never did guess what the mystery ingredient was. That means I win."

"Win what? I don't recall making a bet."

"Sure you did. Mrs. Moto can back me up. You agreed that if you couldn't guess what I put in the dish, you would be in charge of cleaning the bathrooms for the next month, including her litter box."

"I never agreed to any such thing."

"Mrs. Moto, do you hear that? My little panda bear is trying to get out of a bet." The calico darted up to us and deposited a shell at my feet. Then she meowed loudly. "See, she agrees with me," he said.

"I went to the store and got you cat food. Where's the gratitude?"

We sat on a piece of driftwood and watched Mrs. Moto play with her seashell. "So what was it?"

"Cocoa powder. I thought for sure you could taste the chocolaty flavor. It's a Mexican *mole* sauce. Alejandra gave me her mother's recipe."

"Well, you'll have to make that again. It's a winner."

"She gave me some other recipes I want to try out. How does *pozole* sound?"

"It sounds like something I can't spell, but I'm game." I pointed at a young man with spiky green hair and a clipboard who was approaching us. "He seems familiar," I said. I waved at the green-haired man. "Is that you, Simon?"

He looked in my direction and returned the wave. "Hey, Mollie. Fancy running into you here." There were two other people with him—an older woman with short blonde hair and a young woman wearing a baseball cap. All three of them were sporting fluorescent orange T-shirts that glowed in the moonlight. As they neared us, I noticed that their shirts featured a cheerful sea turtle holding up a sign urging people to keep the sea plastic-free.

Simon put his arm around the younger woman. "This is my girlfriend, Fiona. I told you about her at the FAROUT meeting." I did a double take when I heard her name. Nope, a different Fiona than the one Liam had been seeing behind her husband's back.

Simon pointed at the older woman. "And this is Connie." I shook their hands and introduced Scooter and Mrs. Moto. Scooter extended his hand. Mrs. Moto sniffed their shoes. "Mollie is the foremost expert on alien abduction in the whole state," Simon said.

"Are we talking little green men?" Connie asked dubiously.

"Well, some are green, but not all of them," Simon said.

Fiona smiled. "It's something they're passionate about, just like we're into wildlife conservation."

"Well, to each his own, I guess," Connie said. "But we have more pressing problems here on Planet Earth to be concerned with." She gestured at the sky. "Before we start worrying about what's out there, we need to fix what's broken down here."

"From looking at your T-shirts, I'm guessing you're worried about sea turtles."

"You bet we are," Fiona said. "Did you hear there's a resort being planned for this area? They want to knock down those cottages and build a big hotel, swimming pool, restaurants, and a spa. It's going to destroy the delicate ecosystem here."

The older woman chimed in. "Sea turtles come here every year to lay eggs. It's hard enough to protect their nesting grounds as it is. We don't have enough volunteers to monitor and patrol the area. Imagine all those tourists swarming on the beach, shining bright lights, disrupting nests, and killing baby turtles. It has to be stopped at all costs!"

Fiona touched Connie lightly on her arm. "Hey, you're beginning to sound like Ken Choi."

She took a deep breath. "While I don't agree with his methods, at least he's making a stand. All we're doing is filling out forms."

Simon shook his head. "Some might call his methods ecoterrorism."

Connie folded her arms across her chest. "I don't know where you've heard that, but it's just not true."

"It's not just what I've heard, it's what I've seen," Simon said through clenched teeth. "And I don't want my girlfriend caught up in—"

Fiona seized his arm. "Enough, you two. Let's not lose sight of what's important here—the turtles. We did a great job today talking to people about endangered species and handing out educational materials. So no more talk about Ken, okay?" Fiona stared at both of them until they mumbled their agreement.

"We actually live in one of those cottages," I said, trying to steer the conversation toward more neutral grounds. "What can you tell us about this proposed development?"

"Whatever you do, don't sell, no matter how much they offer you," Connie said. "They'll do anything to con you out of your property."

"Who's 'they'?" Scooter asked.

"Norm and Suzanne Thomas. He's orchestrating the deal through a shell company, and she's buying up the property. It isn't the first time they've done it. Remember what happened last year?"

Simon and Fiona nodded.

"But that doesn't make sense," I said. "She posted a listing of our house on her website and put an advertisement in the window of her office. If she were planning on having a shell company buy it, why would she do all that? Why wouldn't she just present an offer from the shell company?"

"If you just had one offer, you might not accept it," Connie said. "So she pretends to be offering it to other buyers, but if anyone shows any real interest she doesn't return their calls. She's even gone so far as to have people pretend to be potential buyers and go to view the property. Then she tells you that the highest offer came from the shell company. You think she did her best to drive up the price, and you happily accept it."

"Wow, that sounds really complicated."

"She's perfected her scheme over the years," Fiona said. "She goes to a lot of trouble to make it all seem legit. She has professional photographs taken, puts listings on her website—"

Connie interrupted. "Coconut Cove isn't the first place she's done this at, and it probably won't be the last. No matter what it takes, she needs to be stopped."

"But wouldn't people get suspicious if the same company kept making offers on neighboring properties?" I asked.

"She sets up a number of them so it seems like a different one each time," Connie said. "She's also been known to get family members to buy properties, then transfer them to her later. Like I said, you should stay away from her. She's a cold-hearted—"

"You do realize she's dead, don't you?" Scooter asked before she could specify exactly what kind of cold-hearted person she had been.

Fiona frowned. "No, I didn't."

Connie shot her fist up in the air. "That means the resort won't go ahead! Wait until Ken hears about this. He'll be over the moon. Remember how he was saying just last week that the only way we could stop this development would be over her cold, dead body?"

"Connie, come on, show some respect. The woman is dead. And besides, Ken didn't mean it literally," Fiona said. "We should probably head back now. It was nice to meet the two of you." She bent down and stroked Mrs. Moto's back. "Sorry, I meant the three of you."

I scooped the cat up in my arms. "Everyone loves you, don't they?" As we walked back home, I asked Scooter what he thought about Ken.

"He seems like a nice guy. Bright, obviously, and passionate about the work he does."

"Yeah, but do you think he could have killed Suzanne?"

"How could he have? You're the one who told me he had an alibi. Wasn't he at a conservation meeting? Now come on. I'll race you back. Last one there has to wash the dishes."

CHAPTER 13
SNOWBIRDS

THE NEXT DAY, I HEADED over to Melvin's Marine Emporium. It was a weekday morning, so I was spared Chad's cheerful greeting when I entered. He was probably acing some sort of math test at school at this moment and trying to convince Tiffany to go out with him.

I had swung by the marina first to get an update on when we could get back aboard *Marjorie Jane*. I almost hated to admit it, but she looked kind of lonely behind the police barricade.

Ben was working on an outboard engine at the other end of the yard. After wiping grease off his hands onto his T-shirt, he told me that there hadn't been any update as to when we'd be able to access our boat.

According to my aspiring-musician and wannabe-pirate friend, Norm had been there earlier in the morning, enraged that he couldn't get on his boat either. He had complained bitterly about the revenue it was costing him. Each day he couldn't work on the boat meant another day's delay getting her launched again and going out on charter trips. Ben wasn't too impressed that Norm was more focused on making money than on the loss of his wife.

With time on my hands, I decided to swing by Melvin's to look at bottom paint. Scooter was busy with work again, which meant that I could focus entirely on the different color options available without being distracted by the latest three-for-one offer that they were running on something we didn't need. I definitely knew we wouldn't be doing Smurf-colored paint again. Despite my lack of fashion sense, even I knew that a bright blue keel and a red hull wasn't a good color combination.

As I examined paint chip samples, I saw Penny walking past a display of fishing tackle boxes. "Hey there," she cried out cheerfully. As usual, she was dressed head to toe in her favorite color. Today's outfit consisted of bright-pink sandals, a ballerina-pink skirt, and a floral-patterned top in shades of fuchsia and salmon-pink. "Come meet Alan. He just bought a boat from me, and I'm showing him all that Coconut Cove has to offer."

Her client's dress sense was more muted—dark-gray shorts and a light-gray polo shirt with a yacht club insignia on it—which went perfectly with his bland features. He kept his eyes focused on the ground and mumbled hello when Penny introduced us.

Turns out Alan already knew all about me. "So, you're the gal who found the bodies in the boatyard," he said in a quiet, monotone voice. He held up his camera and shyly asked if he could take my picture.

I sensed a glimmer of excitement as he listened to my account of the two murders. For a brief moment he made eye contact, then looked away. He continued to ask questions, inching closer to me as I described the murder scenes while at the same time flinching as the details got gorier. He made me think of a timid little mouse who desperately wanted that piece of cheese despite the fact that it was sitting on a lethal trap.

I had been constantly bombarded with questions everywhere I went in town. Printing up some fliers with all the relevant facts to hand out was starting to seem like a good idea. It got old repeating the same story over and over again. So far, I had managed to stay one step ahead of the reporter from the local newspaper and hoped to keep it that way.

"So, if you had to pick one restaurant for Alan to try, which would it be—the Sailor's Corner Cafe, that new Thai place, or Alligator Chuck's barbecue joint?" Penny asked.

"Oh, that's a tough one. Why pick one? Go to the cafe for breakfast, Alligator Chuck's for lunch, and have some Thai food for dinner," I said diplomatically. "Scooter and I have done that before."

"That's a lot of eating out," Penny said.

"I know, but sometimes we're just too busy or too lazy to cook. We're probably going to have to cut back on going out, considering how much money we seem to be spending here at Melvin's."

Alan chewed on his fingernails and mumbled something.

"What was that?" I asked.

He shuffled toward me. "Do you ever order stuff online? There are some discount sites where you can get good deals, probably better than some of the prices here."

"We have," I said. "But we like supporting local businesses when we can. At least, that's the rationale we use when we eat out."

"As a local business owner, I'd have to echo that sentiment," Penny said. She turned to Alan. "You do get a discount at Melvin's for a limited period of time since you bought a boat from me. Plus, the poor guy has been through so much lately that anything we can do to support him is a good thing."

While Penny filled Alan in on more of the details regarding

the loss of Melvin's wife and nephew, I spotted Liam pulling up in front of the store in his sports car. Norm got out of the passenger side and marched toward the door. Liam pulled him back before he could open it. The two of them got into a lively discussion. Norm kept gesticulating wildly at the store while Liam tried to cajole him back to the car.

Alan had crept up to the window and was snapping pictures. Norm caught him out of the corner of his eye, slammed his hand against the window, then pressed his face against the glass and glared at him. The photographer jumped back in surprise.

"I wonder what that's about?" I asked. "Why do you think Liam is trying to keep Norm from coming inside the store?"

"I'm pretty sure I know," Penny said. "Did you hear about Norm's boat? The one at the public docks?"

"What happened?" a quiet voice asked. Alan had managed to creep back toward us unobserved and was standing next to Penny, clutching his camera.

"Well, someone vandalized it the night that Suzanne was murdered," Penny said. "They slashed seat cushions, overturned coolers, broke fishing rods, used bolt cutters to break the padlocks on the lockers, and then threw everything they found in there into the water."

"Was anyone hurt?" Alan asked.

"Thankfully not."

Alan fidgeted with the strap on his camera bag, then asked, "Do they think that lady's murder and the vandalism are connected?"

Penny shrugged. "I don't know for sure, but there was a can of spray paint on the deck."

"What kind of message did they leave?" Alan asked, his eyes shining with excitement. "Was it like the one left by Suzanne's body?"

Penny shook her head. "No, there wasn't a message."

"Oh, that's disappointing." He chewed on his finger for a

moment. "I bet the murderer thought Norm was going to be on the boat and was planning on killing him and leaving a message before he had to flee the scene."

"Or it was just high school kids messing around," Penny said dryly.

While Alan considered this less-than-exciting possibility, the front door swung open and Norm charged toward Melvin's office. "Get out here, you coward!" he yelled. "You're going to pay for what you did!"

Melvin came out of his office clenching his fists. "If you don't leave my store at once, I'm going to call the police." He looked at Liam. "Get your uncle out of here before he causes trouble."

Norm lunged at Melvin, but before he could land a punch, Liam pulled him back. "Don't. You'll just make things worse. There are witnesses."

Norm glared at the small crowd that had gathered to watch.

Melvin crossed his arms. "You should listen to the boy, Norm."

"If anyone is going to listen, it's going to be you," the other man spit out. "How dare you do that to my boat? You're going to pay!"

By this point, Liam had lost all control of his uncle. Norm grabbed Melvin by his shirt. "You vandalized my boat! Do you know how much damage you've done? I've got one boat stuck in the yard, and now the other one is out of commission. Do you know how much business I'm losing?"

Melvin shoved Norm backward. "You? You've got four boats, two of which are still operational. Remember when I used to have four boats? That was until all your dirty tricks caused me to lose all of them except *Nassau Royale*. Finally, you're getting a taste of your own medicine. Whoever did it should get a medal!"

Norm scoffed. "A medal? That's rich." He leaned against

one of the display cases. He seemed calmer, but I was worried that it was only a temporary reprieve. "So how'd you do it?" he asked coldly. "Did you kill my wife, then destroy my boat? Or was it the other way around?"

"Do you really think I would have killed Suzanne?" Melvin asked. "She was your wife. I wouldn't wish that on anyone. Besides, I was at the Tipsy Pirate when it happened. I couldn't have done it."

"Got anyone to back you up?"

"Ask anyone," Melvin said. "How about you? Got anyone to back up your alibi the night of Darren's murder?"

"Yeah, my wife. Except now she's dead."

"I wouldn't have believed a word she said." Melvin walked over to Norm, clutched his arm, and slowly said, "You killed that boy."

Norm stared down at the floor for a beat, then punched Melvin in the gut.

"Would someone like to explain to me what's going on here?" a deep voice boomed out.

The crowd scattered at the sight of Chief Dalton. Officer Moore ushered us outside while the chief dealt with Melvin and Norm.

"Can we stop by the public docks, Penny?" Alan asked. "I'd love to get some shots of the boat that was vandalized."

"I thought you were a wedding photographer?" Penny asked. "Why do you want to take pictures of something like that?"

"Yeah, I do weddings, family portraits, school pictures..." Alan sighed. "It's so boring. I'm really trying to get a break as a photojournalist. But I need to build up my portfolio. I've been trying to take pictures and videos at accidents and crime scenes. I even set up a website to showcase my work." He pulled a phone out of his pocket and showed us shots that he had taken recently. "See, this one is of the big pileup when that truck overturned near here last week. This is one of a fishing boat that was deliberately set on fire in the Keys a couple of weeks ago. And this one is of a—"

"Do you mind going back to that one of the fire?" I asked.

"That woman looks familiar." Alan handed me his phone. I zoomed in on the corner of the photo. "Hmm...I wonder if that's Connie?"

"Who's Connie?" Penny asked.

"I met her last night. She's an environmentalist." I squinted at the phone. "But I can't really be sure if that's her."

"I took a video of the fire too," Alan said. "I was there for a wedding reception when it broke out, so I've got it all on tape. If you want, I'll upload it and send you a link to it. You might be able to get a better look at the bystanders."

"That would be great," I said. I remembered what Simon had said about Ken having been involved in sabotaging fishing boats in the Keys previously. Was there any connection between the two incidents?

***

Mrs. Moto was waiting at the front door when I got home from Melvin's. She knew that the sound of a car pulling up in the drive meant that one of her servants had returned to attend to her every whim. While I pulled my keys out of the lock, she rolled onto her back across the threshold and batted at my foot.

"What, you want a belly rub now?" I picked up the shopping bags that were sitting on the welcome mat and stepped over her. "I've got to get this stuff inside. Maybe later."

She tore in front of me and was sitting on the kitchen counter before I even had time to close the door and set my purse on the entryway table. I placed the shopping bags next to her and opened the fridge to get a can of soda. When I turned back around, she had flipped both of the bags on their side and was pawing through the contents. She knocked the sanding pads I had picked up at Melvin's on the floor and stared at them. Next came the blue tape, followed by the respirator masks. This was a game I was used to. The rules were simple: (1) cat knocks stuff down; (2) humans pick it up; (3) repeat.

As I bent down to retrieve the items, Scooter came into the kitchen. "Oh, are you playing our fur baby's favorite game?" He scratched the cat behind her ears. "Good, that varnish I wanted was in stock," he said before placing the can on top of a cabinet, out of paw's reach. "Did you get anything good to eat?" he asked. "I'm starving."

"There should still be some chicken *mole* left. Why don't we heat that up for lunch? Then I'm going to head to the marina to finish working on my FAROUT report in the lounge."

"Why don't you work here?" Scooter asked as he took a plastic container out of the fridge. "Mrs. Moto can help you."

"Yeah, right. Her idea of 'helping' is lying on top of my keyboard. I think she'd rather keep you company."

Scooter turned on the microwave and leaned back on the counter. "To be honest, I could do without her company for a while. I'm trying to sort through files and paperwork, and she's making a mess of everything. If I close the door to the office, she yowls until I can't take it anymore. You should take her with you to the marina."

"Nah, she'd rather stay here."

We continued our discussion of who should spend quality time with the cat over lunch but didn't manage to come to an agreement. We did manage to agree that *mole* tastes even better the next day.

While we finished off our meal, I filled Scooter in on what had happened at the marine store after the chief arrived on the scene. "Can you believe he actually arrested Melvin?" I asked.

"On what charge?" Scooter asked.

"It's got to be murder, doesn't it?"

"From what you described about the fight between Melvin and Norm, maybe he arrested him on a charge of vandalism."

I leaned back in my chair. "You could be right. I didn't actually hear what the chief charged him with. Officer Moore made us all leave the store. I could only see what was going on through the window. It looked like he took statements from both men, then led Melvin out in handcuffs while Norm gloated."

"See, that's probably what it was."

"But vandalism? Can you imagine Melvin doing that?"

"Look, the man is in mourning. Grief can do strange things to people. And it does sound like he blames Norm for his nephew's murder."

I pushed back my chair. "Let's talk about more pleasant things, like what we're going to have for dinner?"

He shook his head. "You just finished lunch, and you're already thinking about your next meal?"

"I like to be organized," I said as I cleared the table. "How about if we meet up at Alligator Chuck's around seven?"

"Okay. I'm sure I'll have worked up an appetite by then."

After popping the plates and utensils into the dishwasher, I looked around for Mrs. Moto. "Where is that cat? She usually doesn't go too far away when we're eating."

I checked her favorite napping spots—on top of Scooter's pillow, near the sliding glass doors to the patio, and in the bathroom sink—but didn't see her anywhere.

I peeked into the second bedroom. We had turned it into an office for Scooter to run his business from. Seriously, where did that man think he was going to fit all his work-related stuff on a sailboat? Two file cabinets, a large desk, and a floor-to-ceiling bookshelf. We'd have to buy another boat to tow behind us just to hold the contents of this room.

I picked up the files and papers that were scattered on the floor, brushed cat hair off them, and set them on the desk next to Scooter's boring collection of pens. All black, not a single colorful marker. As I was straightening the stack, I noticed one of the documents had my name on it.

"Scooter, can you come here for a sec?" I said.

"What's up, panda bear?" he asked, walking down the hallway.

"Why did you take a life insurance policy out on me? Should I be worried?" I joked.

"Very worried. Why do you think I made dinner last night? Maybe I poisoned it."

"But you ate it too."

"Ah, but maybe I have the antidote and took it before dinner."

"Did you remember to take it before lunch today? We just had leftovers."

Scooter clutched his chest and said dramatically, "My heart! I think I'm dying!" He leaned on the desk, then starting laughing. He picked up the life insurance policy. "Don't you remember talking about this?" He pulled another document out of the pile. "See, here's the policy on me in case I die first."

"But the big question is, who's the beneficiary—me or *Marjorie Jane*?"

He pretended to think about the answer. "Hmm. That's a tough one." He gave me a kiss. "You, of course. Our lawyer also wants us to come by and review our wills too. Now that we have Mrs. Moto, we have to think about what happens to her if we both should pass away at the same time."

"Wow, for someone who didn't even like cats before we got her, you've certainly grown fond of her." I pointed at our adorable fur ball sprawled on his office chair having her afternoon nap. "I think that's why she's made it clear whom she'd rather keep company this afternoon. You."

"But where am I supposed to sit?" he asked.

I shrugged. "Guess you'll have to find another chair. That one's occupied."

* * *

After making a lot of headway on my report in the marina lounge during the afternoon, I packed up my stuff and headed off to Alligator Chuck's to meet Scooter for dinner. I wondered if he had gotten much work done perched on a wooden dining room chair next to his desk, while the cat rested comfortably on his padded office chair.

As I drove down Main Street, I saw an older couple standing in front of Norm and Suzanne's office pointing at something in the window and having an animated discussion. I sent Scooter a text letting him know I might be a few minutes late, pulled into a spot on the next block, and walked back over to see what was going on.

"What do you think about this one?" I heard the woman say loudly. "It's a cute cottage right on the beach. Perfect for just the two of us. It says it's a two-bedroom. We can use one as a guest room when the grandkids come to visit."

"I don't know," the man said in an equally loud voice. "I still think a condo is the way to go. Then we don't have to worry about yard work and maintenance. I've had enough of that over the years. I want to enjoy my retirement."

"Well, let's look at them both. Here, let me jot down the name and number of the real estate agent, and we can give her a call in the morning." She searched in her purse, handing her companion her wallet, lipstick, and reading glasses. "Hmm. I could have sworn I had a pen in here somewhere."

I peered over her shoulder and looked at the window. A familiar sight greeted me—yet another advertisement for our cottage. Had Suzanne printed another copy out and stuck it up here after I threw the last one in the trash?

"Are you interested in that one too?" the woman asked.

"I'm very interested in it," I said. "But it's not for sale."

"It doesn't say anything about being sold or under offer," she said.

"Trust me, it's not on the market."

She tapped on the glass. "Of course it is. It says so right here." She handed her husband a hairbrush, a crossword-puzzle book, and a bottle of hand sanitizer. "Now, where is that pen?"

I briefly considered telling her that I already owned the cottage, but the last thing I wanted was another person trying to come around and buy it out from under me. "Seriously, it's not for sale," I said. "This is a mistake."

The man gestured at the window. "Now wait a minute here, missy. Just because *you* want to buy this place doesn't mean that you should go around trying to pretend it's not for sale. Whoever makes the best offer wins." As he waved his hands wildly to emphasize his point, the lipstick fell on the sidewalk and rolled into the street. "Gosh darn it!" He handed everything back to his wife unceremoniously and went chasing after it.

She struggled to keep everything in her hands. I watched as the hairbrush made its way into the flower box underneath the window. "Hank, how am I supposed to find that pen when I'm holding all this?"

Hank returned, brandishing the lipstick victoriously in his fingers. "Here, give me that." She piled everything back into his hands and rooted around in her purse again.

"Here it is," she said, triumphantly waving a ballpoint pen. She pointed at the hairbrush. "Honey, do you mind picking that up?"

After the two of them managed to put everything back into her purse, she handed the pen to her husband. "Jot down that number, will you?"

"Do you have any paper, Violet?" They both looked at her purse and sighed.

I decided to put them out of their misery before they went through the whole purse charade again. "If I were you, I wouldn't bother writing the number down. The real estate agent is dead."

"Can you believe the nerve of this gal?" Hank asked his wife. "Some people will stoop to any level to get what they want."

The woman clutched her husband's arm. "You should be ashamed of yourself. Saying that someone has passed away just so you can get your hands on that cottage. Come on, honey, let's get out of here. We'll come back first thing in the morning."

"I'm not making it up. I saw the body," I said.

The woman gave me a horrified expression before walking off.

I gazed at the headshot of Suzanne in the upper corner of the window. "Even in death, you're managing to cause problems," I told her. A passerby looked at me oddly, so I waited until he was out of earshot before continuing my conversation with Suzanne's picture. "Did you know we've had people come by at all hours, knocking on the door and asking to see the cottage? The cottage that we never even put up for sale?"

I didn't expect an answer, but it felt good to get that off my chest. I pressed my face up against the window to see if anyone was inside, lurking in the dark. I needed to get that flier down from the window pronto to prevent any future misunderstandings, as well as any other unannounced visitors.

I tried the front door but it wouldn't open, even after jiggling the handle repeatedly. I wasn't going to be able to gain access through the large plate glass window, so I decided to see if there was a back entrance.

As I walked down the dark alley behind the building, I sent my husband another text.

Still running late. Need to sort out paperwork with Suzanne.

My phone beeped right away.

Huh? Suzanne's dead.

Something cold brushed past me. I startled and dropped my phone. I picked it up, turned on the flashlight, and aimed it up and down the alley. Nothing. Probably just a raccoon. I tapped in a reply.

Yeah, I know. But some people still think she's alive.

Thinking about Suzanne's murder was probably too much for Scooter because he changed the subject.

Should I order nachos while I'm waiting for you?

He knows I love nachos. It was clearly a ploy to get me to hurry up. But first things first. I needed to get that ad out of the window. When I got to the rear of the office, I noticed a light on in the back room. Maybe Norm was in the kitchen, hiding out from people staring into the office window. After knocking on the door and not getting a response, I turned the knob, opened the door a crack, and poked my head inside. "Yoo-hoo, is anyone here?" Still no response. Could he be indisposed in the bathroom? I pushed the door open, walked into the hallway, and called out again. Only silence in response.

Since I was already inside, and the office was technically open—after all, the door was unlocked—surely Norm wouldn't mind if I quickly removed the sign. I would actually be doing him a favor. People wouldn't wander by the window, think the cottage was for sale, and annoy him with calls to set up viewings for it.

I walked over to the window and took down the ad. I crumpled it up and took aim at the trash can near Suzanne's desk...and missed. Two out of three, I told myself. I grabbed it off the floor, popped a chocolate from the candy dish next to the computer in my mouth, and tried again.

At least I got closer this time. I took two chocolates this time as a consolation prize. As I got ready to go for my third attempt, I saw something out of the corner of my eye—Violet and Hank were back, along with another older couple.

They were pointing at the spot where the picture of the cottage used to be displayed. When the woman put her face up against the window to try and see inside, I darted behind

Norm's desk and out of sight.

Despite the pane of glass, I could hear their voices. I wondered if they realized that they both needed to replace the batteries in their hearing aids. From their discussion of low-maintenance plants and lawn fertilizers, it sounded like they might be there for a while. Because I had left my purse on the floor next to the window and wouldn't be able to retrieve it without being spotted, it looked like I was going to be there for a while too.

I settled down into Norm's chair while I waited. I swiveled back and forth and pondered my situation. My phone was in my purse, so I couldn't send another message to Scooter letting him know I was further delayed. Plus, I was getting hungry. I really wished he hadn't mentioned nachos in his last text.

Fortunately, Norm also had a candy dish on his desk. Unfortunately, his was full of peppermints. Not nearly as tasty as Suzanne's chocolates, but beggars couldn't be choosers. As I reached across to take one, I accidentally knocked over a cup, spilling tea all over Norm's desk. I quickly wiped up the liquid with tissues, but wasn't fast enough to prevent it from dripping into the top drawer, which was partially open.

I pulled the drawer open. There was a collection of pens, a protein bar, and a handgun on top of a file folder that was sitting in a puddle of tea. I used one of the pens to nudge the handgun to the side—I hate guns and do my best to avoid touching them—and placed the folder on top of the desk. After cleaning up the inside of the drawer, I started to dry off the folder with a fresh tissue. That's when I noticed that it was labeled "Coconut Cove Tropical Resort." It was the same one that had been on Suzanne's desk when I was last in the office, which Norm had complained about because it wasn't locked up.

Curiosity got the better of me, so I leafed through the papers inside. Usually, I find legal documents to be incredibly boring, but these held my interest. The first one was an agreement for the purchase of a house by Sierra Vista Rental Properties. I recognized the address of the property in question immediately. It was right next door to us and owned by our neighbor, Alligator Chuck.

The second document revealed who the owner of Sierra Vista was: Xander Carlton. I didn't know too many men named Xander, so I was pretty sure this Xander was Suzanne's son. It looked like she was using the technique that Connie and Fiona had told us about. She had a shell company, owned by her son, make an offer on Chuck's house. Then the shell company sold the property to the developer of the resort.

I imagine she had planned on taking a similar approach to try to purchase our cottage, as well as Melvin's. We all would have thought they were separate transactions, either bought by individuals or by rental companies. Then once she owned all the cottages on the beach, the construction of the resort could begin, and it would be too late for any of us to protest.

As I flipped over the last page, I noticed an envelope at the back of the folder. Thinking it contained more details about the shady real estate deal, I opened it up. Instead, I found something far more interesting. It seemed that Norm had taken a life insurance policy out on his wife rather recently. And from what I read, it appeared as though he was about to come into a lot of money.

CHAPTER 14
SEEING GHOSTS

AS I WAS PORING OVER the life insurance policy, I heard the front door handle rattling. I froze, hoping Norm wasn't going to come charging in and find me sitting at his desk. I breathed a sigh of relief when I heard a very familiar and very loud voice.

"Someone has to be in there," Violet said. She began banging on the door.

"Honey, no one is there. The lights are off," Hank said.

"Well, how do you explain the fact that the advertisement for the cottage is gone? Someone must have taken it down." She banged on the door some more.

"Violet, stop it. If someone was in there, they would have come to the door by now."

Well, that wasn't exactly true, I thought. I was inside but had no intention of answering the door.

"Where was it exactly, Violet?" another woman asked. I peeked around the corner, making sure to stay hidden in the shadows, and looked at the window. Violet, Hank, and the other couple were staring at the spot where the picture of my cottage used to hang.

"Right there," Violet said, tapping on the glass. "I really wanted you to see it. It's so cute and it's right by the beach. You and Jim really should think about getting a winter place in Florida as well. Think of how much fun we would have. While the guys are off fishing, we can go to the community center. They've got lots of arts-and-crafts classes. I was thinking we'd use the second bedroom as a combination guest room and crafting studio—"

"Violet, come on, let's go," her husband said impatiently. "Jim and Angela don't want to hear about this."

"And we can go for walks on the beach every morning," Violet said, ignoring his interruption. "I was thinking about going with a tropical jungle decorating scheme in the living room to match the palm trees in front of the house." She turned to her husband. "Honey, go knock on the door again."

He shook his head. "I'm telling you, no one is there. We'll come back tomorrow."

"I just don't want to lose out on this place. It's perfect for us." She turned back to her friend. "I think there's going to be a lot of competition for it. There was this woman here earlier who's also interested in the cottage. She's going around telling prospective buyers that the real estate agent is dead. Can you believe that?"

"Well, that takes the cake," the other woman said. "She really must be desperate to get her hands on it."

Her husband took a couple of steps back and glanced up at the office sign thoughtfully. "You know, she may have been telling the truth. I think I saw something about this in the local newspaper. A local real estate agent was murdered recently."

Violet looked crestfallen. "Dead? How are we going to view the property now?"

Her friend gasped. "Did you say the advertisement was

hanging right here?" Violet nodded. "And when the woman told you the real estate agent had been murdered, you didn't believe her?" Violet nodded again. "Well, don't you see what that means?" Violet shook her head. "Her ghost was here. *She* tore down the sign. The recently departed don't like it when people make light of their passing, especially ones who have been murdered!"

The blood drained from Violet's face. "A ghost? Do you think she could haunt the cottage? Maybe this office is haunted too!" she said, clutching her friend's arm. Their husbands looked at each other and rolled their eyes.

I rolled my eyes right along with them. Ghosts? Haunted houses? Who believed in this kind of nonsense?

I stopped my eye-rolling when I heard Norm's voice. "Can I help you folks? Did you stop by to sign up for a fishing charter?"

"No, we were just looking at the signs in the window," Violet said.

"Oh," Norm said. After a long pause, he added, "My wife was the real estate agent. She recently passed away." The two couples murmured their sympathies. Violet started to ask something about ghosts, but her husband put his finger on her lips.

"Was there a particular property you were interested in?" Norm asked. He sounded awfully businesslike for someone who had just lost his wife. But maybe getting a hefty insurance payout sped the grieving process along.

"Definitely not the cottage on the beach," Violet said. "Right, honey?"

"The cottage on the beach? There's four of them." Norm pursed his lips. "There's already an offer on two of them." I glanced at the file folder in my hand. I knew exactly what he was talking about—Sierra Vista Rental Properties, aka Xander Carlton.

He scratched his head. "We're still in negotiations with the owner of one of the cottages, but I expect he'll be heading back to the Bahamas soon and will put it on the market then." The way Melvin felt about Norm, I couldn't imagine any scenario where he'd list his property with him.

"The Bahamas. How exciting. We went on a cruise there last year," Violet said loudly.

Norm rubbed his ear and took a step back. "There's another one up for sale at the moment, but I think there's already a potential buyer."

Violet nudged her friend. "I bet it was that awful woman who was here earlier."

"What awful woman?" Norm asked.

"We didn't catch her name, but she was short with medium-length brown hair. Nothing really stood out about her."

I breathed a sigh of relief. I was pretty sure Norm wouldn't figure out it was me based on that nondescript description. Then I got slightly miffed. What did they mean that nothing stood out about my appearance? I was wearing some really cute earrings.

"Tell you what, why don't you give me your name and number, and I'll give you a call tomorrow once I've had a chance to go through Suzanne's things?" Norm said.

Thankfully, he entered their details into his phone rather than asking Violet to get a pen and paper out of her purse. They asked him where a good place in town was for breakfast the next morning. While he walked with them a few steps away to point out the Sailor's Corner Cafe, I dashed over to the window, grabbed my purse, and exited through the back door before Norm could catch me in the office.

* * *

I slid into the booth across from Scooter. "Sorry about being late. I got held up with some work stuff." I tucked my purse and the file folder next to me on the bench seat. Yes, before you ask, I took the folder with me. After all, it was evidence that I'm pretty sure Norm forgot to mention to the police.

"Did you order already?" I asked.

"No, I thought I'd wait for you. Besides, I can't decide. It's a toss-up between the baby back ribs and the gator."

"Alligator? That's adventurous."

"Well, we've lived in Florida for a while. I figured it might be time we tried it."

"By *we*, I'm going to assume you mean *you*. I have no intention of eating something with that many teeth."

A tall man wearing an apron and chef's hat came up to our table. "Mollie, Scooter, it's nice to see you!" he said.

"You too, Chuck," Scooter said, shaking his hand. "It's hard to believe we're neighbors. The only time we ever see you is when we're here at your restaurant."

"This place sure keeps me busy," Chuck said as he handed us a couple of menus. "If you want to see me going forward, you're going to have to come here more. I'm selling my property."

"Both your cottages?" Scooter asked. "Even the one you're living in?"

"Yep. It's too much of a hassle to manage the one that's a rental property, and I can't keep up with the maintenance on my own cottage, let alone two of them. I'm buying a place at the Tropical Breeze condos."

"That's pretty lucky that you found two buyers," my husband said.

"No, it's just one buyer. It's a company that manages a lot of rental properties in the area. Suzanne told me they liked the idea of the two cottages being next door to each other. Sometimes, large families like to rent two adjacent properties and go back and forth between them."

"Is it Sierra Vista Rental Properties you're dealing with, by any chance?"

"That's the one," Chuck said. "You know them?"

"I've read about them." I leaned against the corner of the booth to hide the file folder from sight. "Are you sure they're going to keep them as rentals? Rumor has it someone wants to develop a resort right where our houses are."

"Oh, I've heard that too. I asked Suzanne about it, but she said it was just that, a rumor." He shrugged. "But to tell you the truth, maybe something like that would be good for business. More visitors to town means more customers."

"I guess there are pros and cons to that sort of thing," Scooter said diplomatically.

I felt my purse begin to slip. I wedged myself against it to keep it on the seat.

"Why are you so fidgety?" Scooter asked.

"Me? I'm not fidgety. Just hungry, I guess. I thought there would be nachos waiting for me."

Scooter pointed at an empty plate. "You snooze, you lose."

"Did you want to go ahead and order dinner? Do you know what you want?" Chuck asked.

"Can you give me a few minutes to look at the menu?" I asked.

"I was thinking about gator," Scooter said. "But my little panda bear turned up her nose at the idea."

"Too many teeth," I said.

Chuck smiled. "Ah, you're a vegetarian. No problem. We just added veggie burgers to the menu."

Scooter snorted. "Trust me, she eats meat. She's just picky about it. Besides, I think she'd make the worst vegetarian ever. She'd probably just subsist on chocolate and cheese."

"Sounds good to me," I said.

"Why don't you take a few minutes, check out the menu, and a waitress will be by to take your order. I'd better head back to the kitchen. Those gators aren't going to cook themselves."

Two couples came into the restaurant, chattering loudly.

"There's only one table left. We'd better grab it before someone else does, Hank," I heard a familiar woman say.

"Violet, cool your heels. The hostess will be right back."

"Oh no," I said, scrunching down in my seat.

Scooter turned around. "Who are you hiding from?"

"Hiding? I'm not hiding."

"Yes you are."

"Can you just move a little that way?" I indicated which direction with my hand so that his back would block me from view. "That's better," I said.

"Care to explain?"

"Oh, it's just that I had a little…run-in with one of those couples earlier."

"Run-in?"

Our waitress came over to our table and set down two glasses of water. "I'll be back in a few to take your order," she said.

"Go on," Scooter said.

"It was just something to do with a ghost."

"I thought you didn't believe in ghosts."

"I don't, but they do." I unfolded my napkin and placed it on my lap. Scooter gave me a meaningful look. "They think Suzanne's ghost is haunting her office and our cottage."

"Why do they think that?"

"They were checking out the sign for our cottage in the window. She thought it would be the perfect house for their retirement. Then when they came back to show their friends, the sign had disappeared."

"And they think a ghost was behind it?" I nodded. Scooter leaned forward and stared at me. "I'm going to go out on a limb here and guess that a ghost wasn't involved. Exactly why were you late for dinner?"

"Oh, look, there's Ken and Leilani," I said, pointing at the door. "There aren't any empty tables. Maybe we should ask them to join us." I waved them over enthusiastically. "Come sit with us," I said.

"Thanks," Leilani said as she sat next to me. "We appreciate it. This place is really packed tonight."

Ken snagged one of the menus and handed the other to his wife. "So, what have you two been up to?"

"Oh, my adorable wife was just telling me some ghost stories," Scooter said with a smirk.

"You're kidding, right?" Ken said.

"Of course he's kidding," I said quickly. "I was walking down an alley in the dark earlier tonight, and I felt something cold brush against me. I was just joking, saying that it must have been a ghost."

"Dark alley?" Leilani asked, raising her eyebrows.

"Taking a shortcut. Anyway, it was probably just a raccoon. No big deal."

Scooter leaned back with a big grin on his face. "Why don't you tell them about the time you tried to teach raccoons sign language?"

I put my head in my hands. "You promised not to ever bring that up again." When I glanced up, Leilani and Ken were looking at me quizzically. Scooter was laughing. "Tell you what, why don't we change the subject? Did you know that Chuck is selling his two cottages?"

Ken slammed his fist on the table. "What? That traitor! I've talked to him numerous times about the importance of protecting the turtle nesting grounds." He snatched Leilani's menu from her hands. "Come on, let's get out of here. I refuse to patronize his restaurant."

"No, we're staying here," she said firmly. She took the menu back. "I'm tired and hungry. We're not going to run around town trying to find another place to eat that meets your standards."

Ken folded his arms. "My standards?"

Leilani sighed. "Look, not everyone is as passionate about the environment as you are. But lashing out at everyone isn't going to help. Remember, you can catch more flies with honey than with vinegar."

"Hey, folks," our waitress said as she deposited a basket and small bowl on our table. "Alligator bites and swamp sauce, on the house. I'll be right back."

Leilani pushed the basket toward Ken. "Go on. You know how much you love these."

He pulled a breaded nugget out, dipped it in the sauce, and popped it in his mouth. "They are good."

Before he could grab another one, Leilani placed the basket in front of me. "Better get some now before Ken eats all of them."

"Um...I'll pass. I'm not sure I want to eat anything that comes with something called swamp sauce."

Leilani laughed. "It's just a type of barbecue sauce."

"That might be okay, but maybe with chicken strips instead."

Ken reached across the table and pulled the basket back. "Good. More for the rest of us."

After the three of them had polished off the appetizer, I asked, "Ken, what would happen if there was, say, some proof that Norm and Suzanne were involved in the resort development?"

Ken wiped his mouth with a napkin. "That's the problem. I don't have any proof. I know they're in it up to their necks, but it's all just hearsay. But if there was proof, that would make a huge difference." He looked at me curiously. "Why, do you have some?"

I smiled mysteriously. "You never know. Something might turn up."

* * *

The following evening was the night of the weekly barbecue and potluck at the marina. It was hard to believe so much time had gone by already. In the span of just seven days, two people had been killed, Mrs. Moto had "lost" two more collars, I'd managed to get through my first public speech, and I had uncovered a real estate scam.

What I hadn't managed to do yet was discover who had murdered Darren and Suzanne. The thought of Chief Dalton beating me to the punch was more than I could stomach. As I looked around the patio, I wondered if someone here had done it. Was there some clue I was missing?

I saw Liam at a table with a couple of other young guys laughing, drinking beer, and checking out girls as they walked by. His uncle was over at the barbecue giving Ned unsolicited advice on how to get the chicken skin crispy without burning it. Ken was at the buffet table ladling baked beans and potato salad onto Leilani's plate. Melvin was sitting in the corner by himself, sipping on a soda.

"Penny for your thoughts, Mollie." I glanced up and saw Ben smiling at me. "Can I join you?"

"Of course. Have a seat. I'm just waiting for Scooter to get here."

He set a six-pack of beer on the table. "Want one?" When I passed, he cracked one open, took a swig, then leaned back in his chair. "I'm so glad it's Friday," he said. "It's been such a long week. We've been so busy in the boatyard."

"Is there any word on when we'll be able to get back to our boats?" I asked.

He shrugged. "I haven't heard anything. You should probably ask Nancy. She's been on the phone every day to Chief Dalton, chewing his ear off."

"That sounds like Nancy," I said. "I'd love to see how he reacted to that."

"Not well, I would imagine," Ben said. "There are very few people who will stand up to her."

"Ned seems to have developed a bit of a backbone as of late."

"I heard about that. Something to do with his movie collection." Ben finished his beer and opened another. "Well, it just goes to show you that there's a line everyone has that you don't dare cross."

I looked at him thoughtfully. "It does make you wonder what would cause someone to snap and murder Darren and Suzanne."

"I try not to think about it," Ben said. "I thought when the chief arrested Melvin, that was who did it. But then they released him last night."

"I spoke with him earlier," I said. "He was really cagey about the arrest. He told me he didn't want to talk about it, and then he walked off and sat at that table by himself."

Ben shrugged. "Maybe it was just about vandalizing Norm's boat."

"I hope so. I mean, I don't really hope so. It's just that I hope that's why they arrested him, not because he's a murderer. Does that make any sense?"

"Yeah, makes total sense. Melvin's a nice guy. No one wants to think he killed someone. You want the bad guys to be...well...bad guys. But I guess that's why neither of us is in the police force, Mollie. We can't be objective when it comes to this kind of thing."

"You think Chief Dalton is objective?"

"Sure, why wouldn't he be?"

"It's just that he's such a pain in the you-know-what sometimes." I thought about the colored-marker incident. "Actually, make that all the time."

Ben laughed. "Maybe that's why they have an anonymous tip line. So people don't have to talk directly to him."

"There's an anonymous tip line?"

"Sure." Ben leaned forward. "Why? Do you have a tip for the police?"

"Me? Of course not," I said, thinking about the file folder I had tucked away in the drawer of my nightstand. That might solve the problem of how to get the information about the real estate scam to the police without revealing exactly how it was found.

"Earth to Mollie," Ben said. "You're lost in thought. Come on, you can tell me. What have you found that you want to tip the police off about?"

"Nothing. I was just thinking about dolphins. I see you've got your dolphin T-shirt on again."

Ben's face turned a little pink. "Alejandra said she liked it last week."

"She won't be here tonight. She's at a friend's wedding this weekend."

"Oh," he said glumly.

"But I like your shirt."

"Thanks, I guess."

A loud commotion over by the buffet table interrupted Ben's thoughts about Alejandra and my thoughts about how best to disguise my voice when I called the tip line.

"Get out of here, you mangy cat!" Nancy was waving a broom as a streak of fur bolted past her and hid underneath a table.

"I'd better go see what trouble Mrs. Moto has gotten into now," I said.

I walked over to the table, crouched down, and gave her a stern look. "Nancy is mad at you. You really don't want to get on her bad side."

As I was trying to convince the cat to come sit over at our table, my phone beeped, alerting me to a new email. Alan had sent me a link to the video from the fishing boat fire in the Keys. I held the phone with one hand while scratching Mrs. Moto under her chin with my other. The first part of the video showed the wedding reception that he had been there to film. The happy couple was posing on one of the docks with their bridal party when a boat burst into flames behind them. They screamed and ran back up to the clubhouse while Alan stayed behind and continued to capture footage of the fire.

After watching the video a couple of times, I was convinced that Connie was in the background by the boat that went up in flames. And the man standing next to her looked a lot like Ken.

CHAPTER 15
HARASSING SEAGULLS

"ENOUGH, ALREADY!" I SAID AS the third sanding belt of the day broke. I had spent the past five hours working on *Marjorie Jane*'s bottom, and nothing had been going right. I was exhausted, frustrated, and ready to pay the next person who walked by a hundred dollars to take the boat off our hands. I pulled back the hood of my Smurf suit and knocked on the hull. "Hey, is anyone in there? I'm ready to go home, get something to eat, and wash all this grime off me."

"Wow, are you done sanding the bottom already?" Scooter asked, leaning over the side of the boat.

"No, but I'm through for the day."

Scooter looked down at his watch. "But it's only two."

"I can't take any more torture today." I wiped grit off my lips, which were desperately in need of some sort of industrial-strength lip balm. "Besides, Mrs. Moto needs to be fed."

"Oh, come on, she can hold out for a little while longer. This is the first day we've been able to get back in the boatyard and work on *Marjorie Jane*." He wiped the sweat off his brow. "Did you see Nancy go after Chief Dalton at the barbecue last night? It's thanks to her that we're finally able to catch up on all the work we need to do on the boat."

"Did we sign up for a race that no one told me about?"

"Well, not exactly."

"So there aren't any real deadlines other than the ones you decided to set for us?"

"But the sooner we finish up in here, the sooner we can splash the boat in the water, the sooner we can get her ready to go, and the sooner we can sail off to the Caribbean."

"Wow, there's a lot of 'sooners' in that sentence. If you checked a thesaurus, there would be a lot of helpful alternatives like, 'the more *speedily* we go home and feed Mrs. Moto, the more *quickly* I can have a nice bubble bath, and the more *rapidly* you can give me a foot rub.' See how much better that sentence sounds? It just rolls off the tongue."

Scooter smiled and held his hands up. "Okay, I know when I've been beaten. Why don't you head back home, and I'll give you a call later so you can come back and pick me up? That'll give me time to finish up a few things."

"Okay, sounds like a plan." I unzipped my suit, wadded it up into a ball, and threw it into the trash.

After I walked back to the boat, Scooter said, "Actually, you know what? Why don't I sleep on the boat tonight? That way you can just relax and don't have to worry about coming back here."

"You want to sleep here? It's a mess down below. The floorboards are still torn up. The lights aren't working. Neither is the toilet. Are you some sort of masochist?"

"I don't mind roughing it."

"Fine, I'll tell Mrs. Moto you chose *Marjorie Jane* over her. We can have a quiet girls' night together. I'll have a glass of wine, she'll have some catnip, and we'll watch a movie."

Scooter pointed over at *Mana Kai*. Leilani was sitting in the cockpit of her catamaran working on her computer. "Why don't you ask Leilani to come over? You were saying it would be fun to get together with her again."

"That's a good idea. Maybe she'd like a break from her boat as well." I knocked on their boat and shouted, "Hey, Leilani! Fancy some wine and Thai carryout?"

She didn't respond, so I climbed up a few rungs of their ladder and knocked again. Still no response. I didn't want to go the rest of the way up and hoist myself on deck to get her attention—it's a little like opening someone's front door and walking in uninvited—so I tried knocking one more time, bruising my knuckles on the fiberglass in the process.

"She probably can't hear you." I looked down and saw Ken standing at the bottom of the ladder. "She's always listening to those audiobooks of hers. I can drop an entire toolbox on the floor, and she wouldn't hear a peep. Here, let me try."

I watched as he ascended the ladder, walked across the deck, and tapped her on the shoulder. She lifted up her head and gave him a smile. He removed the headphones she was wearing. "Mollie was trying to get your attention," he said, pointing down at me.

"Oh, she was? I didn't hear her." She leaned over the side of the cockpit and waved at me. "Sorry about that. My book is getting to the good part," she said. "I'm determined to finish it tonight and find out whodunit."

"Ah, I understand. I was going to see if you wanted to come over later for a girls' night, but maybe another time."

After Leilani and I settled on a date for the following week, I asked Ken to tell me more about the volunteer work he did with Connie. I mentioned that I had heard the two of them had worked on a project in the Florida Keys a few weeks ago. Of course, I hadn't heard that so much as possibly seen the two of them on a video next to a boat on fire.

Ken squirmed and looked at me uncomfortably. He told me that he hadn't been down in that part of Florida in months and that the only work he did with Connie was related to public lectures and films. The conversation ended abruptly when he went inside their boat without saying goodbye. Leilani tried to apologize for his behavior, saying that he was under a lot of pressure trying to secure grant money, but I wasn't convinced that was the reason why.

* * *

Mrs. Moto and I enjoyed an early dinner for two, probably better described as "linner"—that meal you have between lunch and dinner. Personally, I could see making this a regular part of my day. Like my feline companion, I function so much better when I have frequent feedings.

We both had tuna, except hers came out of a can, while mine came out of the freezer. Despite what Mrs. Moto would try to lead you to believe, one can is a perfectly adequate serving for a cat of her size and age. I even showed her the label to prove it to her, but she still wasn't having it. I was finally able to appease her, but only after I put a tiny piece of my own tuna on her plate.

Afterward, we went for a walk on the beach. As usual, she dashed off in pursuit of gulls. While she terrorized the birds, I paused and breathed in the salt air. Why would Scooter voluntarily choose to spend the afternoon and evening working on a dilapidated boat when he could be here listening to the gentle lapping of the waves on the shore?

My peace and quiet was interrupted by the loud shrieks of two boys running down the beach chasing Mrs. Moto. The birds had scattered and were watching smugly from a safe distance. The tables had finally turned in their favor. The cat was the one being chased, not them.

"Get over here right this second!" a harried-looking mother screamed. "Leave that poor cat alone."

She seized the boys by their hands and led them back to their beach towels, muttering something about taking away their Xbox privileges. Poor things, I thought as I walked past them. I knew all about maternal threats, except in my case, we didn't have all the electronic gadgets kids had nowadays—although the mention of taking away my collection of Barbie dolls always elicited good behavior. For a while, at least.

I looked around for Mrs. Moto, but there was no sign of her. The seagulls were still enjoying their reprieve from their furry stalker. "Here, kitty, kitty," I shouted as I walked down the beach. "Come on out from where you're hiding, and I'll give you some extra tuna." Still nothing.

The two boys had escaped the clutches of their mother again and were running toward a very impressive-looking sandcastle. "If you don't get back here this instant, there won't be any ice cream for dessert," she shouted. That did the trick. They galloped back, grabbed their plastic sand buckets and shovels, and obediently made their way up the path toward the parking lot.

As I paused to examine the sandcastle more closely, admiring its four large turrets decorated with seashells and seaweed, I saw two pointed ears and a pair of green eyes peeking over the top of the moat.

"Don't worry, they're gone," I told the feline. She gave a faint meow. I motioned her over to a piece of driftwood. "Come on, let's sit here for a while and make sure there aren't any more small humans waiting to attack you before we head back." She curled up by my feet while I kept a lookout.

"Is that you, Mollie?" a woman called out.

Mrs. Moto gazed at the intruders with a mixture of curiosity and wariness.

"It's okay. This is Fiona and Connie," I said. "You remember them, don't you? We met them the other day when they were with Simon, that nice guy from FAROUT. They're not going to chase you. They're turtle people. They love animals."

She padded over to them and sniffed at them cautiously. Fiona won her over completely when she picked her up and gave her a few scratches under her chin.

"What are you two doing here?" I asked.

"We were passing out these," Connie said. She reached in her backpack and handed me a pamphlet. "Trying to raise awareness about turtle conservation."

"You guys are so dedicated. It's really great that you have a cause you believe so much in."

"Well, we do what we can," Fiona said. "We have to try to reach the public in lots of different ways to get the message across. These work for some people." She pointed at the pamphlet in my hand. "But others throw them away."

"At least people take them from you. Maybe they read them before they toss them. We've got a much harder time trying to hand out stuff for FAROUT. All you have to do is mention alien abduction, and for some reason, people just walk away without hearing what you have to say. Even the offer of a free bumper sticker doesn't do it."

"Yeah, well, talk of little green men will do that," Connie said dismissively. "But when it comes to serious causes, I really think Ken has the right idea—videos."

"Ken Choi?" I asked.

"Yep, him. He's over there right now filming. He's making a video about how the toxic red tide we've been having on the coast is impacting sea life."

I looked over where she was pointing and could just about make out someone standing near the shore holding up a small camera on a selfie stick.

"He makes short videos for his YouTube channel, but he's also been involved in making longer films," Connie said.

"Speaking of films, I think I saw you on a video of a wedding that took place a few weeks ago in the Florida Keys."

"Me?" Connie asked. "Couldn't have been. The last wedding I was at was for my niece last year."

"Are you sure? The lady looked a lot like you. A fishing boat caught on fire during the reception."

Connie frowned. "Must have been someone else. I think I'd remember that. Probably just someone who looked like me. What are you doing watching wedding videos anyway? Unless you're the one getting married, they're so boring. Now, films about protecting wildlife, like the ones Ken makes, are much more interesting."

"Didn't he just show one the other day at the Florida Turtle Trust meeting?" Fiona asked.

"Yeah. He introduced it and then led a Q&A afterward," Connie said. "That turned out to be a huge disaster."

"Why, what happened?" I asked.

"Right after the film started, I saw him take off in his car. We couldn't find him anywhere when it ended, so we improvised by serving refreshments while we waited for him to show up."

"So he wasn't there the whole time?"

"No. I tried to ask him where he was going, but he said he had something urgent to take care of."

"How long was the film?" I asked.

"About two hours."

"And how much longer after it finished before he turned up?"

Connie scratched her head. "I don't know. I guess thirty, forty-five minutes? Why are you so curious about Ken? I was ticked off that he left, but it all worked out okay in the end."

"Just one last question. What time did the movie begin?"

"Eight," Connie said. "Listen, if you're interested in future film showings, I've got another pamphlet that lists them all." She bent down and started to stick her hand in her backpack. A furry paw reached out and swiped at her.

Fiona laughed. "Looks like you have a hitchhiker."

The older woman did not appear to be amused. She coaxed Mrs. Moto out of the bag, zipped it up, and slung it over her shoulder. "Come on, let's get going," she said to Fiona.

"Hey, something fell out," I said, running after them. As I

handed Connie her MP3 player and earbuds, it all clicked into place. I knew who had killed Darren and Suzanne.

* * *

I sat there for a while thinking about what Fiona and Connie had said. Ken wasn't at the Florida Turtle Trust event the entire night, which meant that he didn't have an alibi for Suzanne's murder. And his alibi for the night of Darren's murder didn't hold up either. Because Leilani had been working in the aft cabin with her headphones on, drowning out any other noise, he could have easily left his boat and killed the young man without his wife being any the wiser.

"Come on, Mrs. Moto. It's time to go home," I said, scooping her up in my arms. "I think I left my phone on the counter, and we need to call the—"

"Who do you need to call?" I turned and saw Ken standing behind me, holding his camera.

"Just my mom. You know how moms are," I stammered.

"Oh, your mom will be fine. You can call her later. I'm making a video, and I thought you could help me with it. You were so interested earlier today in the work Connie and I did in the Florida Keys that I think you'll like this one."

"Sorry, I really have to go and call her. She gets worried when I don't check in every night at this time." I laughed nervously. "She might even call the police to check up on me." I backed up a few steps toward the sandcastle and stumbled. Mrs. Moto leaped out of my arms and dived into the sandcastle's moat.

Ken grabbed my arm and pulled me toward him. "I said, I need your help with my video."

"I really need to get back. Scooter is waiting for me at the cottage."

"No, he isn't. I heard him tell you that he's staying on the boat tonight, remember?"

He reached behind his back, pulled a handgun out from the waistband of his shorts, and jammed it into my side. "Now, start filming." He shoved the camera into my hand and stepped back, keeping the gun pointed at me.

I looked behind me at the sandcastle. Mrs. Moto had crawled down into the moat. Her ears were flattened, her back was arched, and she was growling. Ken waved the gun at her. "Go on, get out of here," I yelled. She stood her ground, growling louder.

"Stop staring at that cat," he hissed. "Press the Record button, and aim the camera toward me." While I tried to keep my hands from shaking, Ken coldly recounted why Darren and Suzanne deserved to die and that anyone else who stood in the way of the environment would also suffer retribution.

"You killed them to protect the environment? How is that going to win anyone over to your cause?" I blurted out. "Ecoterrorism is bad enough, but murder?"

Ken took a step toward me, pointing the gun at my chest. "An ecoterrorist? Is that what you think I am? Someone has to protect innocent wildlife from humanity. Handing out pamphlets and giving lectures isn't enough. It doesn't stop the poaching. Everyone knows it's going on, but no one does anything about it. But I'm stepping up to the plate. I'm taking care of it!"

"Is that why you've set fishing boats on fire?"

Ken gave a humorless laugh. "If they don't have a boat, they can't go out poaching, now, can they?"

I flinched as he took another step forward. "Vandalizing property is one thing," I said cautiously. "But killing people?"

Ken lowered the gun and looked over at the sun setting on the water. "I didn't have a choice," he said softly. "Darren had overheard Connie and me talking about setting those fishing boats on fire. He recorded the whole thing on his phone and threatened to go to the police with it unless I paid him off. He even had some pictures that he got off a website of the two of us next to a boat we torched."

"Is that what you got in the mail the other day at the turtle sanctuary? Pictures?" Ken nodded. "But couldn't you have just turned him in for poaching?"

"With what evidence?" Ken asked sharply. "And even if I did have any, all they would do is make him pay a fine. This way, I could keep him from blackmailing me and stop the poaching."

"So why Suzanne?"

Ken waved the gun toward the shoreline. "Because of this. She was going to destroy the turtle habitat with her resort development." He narrowed his eyes and looked intently at me. "Everyone who is complicit with the resort development—people like you and Chuck, agreeing to sell your cottages to her—are in on it!"

"But we don't want to sell," I stammered.

"I've heard Scooter talk about selling." Ken pointed the gun at me again. My legs started trembling. I tried to scream for help, but I couldn't get any words out. "Don't even think about yelling. If you do, I'll shoot you. Besides, the sun has set and the beach is deserted. No one would hear you." He gripped my arm and spun me around, pressing the gun into my side. "Now, here's what we're going to do. We're going to walk over to your house, slowly. Any false moves and...well, you know what will happen."

I stumbled as he pushed me forward. As I tried to regain my balance, I saw a ball of fur flying through the air and heard Ken scream. Then I felt a sharp pain in my leg, collapsed on the sand, and everything went black.

* * *

I felt something scratchy on my face and opened my eyes. Mrs. Moto was standing on my chest. She licked my nose, meowed loudly, then pawed at the side of my head. "Hey, that hurts!" I rubbed my eyes and took in my surroundings. I was on the beach, my head propped up against a piece of driftwood.

How did I get here? I wondered. Then I saw the large sandcastle and remembered. When Mrs. Moto had attacked Ken, he'd dropped the gun and it had gone off. I glanced down at my leg. Blood was dripping down it, and although I was in agony, the bullet appeared to have just grazed it. I slowly got to my feet and looked around in a panic. "Where is he?" Mrs. Moto yowled and tore down the beach toward our cottage. That's when I smelled it—the fire.

I hobbled after her, keeping an eye out for Ken and doing my best to ignore the pain in my leg. My heart was racing, and I was struggling to breathe, but I kept pounding my feet in the sand, trying to catch up with my cat and keep her safe from that madman. Finally, I saw her, sitting quietly on the beach. She stared at me with those green eyes of her, meowed softly, then looked straight ahead of her.

I followed her gaze and saw what was burning. Our cottage. Our home. Our everything.

CHAPTER 16
BLING FOR MRS. MOTO

"MOLLIE AND SCOOTER ARE HERE, everyone!" I heard a voice shout as we walked into the Tipsy Pirate. A crowd swarmed around us, giving us hugs and asking us a million questions.

"Let them breathe, folks," Ned said, gently pushing people aside. "We saved you some seats at our table." He pointed at a spot near the stage where Penny, Ben, Alejandra, and Nancy were sitting. "You two must be so stressed out and exhausted after everything you've gone through. Come on, let's get you a drink."

"Drinks are on me tonight," a nasal voice said behind us. I turned and saw Norm holding his hat in his hands. "It's the least I can do," he said. He lacked his usual bluster, probably because he was now under investigation for his role in the real estate scam. Before we could thank him, he walked over and told the bartender that he would be picking up our tab. I hoped he didn't think that would get him out of our bet. I was still determined to finish the bottom paint on *Marjorie Jane* and then throw a boat renaming party when Norm changed the name of his boat to *ET.*

"You look really good, Mollie," Penny said as I sat in a chair between her and Alejandra. "Is your leg doing okay?"

I glanced down at the bandage wrapped around my calf. "A little sore, but it's fine."

"It's hard to believe it was just yesterday that Ken had you at gunpoint, you got shot, and your cottage burned down," Alejandra said.

"You probably didn't sleep well last night," Ben said. "You have some dark circles under your eyes."

Alejandra gave him a warning look. "No, she doesn't. She looks great. I like your top. Pink's a good color on you. Don't you like her top, too, Ben?"

Ben shrugged. I noticed he was sporting his dolphin T-shirt again, probably hoping Alejandra would notice that instead of what I was wearing.

"Thanks. Penny lent it to me," I said. "We haven't had a chance to go buy new clothes yet. Everyone has been so great helping us out."

Ben leaned forward. "I want to hear all about how you solved the case."

"Well, I wouldn't really say I solved it. I didn't figure out who did it until it was too late." I bit my lip. "Too late to save our cottage."

"But you put all the puzzle pieces together," he said. "Come on, tell us how you did it."

Nancy scowled. "For goodness' sake. She's not a detective. If you want to know what happened, ask Chief Dalton."

Ben rolled his eyes. "Yeah, that'll be the day."

"I'd actually be interested in hearing what Mollie has to say," Alejandra said.

The waitress handed me a gin and tonic. I took a sip, then glanced at Scooter. "Are you okay if I tell them what happened? I promise I'll leave out any gory details." I reached into my purse and handed him a pack of M&M'S. "But just in case, these should help."

"We should probably start buying these in bulk," he said with a smile.

I leaned back in my chair. "Well, at first, when it was a question of just one..." I looked at Scooter and watched him pop some candy in his mouth. "Of just one...um...victim, I thought Liam might have done it. I wasn't sure why, though. It could have been because Darren was involved in poaching with Liam. Apparently, he had been blabbing about it all over town. Maybe Liam wanted to put a stop to that in a permanent sort of way."

"Did you hear Darren talking about the poaching?" Penny asked.

"Not exactly," I said. I glanced at Ben. "I happened to overhear you talking about it with Liam out there on the deck last week."

Nancy peered at Ben over her reading glasses. "So, you knew about the poaching, and you didn't tell anyone."

Ben squirmed in his seat. "I didn't know for sure. It's not like I had any proof," he said. "Besides, these guys were buddies of mine."

"Leave the boy alone, Nancy," Ned said. "It's hard to rat out your friends. Anyway, it's all out in the open now. Liam is going to pay the price for what he did." He looked at me. "You said you weren't sure why Liam might have done it. What other theory did you have?"

"Well, there was obviously no love lost between Melvin and Norm. Liam told me that he often had to do his uncle's dirty work. What if he killed Darren on his uncle's instructions to drive him out of business? The loss of his nephew was devastating to Melvin. He's even been talking about getting out of the fishing charter business as a result."

"I talked to him earlier," Penny said. "He's decided to sell *Nassau Royale*. It's just too hard for him to manage now that Darren is gone."

"Is he going to go back to the Bahamas?" Alejandra asked.

"No, he's decided to stay and focus on the marine store," Penny said.

"Fortunately, he didn't lose his cottage in the fire," Scooter said. "That probably would have been the last straw. All four of the cottages on the beach are right next to each other. It's really lucky they didn't all go up in flames." He finished off his drink and motioned to the waitress for another one. "Ken Choi," he said, shaking his head. "I can't believe we actually started to become friends with that guy. First, Darren and Suzanne, then setting fire to our place. Not to mention the cold-hearted bastard was responsible for my wife getting shot," he said through gritted teeth.

"That's something I was wondering about. Why did he burn your place down?" Alejandra asked.

"He was convinced we were going to sell our cottage. So he set fire to our and Chuck's properties for what he saw as our role in the resort development."

"But weren't they planning on tearing down the cottages to develop the resort?" Penny asked. "What would it matter if they were burned down?"

"The man was completely unhinged," Scooter said. "He just wanted to make a grand statement about what happens to people he thinks are abetting the destruction of the environment."

"Do you mind going back to the part about Liam?" Alejandra asked. "I thought he had an alibi for the night of Darren's murder."

"Well, it wasn't a really good one. He said he was at home watching a basketball game. But no one was with him."

"He knew everything that happened in the game when I talked to him about it," Scooter said.

"He could have read about it online," Ned said. "I always check out the sports news every day. Sometimes, I even watch replays of games I missed."

"True," I said. "To be honest, even if you have someone to back up your alibi, it doesn't mean the other person is telling the truth. Take Norm, for example. He definitely had motive to kill Darren because of Melvin, but Suzanne said the two of them had been at their office all night." I leaned forward. "Turns out he had actually left during the time Darren was killed, only no one knew about it."

"How did you find out about that?" Alejandra asked.

"Officer Moore might have let it slip when I saw her earlier today at Penelope's. We bonded over our love of cinnamon mochas. Norm was actually meeting with an insurance agent that night. I happen to know that he took out a very hefty life insurance policy on Suzanne."

Penny raised her eyebrows. "That would give him a great motive for her death."

"Hang on," Alejandra said. "Let's focus on Darren's murder first. Who else did you think could have done it?"

"Well, I thought Suzanne might have been a suspect when Mrs. Moto found one of her charms near the crime scene. But when I returned it to her, she seemed really calm about it and genuinely perplexed about how it had ended up there. And besides, I couldn't picture her setting foot in the boatyard in those heels of hers, let alone killing someone and risking getting blood on her clothes."

"It took a threatening note to get her to go into the boatyard the night she was, you know..." Scooter said. He took a deep breath. "It was probably the first time she had ever been there."

"And of course Melvin couldn't have done it," Alejandra said. "He was his nephew."

I looked over where Melvin was sitting in the corner with a few of his friends. "I thought so too. But I found out that he knew Darren was mixed up in poaching, and he was furious about it. Tiffany overheard them arguing about it at a basketball game."

"Fortunately, he wasn't furious enough about it to kill him," Penny said. "He was his own flesh and blood, after all."

"That's what everyone assumed, myself included. But when I think about it objectively, did I assume that because I liked him? After all, I thought Norm might have killed his own wife."

"Okay, tell us about Suzanne's death," Alejandra said. "Who had an alibi for that one?"

"Liam was with a woman that night. She's married and was hesitant to come forward at first to vouch for him."

Nancy frowned. "What was he doing with a married woman?"

I smiled, thinking about the texts I had seen on Liam's phone. "You don't want to know."

Ben shook his head. "That guy just can't keep his hand out of the cookie jar." He glanced at Alejandra. "Aren't you glad you didn't go out with him? You deserve a one-woman kind of guy," he said with a hopeful look on his face.

"So, what about Norm?" Alejandra asked without meeting Ben's eyes.

"He claimed he was at the Tipsy Pirate when the murder took place. Officer Moore said there were a number of people who could vouch for him," I said.

"Melvin told me the same thing," Penny said.

"Yeah, he told me that too, but..." I glanced at Melvin again. He was staring into his beer, oblivious to his friends chatting away around him.

"But what?" Penny asked.

"Melvin wasn't at the Tipsy Pirate. Office Moore told me he was at the waterfront park that night getting some fresh air and thinking through everything."

Penny gasped. "So was he the person who vandalized Norm's boat?"

"No," I said. "But he saw the whole thing and didn't call the police. He honestly believed Norm killed his nephew, and he was so upset about it that he practically cheered the vandals on."

"So, who did do it?"

"A woman named Connie. She shares Ken's views on taking extreme measures to protect the environment, including sabotaging boats involved in poaching." I took a sip of my drink. "Oddly enough, it turns out that both Liam and Melvin ended up vouching for each other at the time of Suzanne's death. Liam was at the park as well with his lady friend."

"But didn't Liam see Melvin?" Penny asked.

"No, Liam was a little too distracted by other things, if you know what I mean," I said. "Did you know that Leilani and I had actually seen Liam and this woman earlier that night when I was dropping her back off at the marina after the FAROUT event? The two of them were having a fight on the street by the marina entrance. He chased after her, and then they went to the park to talk things through. Melvin was sitting on one park bench thinking about the death of his nephew, and they were on another one making up." I shrugged. "Liam did have a good reason to kill Suzanne. He was tired of her lording her son over him, but he didn't do it."

Alejandra swirled the ice around in her drink with a swizzle stick. "So, Liam and Norm had alibis for Suzanne's death. I guess that brings us to Ken."

Scooter reached across the table and squeezed my hand. "The thought of him holding a gun at you and you getting shot." He turned pale and shuddered. I looked at the empty M&M'S bag on the table.

"Why don't we stop off and pick up some chocolate ice cream to take back with us to the hotel tonight?"

He leaned back in his chair and nodded. "Good idea."

Everyone at the table was watching me expectantly. "So, Ken. Well, he had alibis for both murders. Leilani and he were both on their boat the night of Darren's murder. But she was in the back cabin and had her headphones on. Her husband was able to sneak out without her knowing. Darren had been blackmailing Ken about his ecoterrorist activities. The two of them had arranged to meet that night, and Ken was supposed to pay him off. But he did more than that—he killed him."

"All because he was blackmailing him?" Alejandra asked.

"That was just part of it. Ken was enraged that Darren was poaching. Saving the environment was very important to him."

Scooter scowled. "So important that he'd kill for it."

"How did Suzanne's charm end up in the boatyard?" Penny asked.

"Ken went to her office to confront her about the real estate scam they were running. You know, the one where they were secretly buying property up in order to develop a large resort. It must have fallen off her bracelet onto the floor. He picked it up, thinking it might come in handy at some point. So he left it at the murder scene. But when I found it, it was outside of the cordoned-off area, and the police hadn't found it during their initial investigation." I thought about how Mrs. Moto loved to bat objects around. "Ken was probably wondering why Suzanne was never arrested for Darren's murder after he tried to pin it on her."

"So is the property deal what drove him to kill Suzanne?" Penny asked.

I nodded. "It is. When he heard she was still trying to buy property in Coconut Cove, including our cottage, he snapped. He sent her a note threatening to expose her and told her to meet him at Norm's boat. And...well...you know what happened."

"But he didn't stop there," Scooter said. "He held you at gunpoint, you got shot, and he burned our house down."

"Thankfully, you weren't hurt too badly, dear," Nancy said gently.

I felt my eyes well up. "It could have been worse. I was sure he was going to kill me." I took a deep breath. "But Mrs. Moto saved the day. When he kept waving the gun at me, she jumped out from the sandcastle she was hiding in, hurled herself at his leg, and sunk her claws and teeth in. He was so startled that he dropped the gun. That's when it went off, and the bullet grazed my leg. Then he ran off to torch the cottages."

"But you didn't see him set them on fire?" Alejandra asked.

"Uh...no, I didn't."

"That's because my little panda bear fainted from the shock of it all," Scooter said, squeezing my hand.

"Should we talk about the time you fainted?" I asked Scooter with a smile, remembering what had happened when he'd seen Darren's body.

Fortunately for Scooter, Norm came over and handed me an envelope. "Here, we all took up a collection for the two of you. You'll probably need a little help getting back on your feet."

My eyes grew wide when I looked inside the envelope. "We can't possibly accept this," I said as I handed it to Scooter.

"No, we can't," he said. "It's a very thoughtful gesture, but we're fine. We've got insurance and savings." He pointed over to the bar where a couple of off-duty volunteer firefighters were standing. "I've got an idea." He leaned across the table and filled me in on his plan. Then he pointed at the stage. "Go on, tell everyone."

"Oh no, not me. Why don't you do it?"

"You can do it. You're experienced at public speaking now."

I reluctantly got up on stage, picked up the microphone, and thanked everyone for their donations. When I suggested that we give the money to the fire department instead, everyone cheered.

* * *

"You did great, my little panda bear," Scooter said, giving me a big hug. "I have a feeling you're going to be in demand as a public speaker. Next stop, Mollie's World Tour!" He stepped back and gave me an appraising look. "Hey, are you okay?"

"I just need a minute," I said. "I'm going to go get some fresh air. I'll meet you at the car."

"All right, just don't take too long. Mrs. Moto is waiting for us back at the boat."

I walked out onto the deck, leaned up against the railing, and took a few deep breaths. I was feeling overwhelmed by all the love and support everyone had shown us. Coconut Cove really was a special place. People looked out for one another. Sure, they might know a little too much about your personal business—you certainly couldn't hide anything in a town this small for very long—but that also meant that they genuinely cared when something tragic happened in your life.

As I gazed out across the water, I had to admit that Ken had been right about one thing. Big developers coming in would ruin the quirky charm of Coconut Cove. There had to be a way to bring more revenue into the area while retaining our small-town identity and appeal. Next month's boating festival would be a good test of this. It was sure to draw lots of tourists, but it would also highlight locally-owned small businesses, like Penelope's bakery, Chuck's restaurant, the Sailor's Corner Cafe, and the Tipsy Pirate. I hoped nothing would ruin it.

I took a last look at the sun setting over the water. When I turned to head back inside, I noticed Ned and Nancy at the far side of the deck, holding hands. This was a first—I don't think I had ever seen them be affectionate toward each other in that way before. Nancy probably thought it would come across as a sign of weakness.

They walked toward me, whispering to each other. Nancy even giggled at one point. As they passed me, she noticed me watching. She dropped Ned's hand, then fixed her piercing blue eyes on me. "What are you looking at, Mollie?" She pursed her lips and continued to glare at me. "Are you going to stand there all day? You're blocking the entrance." I took a step back and she whisked past me. "Come on, Ned, let's go," she said over her shoulder.

Ned started to follow his wife, then paused and gave me a big smile. "She apologized. Can you believe that?"

"That's terrific," I said. As he walked inside, I muttered under my breath, "Enjoy it while it lasts."

Before I met Scooter at the car, I had one last thing to do—pay a visit to my old friend, Coconut Carl.

"Hey, Carl, remember me? It's Mollie. I just wanted to say thank you for everything you did. My FAROUT speech went great. Now I have another little favor to ask. We could really use some good luck when it comes to finding a new place to live. Do you think you could help out with that?" I rubbed his belly three times, clockwise.

As I was about to give some tourists their chance with Carl, I remembered something. I stepped back and whispered in his ear. "By the way, I wasn't talking about living on *Marjorie Jane*. Just thought I should make that clear." I threw in a few extra belly rubs for good luck.

* * *

"Mrs. Moto, where are you?" I called out. A furry face peeked over the side of the boat and watched me climb up the ladder, her whiskers twitching. Once I clambered onto the deck, she rubbed against my legs and purred loudly. Then she padded back to the side of the boat and watched Scooter make his way upward. As he neared the top rung, she leaned over and quickly licked his forehead before darting into the cockpit.

"Yuck. What was that about?" he asked as he wiped the remnants of her kiss off.

"I think she's worried about us. She's afraid we might fall

down and get hurt." I gave her a scratch on the head. "Or worse," I added.

Scooter rolled his eyes. "I think that would only upset her if it meant we couldn't open a can of her favorite cat food at least twice a day."

He sat in the cockpit and stretched his arms behind his head. "It's a nice night out. I love a full moon, don't you?" He put his arm around me and pulled me close. Mrs. Moto climbed onto his lap. "It wouldn't be so bad living on the boat, would it?"

I pulled back and stared at him. "You're joking, aren't you? There's barely enough room to move, the floorboards are torn up, the toilet doesn't work, and I can't even begin to imagine cooking down below." Mrs. Moto yowled loudly. "See, Mrs. Moto agrees with me."

"You're right. It doesn't make sense to move aboard. At least, not yet." I leaned back and gave him a pointed look. He tried again. "At least not for a while?" I raised my eyebrows. "At least, not until it's your idea?"

"That's better," I said.

Scooter smiled. "I thought you'd feel that way. Fortunately, I think I found us a place to live. A place that's on land with a working kitchen and bathroom."

"That's great! Where?"

"There's a unit available for rent at the Tropical Breeze condos. It's fully furnished, so we can move in right away." The calico meowed. "And yes, pets are allowed," Scooter said, giving her a scratch on her head.

He sighed. "I guess it won't be a big deal to move, considering we've lost everything."

"I'm really going to miss my boots."

"I'm going to miss my comic book collection," Scooter said in a strained voice.

I squeezed his hand. "Hey, are you crying?"

Mrs. Moto stood and looked at him curiously. She reached

up and put her front paws on his shoulder. He picked her up and rubbed his face against her fur. "I'm fine. I think it's just my allergies acting up."

Mrs. Moto squirmed in his arms and stuck her paw into his shirt pocket.

"Looks like she found another clue," I said jokingly.

The calico kept poking in his pocket insistently.

Scooter smiled. "Actually, she found something better than a clue in the bilge earlier today. Of course, she may have been the one who put it there in the first place." He picked her up and gazed into her eyes sternly. "You're going to have to stop knocking stuff off tables and counters." She leaned forward and licked his face. "Hey, stop that."

He set the cat on the seat next to him, reached into his pocket, and pulled out my diamond necklace. I put it around my neck and gave Scooter a kiss. "Thank goodness. I thought it had been lost in the fire!" Mrs. Moto meowed. "Yes, of course you deserve all the credit. What would we do without you and your uncanny ability to find things?"

Scooter smiled. "I suppose she isn't too bad." He looked at our little fur ball. "But I don't really think that collar suits her, do you? It's just too ordinary for such a clever cat."

I stroked Mrs. Moto's neck and inspected the plain navy collar. "Well, it's not like it's going to last long. She'll mysteriously lose this one soon too."

Scooter pulled a small bag out of the pocket on his cargo shorts and opened it up. "I think the reason she hasn't been happy with her collars is that she's jealous that you get to wear a sparkly necklace with a diamond and she doesn't." He pulled out a glittery silver collar encrusted with rhinestones. "See, now you've got some bling too," he said, fastening it around her neck. Mrs. Moto started purring loudly. I think she approved.

Scooter smiled at her reaction. "You know, it doesn't really matter about the cottage. Things can be replaced, Mollie.

What's important is that I've still got my favorite girl." Mrs. Moto meowed. "Sorry. Of course I meant my two favorite girls." Then he rubbed his hand along *Marjorie Jane*'s woodwork. "Make that my three favorite girls."

MOLLIE'S SAILING TIPS

I asked Mollie if she wouldn't mind sharing her thoughts about downsizing and moving onto a sailboat. "Living on a boat is Scooter's dream, not mine," she said while petting Mrs. Moto. The Japanese bobtail cat meowed loudly in agreement. "It's not her dream either," Mollie said with a smile. "She likes to have plenty of room to play with her catnip mice."

When I explained that some of our readers might be interested in a liveaboard lifestyle, she agreed to share some downsizing tips that she had picked up from people at the marina.

After taking a sip of coffee and nibbling on a brownie, she sighed. "Of course, if you are going to downsize, don't do it the way we did it. Losing everything in a fire was absolutely devastating."

***

Mollie's Thoughts on Downsizing & Moving onto a Sailboat

1—Think Small

Our cottage was so spacious in comparison to *Marjorie Jane*. To be honest, it was quite a shock to the system to find myself living in such a tiny space. Only one person can be in the kitchen (aka galley) at a time, Scooter can't stand up in our bedroom (aka aft cabin), and there's a distinct lack of closet space. If you're going to move onto a sailboat the size of ours, you'll have to do some serious downsizing.

2—Multi-Function Items

Since you won't have much room, look for items that can serve more than one purpose. For example, when we lived in our cottage, we used to have different glasses for red wine, white wine, and champagne. Now we have one set of glasses and we use them for everything—water, soda, juice, wine, beer etc. Oh, and they're not even made of glass, they're plastic because when your sailboat gets tippy (aka heeling to one side), things get broken.

3—Scan Photos and Documents

Some of the ladies in my sailing class told me that they scanned their photos and important documents and saved them on a hard drive or up in the cloud. It saves a ton of space on board, plus if you have water leaking into your boat, your papers won't get all soggy.

4—Do You Really Need It?

Some of the cruisers we've talked to told us that they found that there were lots of things that they had on land that they ended up not needing once they moved aboard. One of the guys tried to tell me that I could get by with just one pair of shoes and two pairs of underwear on-board. Yeah, like that's ever going to happen. This girl likes her shoes and underwear isn't something you should ever skimp on in my opinion.

5—E-readers

One of the things I was most upset about losing in the fire was my collection of books. While I like my e-reader, there's something special about holding a real book in your hands and turning the pages. But, if you live on a boat, storage space for books is at a premium, so it makes sense to switch to e-books.

6—Storage Units

One couple we know decided to rent a storage unit for the first couple of years they lived aboard their boat. They weren't sure if the cruising lifestyle was going to work for them and they hated the idea of getting rid of precious keepsakes and family heirlooms in case they decided to move back on land.

7—Save Space for Cat Stuff

Mrs. Moto wanted me to make sure to remind everyone that the most important thing to do when downsizing is to remember that you need to leave plenty of room on your boat for cat food, toys, and litter. In her opinion, humans can get by just fine with one pair of shoes and two pairs of underwear which leaves more space for catnip mice.

AUTHOR'S NOTE AND ACKNOWLEDGMENTS

Thank you so much for reading my book! If you enjoyed it, I'd be grateful if you would consider leaving a short review on the site where you purchased it. Reviews help other readers find my books and encourage me to keep writing.

My experiences buying our first sailboat with my husband in New Zealand (followed by our second sailboat in the States), learning how to sail, and living aboard our boats inspired me to write the *Mollie McGhie Sailing Mysteries*. There's a little bit of Mollie in me.

Be on the lookout for the third book in the series, *Poisoned by the Pier*. You can sign up for my free newsletter at ellenjacobsonauthor.com for updates on new releases.

I want to thank my wonderful beta readers who were so generous with their time, graciously reading earlier drafts and providing insightful and thoughtful feedback: Alexandra Palcic, Duwan Dunn, Elizabeth Seckman, Greg Sifford, Liesbet Collaert, Rebecca Douglass, and Sara Barnard. I also want to thank Tina Riley and Tyrean Martinson for their support and advice. Most of all, I want to thank my husband, Scott Jacobson, for his input and encouragement throughout the process. I couldn't do it without him.

The staff and boaters at Indiantown Marina in Florida deserve a special shout-out. The community at the marina is wonderful. It's been a lovely place to write both *Murder at the Marina* and *Bodies in the Boatyard*.

The followers of my blog, *The Cynical Sailor*, have been a huge source of inspiration. Their kind words and encouragement motivated me to publish my first book and continue writing. I've been fortunate to have made good friends (both virtual and in-person) through the blogging community.

Thank you to everyone who made suggestions about murder weapons and methods on Facebook, my blog, via e-mail, and in person. Everyone had such great ideas that it was hard to decide how to kill off the victims in *Bodies in the Boatyard*. In the end, I went with a couple of suggestions made by more than one person.

As always, many thanks to Chris Brogden at EnglishGeek Editing (englishgeekediting.com) for his keen eye, thoughtful edits, and support. He goes above and beyond the call of duty, for which I am very grateful.

Any many, many thanks to all of my readers. Your support and encouragement means everything.

ABOUT THE AUTHOR

Ellen Jacobson is a writer who lives aboard a 34-foot sailboat, *s/v Tickety Boo*, with her husband and an imaginary cat named Simon. Her cozy mystery series, *The Mollie McGhie Sailing Mysteries*, featuring a reluctant sailor turned amateur sleuth, is inspired by her own sailing adventures and misadventures.

In addition to murder mysteries, she also enjoys writing sci-fi and fantasy stories. When she isn't killing off characters, creating imaginary worlds, working on boat projects, or seeking out deserted islands, she blogs about her travel adventures and daily life living aboard a sailboat at thecynicalsailor.blogspot.com.

If you would like updates on current and future releases, please see her website at: ellenjacobsonauthor.com.

You can also follow along on Twitter: @Ellen__Jacobson and Facebook: @EllenJacobsonAuthor.

ALSO BY ELLEN JACOBSON

The Mollie McGhie Sailing Mystery Series

Robbery at the Roller Derby (Prequel)
Murder at the Marina (Book #1)
Bodies in the Boatyard (Book #2)
Poisoned by the Pier (Book #3)
Dead in the Dinghy (Book #4)

Printed in Great Britain
by Amazon